PRAISE FOR

The Book Borrower

"In deceptively quiet, guileless prose, she has described the mind-numbing routine of child-care and the fraught, complex relations of men and women. Only Margaret Atwood (in *Cat's Eye*) has written as knowingly about the friendship between women. Emotionally wrenching, beautifully realized work."

—*New York Times*

"This excellent novel weaves the story of a 1921 trolley strike. . . . Mattison is concerned with the small decisions and coincidences that alter the course of our lives. Are they accidents, or impulses born of something deeper? Mattison's observations are so minutely compelling that each feels like a shiny object, once lost but found unexpectedly."

—*The New Yorker*

"Extraordinary."

—*Washington Post Book World*

PRAISE FOR

Men Giving Money, Women Yelling

"Alice Mattison is a charmer. She's one of those uncommon writers who are genuinely tickled by the ids and egos they commit to paper, and her characters bask—rather than squint—in the sunshine of her affectionate scrutiny. *Men Giving Money, Women Yelling* (is there an award for book title of the season?) is Mattison's third collection of short fiction, and it's crammed with characters—teachers, lawyers, social workers—who pop cleanly, if a bit frantically, off the page."

—*New York Times Book Review*

Edward Mattison

ALICE MATTISON is the author of two other novels and three collections of short stories, as well as a book of poems. Her work has appeared in *The New Yorker*, *The Threepenny Review*, *Boulevard*, and elsewhere, and has been reprinted in *The Pushcart Prize*. She lives in New Haven, Connecticut, and teaches in the graduate writing program at Bennington College.

Hilda
and Pearl

Alice Mattison

Perennial

An Imprint of HarperCollins*Publishers*

A hardcover edition of this book was published in 1995 by William Morrow.

HarperCollins books may be purchased for educational, business, or sales promotional use. For information please write: Special Markets Department, HarperCollins Publishers Inc., 10 East 53rd Street, New York, NY 10022.

First Perennial edition published 2001.

Designed by Jessica Shatan

The Library of Congress has catalogued the hardcover edition as follows:

Mattison, Alice.
    Hilda and Pearl : a novel / by Alice Mattison.
       p.   cm.
    ISBN 0-688-13127-1
    I. Title.
PS3563.A8598H5   1994
813'.54—dc20   94-2634   CIP

ISBN 0-06-093693-2 (pbk.)

01 02 03 04 05 PSI/RRD 10 9 8 7 6 5 4 3 2 1

FOR JANE KENYON
AND DONALD HALL

Hilda and Pearl

I ⁊

HILDA SAID SHE'D TAKE THE PLUMS BACK TO THE COTTAGE with her, because if she left them at the lake no one would remember to bring them. They were the tart red plums of July. Frances, who had eaten one a while ago, didn't care whether her mother took them.

"Come on," said Aunt Pearl, who had started quickly up the hill but then turned to wait, watching Frances's mother, who didn't hurry. Aunt Pearl's freckled arm was raised and her hand shielded her eyes. She looked restless to Frances, who was watching from a little way into the water. Aunt Pearl didn't wear a beach jacket, just her blue bathing suit, and when she was ready to leave the beach, all she had to do was walk away, but Hilda put her terrycloth jacket on over her bathing suit, then gathered up her knitting. Next she leaned over for the paper bag of plums, which was on one of the Adirondack chairs.

When Hilda leaned over, her beach jacket opened and her breasts looked big. Frances, who was eleven, did not yet have breasts.

Hilda caught up with Aunt Pearl, and Aunt Pearl stretched her hand out: she wanted a plum. Frances knew that she would eat two or three on the way back to the cottage, her free hand under her chin to catch the juice. Now Hilda fed her the first one, reaching up to offer it. Aunt Pearl was tall.

They hadn't suggested that Frances come along. Of course, they were only going to the cottage to change their clothes and start supper. Her mother wanted to eat early because people were coming from one of the other cottages after supper to sing or play cards.

Frances's teenage cousin Simon, Aunt Pearl's son, stood at the edge of the lake in his shoes and socks and trousers and shirt, looking straight ahead at the water, not answering when Uncle Mike shouted at him. "Stupid," said Uncle Mike, and Frances's father, Nathan, who was sitting in an Adirondack chair at the edge of the beach, flinched. Uncle Mike had stopped shouting for a while but now that the women had gone up the hill he began again.

Frances liked sitting on the rock because her feet stayed wet. She liked listening to Uncle Mike too. She didn't mind when he shouted at Simon, though she knew she ought to be angry with him. Mostly she found it interesting, and waited almost eagerly for the next thing he'd say. Her parents would never talk that way. It gave her the edgy, excited feeling that some permission had been granted—to both herself and Simon—though Uncle Mike shouted at him *not* to do things. She had stayed in the water longer than she would have if Uncle Mike hadn't been criticizing Simon for not going swimming at all.

Simon stood so close to the water that although his shoes looked dry, Frances thought there wasn't room between his shoes and the water for so much as a pine needle. He would not go into the water or even put on a pair of swimming trunks, though his parents had gone to the trouble and expense of buying a bathing suit and bringing it from the city. His family had been at the lake for three days—visiting Frances's family, who stayed for a month—and so far Simon hadn't gone into the water once. It was shameful not to learn to swim, and Simon could barely swim. It was hot, and anyone with sense would want to cool off in the water. Uncle Mike shouted all this at Simon's back.

Years earlier, Frances had been lying in bed one night, supposedly asleep, listening to her parents talk through the slightly opened door. "Mike takes his belt to Simon," her mother had said.

"No," said Nathan. Frances had known what her mother had meant. It was a strange way of talking, to take your belt to someone. It could mean that Uncle Mike carried his belt across the room and gave the belt to Simon, but it didn't. She had wanted to question Simon about this subject, but she never did. She was five years younger than he was, and he was kind to her, but they didn't talk much.

She was facing the shore. When she looked up she saw her mother and aunt, now far along the dirt road that went to the cottages. There were many cottages, and theirs was far away. She knew how her mother and Aunt Pearl would walk: slowly, talking all the time, sometimes giving each other a push if one of them made a joke. They would stop when Aunt Pearl wanted another plum, and Hilda would open the bag and hold it for her, teasing about how much Pearl ate.

Simon was looking out at the lake. Frances thought he was trying

3

to look as if he had something on his mind and hadn't troubled himself to notice who Mike was talking to. At the edge of the beach, near where the grass started, Frances's father turned his hands over and over on the arms of the Adirondack chair.

Nobody but their family was at the lake, even though there were many cottages and it was a hot day. It was after five o'clock, that was one reason, but none of them could figure out any other reasons. She and her parents sometimes talked about what the other people were missing. Frances's father liked the beach the most. He would take a long swim and then sit in the sun, moving his chair as the shade advanced in the afternoon. He said he needed many hours of sun to bake the winter out of him, and Frances pictured him in his classroom at Erasmus Hall High School in Brooklyn, where they lived, teaching history in his suit, always chilly, waiting for summer, when he could spread out his bare arms. He was glad to see his brother, Mike, and Mike's wife, Pearl, and their son when they visited, but now he looked unhappy, studying Simon's back as if he were trying to read something written on it.

"Worthless," said Uncle Mike. He hadn't said Simon was worthless, but something else. Frances ran her mind back to see. Uncle Mike had said it was worthless to talk to Simon. Just then, carefully timing his first movement to a moment when it would not seem responsive to anything his father had said, Simon turned around and began to walk back toward the cottages.

Uncle Mike snapped his head around quickly, watching Simon. Sometimes he looked like a young man. He was much younger than his brother, Nathan, and he looked younger than he was. His hair was not gray, and it swooped sideways across his forehead. His bathing suit was the tight kind with a bulge in front, not like Frances's father's trunks, which were loose like shorts. Mike was smoking a cigarette, and now he dropped it and kicked sand over it with his bare foot. For a moment he looked as if he might order Simon to stop walking, but he didn't. He moved forward now and stood at the edge of the lake where Simon had stood. When Simon turned around, Mike had been in mid-sentence, saying, "I'm not the kind of father who . . ." but he stopped and seemed to swallow the sentence like something coming out of his mouth that he'd now rather keep.

His face worked as if he were going to speak again.

"Daddy," said Frances, "do you want to watch me float?"

Now she would have to get wet again. She didn't know why she had said that. Her father stood up slowly and came toward the edge of the water, and Frances got off her rock and pulled her bathing suit down where it had crept up on her backside. She walked out to where the water reached her knees. This part of the lake was in shade now, in a shadow cast by trees at the side of the beach, and the water was dark, but it felt warm. She lay down, arching her back, tipping her head backward. Her hair streamed out. She held her body as still as possible. She could see one cloud, a rough triangle, and trees far away across the lake behind her.

"Very good," her father said sadly, but loudly and slowly, so she could hear.

She stayed still as long as she could. Sometimes her legs would go down and she would give a little kick. After a while she heard Uncle Mike's voice again. Her ears were in the water and she couldn't hear what he said. Now her father spoke again and this time she couldn't hear him either. They were angry. They were probably arguing about

Simon. Frances rolled over and began to swim. She would do more laps, slowly and carefully, keeping her elbows close to her body when her arms were underwater. She swam back and forth next to the rope until she was tired. As she swam, she wondered if Uncle Mike might praise her, but when she finished and stood up—so tired that her legs were unsteady for a moment—neither of them was paying attention to her. It had to be late. There were deep shadows.

"A whole way of looking at things," Mike was saying. "An entire way of looking at things. It's not just McCarthy."

Frances came out of the water and wrapped a towel around her shoulders. She was cold. She tied the laces of her sneakers together and put them over her shoulder, one in front, one behind. She didn't want to hear about McCarthy. Uncle Mike was holding an imaginary saxophone in his hands, his feet planted far apart as if he were playing, his fingers moving. But he was talking. "*Never* understood the way you look at things. *Never* could see it."

Mike had a regular job but he had wanted to be a musician. He had played saxophone in a jazz band during the Depression, when he was a young fellow, but he couldn't make money at it. He still played with some friends, not often, or he practiced at home. But his hands often played an instrument that wasn't there.

Frances started to walk, and the sneakers bumped her chest and back rhythmically as she climbed the short rise away from the beach. In a book about old times, a girl might walk barefoot on a dirt road with her shoes bumping her chest and back. The towel could be a shawl. The road was hot and stony. Frances had to place her feet gingerly when she took a step, and that seemed wrong for what she was imagining, for the girl walking barefoot.

Frances moved to the edge of the road, where the lawn started, because it would be cooler and more comfortable, but it was the dirt and stones that had made her feel like an old-fashioned girl. Her suit was still wet and the middle of her body was cool, but her arms and legs felt hot now. She came to a shaded place and she stepped off the lawn even though the stones would hurt her feet. She almost wanted the stones to hurt her. In front of her, a little to the side, a brown striated stone stuck out of the ground and came to a point. Frances deliberately ran her foot over that stone, and put her weight down so the point pressed into her arch. It hurt. If the stone cut her, she could get blood poisoning and even die.

It was dishonest to imagine dying—though it was interesting. One day, when Frances was on her way to Macy's with her mother to buy a coat, she had heard a woman crossing a street in New York say, "Nobody believes he's going to die." When Frances looked into her mind, she discovered it was true of her: although she knew everyone died, she didn't believe *she* would die. She didn't know it in the obvious, ordinary way she knew that she lived on the third floor of an apartment house, the way she knew that if she rang the doorbell, her mother, Hilda Levenson, would open the door.

It seemed wrong not to believe in something true. Whenever she thought of dying after that, she made sure to tell herself over and over that someday she was going to die. Once, she had felt herself just about to believe it, and to her surprise had pulled her mind away quickly the way she might pull her foot from a stone.

She was almost at the cottage. She came to a place where the road was soft sand and easy to walk on. "I'm going to die," she said out loud in a low voice, and with some excitement she heard herself differently, as if another ear had opened in her body. The words went straight in and she knew they were true. She looked at the trees and the gray cottages, and still knew she was going to die, and didn't have to keep telling herself. She had thought that if she ever believed it, it would be for only an instant, and if she wanted to believe it again, she'd have to work just as hard.

She crossed the short lawn in front of their cottage. Her mother's brown slippers, which she wore to the beach, were drying on the step. Frances climbed the wooden steps and caught the screen door just before it banged.

The cottage was dim and quiet. Simon was not lying on the cot where he was sleeping this week, on the screened porch. In the living room, the daybed where his parents slept was closed, and nobody was there. Frances dropped her sneakers in the living room and went to the doorway of her bedroom, but as she stepped inside she saw Simon stretched out on her bed, apparently reading, looking as if he'd been there for a long time, propped on one elbow with his back to her. He didn't turn around. "I'm going to die," she said in a low voice, but his back, in a white shirt, seemed to be telling her in a quiet but clipped voice to go away. His legs were bent at the knees, and behind him on the bed were her clothes, her shorts and halter and her underpants on top. Maybe they were where she had left them, and maybe he had pulled the pile of clothes closer to the end of the bed so he'd have room to lie down. Frances stepped forward, just to take the pile of clothes. She would go into her parents' bedroom, which was on the other side of the living room, the side that got the sun in the afternoon. Frances opened the door without knocking, then remembered her mother and Aunt Pearl.

The yellow cotton curtain had been pulled across the screen, and the room was dim and still. Heat struck Frances's face as she stepped in, as if someone had reached out a flat palm. There was the sweet smell of talcum powder, and a cloud of it in the air. Frances's mother was facing away from the door, naked, her fingers curved and close together. She was going to apply powder to Aunt Pearl's back. Aunt Pearl, also naked, had her back to Hilda. Her skin was red on either side of the white lines of her bathing suit straps, and in between the lines. Now they both turned slowly and some of the powder in Hilda's hand drifted to the floor. She leveled her hand to save it and applied it to her own body, lifting her breast and stroking her chest underneath it. "What is it, baby?" she said.

"I need to change out of my bathing suit," said Frances. "Simon's in my room." Her mother's breasts were larger than Aunt Pearl's, and hung down, so there were those little rooms under them, secret places. Her mother's belly was round and full of folds, and her belly button, in the middle of it, seemed mournful.

"Come on in," said her mother. "We were just taking a little nap." The air was rich with sleep. It seemed to Frances that it would be easy and delightful to lie down on the rumpled, bare sheet—the blankets had been pushed to the floor—and fall into her mother's nap, Aunt Pearl's nap. The sun was coming through the curtain and the air was yellow, and it did seem as if yellow was the color of naps, and if she just pulled off her wet suit and lay down, she could enter the nap where Hilda and Pearl had left it.

But she felt small and naked, even though she was wearing her bathing suit and Hilda and Pearl were not wearing anything. They were wearing their flesh. Aunt Pearl was tall, with short blond hair.

Her breasts were smaller than Hilda's and her belly was not so large, but her rear end was large. Her body swelled below her waist, and her buttocks were like a chair, firm and broad, yet with that line down the middle that looked childlike to Frances.

She hesitated. If she left, there would be nowhere to change but the bathroom, and there the floor would be wet, and she would see a spider while she was undressed and have to put her clothes on before she could run away.

"Are you sunburned?" said Aunt Pearl. "You look as if you're peeling a little." And she stepped forward and turned Frances around to examine her back and shoulders.

"Do you want some powder, honey?" said her mother, and now it was as if Frances had been standing on a step or a little stool, just above the room, and she deliberately stepped off it into something fragrant and soft. "My stomach hurts," she said, making her voice sound as if she were younger than she was.

"Are you constipated?" said her mother. "Did you go to the bath-room today?"

"It's not that," said Frances. "It's like something rubbed on my stomach and made the outside hurt." Her bathing suit had cotton ties that went into loops and made a bow behind her, and she reached back and undid the bow, and then worked the suit down her body.

"Is it a mosquito bite?" said her mother.

"I don't know." There was a bite on her stomach, and her mother squatted in the dimness to look at it and said that was it. Frances wanted to lie down on the bed but she didn't. She sat on the bed and Aunt Pearl sat down next to her. She was still behaving as if she were younger than she was, younger than eleven. "Mommy's fat," she said.

"No, she's not," Aunt Pearl said. "I'm fat. I have a fat tush."

"Mommy has a fat stomach."

"I think it looks nice," said Aunt Pearl. The truth was that Frances thought it looked nice, too.

Frances's mother stood in front of the mirror and looked at herself, but the mirror was too small, it showed only her head. She picked up her hair. "I used to be thin," she said. "When I was in high school, I had to have an extra hole made in my belt."

"Well, I never had to do that," said Aunt Pearl.

"You're *still* thin," said Hilda.

"Except for the backside," Pearl said. "That was pretty small, too, until I had a baby."

Frances tried to imagine Aunt Pearl pregnant. She had been pregnant with Simon. Her belly would swoop out in front, but Frances didn't see why her backside would get bigger. There was a towel lying on the bed and Frances dried her stomach and what she could reach of her back. She was only a little damp. Aunt Pearl took the towel, though, and dried the part of her back Frances couldn't reach. Then she rubbed powder on Frances's back. Her hand felt large.

"It's not so big," said Hilda.

"Yes, it is," said Pearl. "If I had another baby, I'd have a behind like an elephant."

Frances began to get dressed. "I don't think so," said Hilda vaguely, as if she was thinking about something and had lost track of the conversation.

Then Hilda said, "I gained most of the weight the first time," which didn't make sense, because Frances was an only child.

"You were pregnant only once," she said in her regular voice, no longer pretending she was a little girl.

Her mother turned toward the chair where she had left her clothes. She glanced at Frances but didn't answer for a moment. "I said I got big when I was pregnant," she said.

"No, you didn't," Frances said. "You said you got big the first time."

"It's the same thing."

Frances was annoyed. "That doesn't make sense. Why would you say it was the first time if there was only one time?"

"Well, that was the way I said it," Hilda said, with a laugh, as if she often said silly things.

Frances knew the answer. Her mother had had a miscarriage. Simon had said once that her mother had had a miscarriage, one of the rare times they talked at any length. Frances had asked her mother what a miscarriage was, and her mother had said it was when a baby died before it was born. Frances didn't feel she could ask whether that had happened to Hilda. Now she knew it had. She thought it must have been before she was born. She'd remember if her mother had had a dead baby when she was around.

Her mother put on her underpants and fastened her brassiere, reaching behind her back and leaning over. Frances quickly finished putting on her clothes. Aunt Pearl was wearing her bathrobe. She said she had changed her mind and was going to take a shower, even though she'd already used all that powder. There was a snap and a thud from outside, and Aunt Pearl shook her head. "My hunter is home from the hill," she said. Now Frances remembered that she had heard the screen door, and a voice, her father's voice. She couldn't remember what he had said to Uncle Mike. "Juice," that was it. While Aunt Pearl was putting powder on her. He had offered Uncle Mike some juice.

The snap was Uncle Mike's slingshot, which he'd made the night before. There were insects in the cabin, big shadowy long-legged drifting insects that Hilda said were baby wasps. Her father swatted them with a newspaper, but they always seemed to float away before the folded paper hit the wall. When Aunt Pearl and Uncle Mike had arrived, Uncle Mike said he knew how to get rid of the baby wasps. He walked up and down outside the cabin until he found a forked stick. He broke off the prongs so it was the right size, and peeled off the bark. Hilda bought blueberries in boxes that came with rubber bands on top, and Mike cut a rubber band and fastened it to the forked stick, making a slingshot. He was still experimenting with ammunition. So far he was tearing up newspaper and making wads. He'd killed two baby wasps but said he could do better if he could make the slingshot work just right.

When Frances came out of the bedroom in her shorts and halter, Uncle Mike had made half a dozen wads of newspaper and he was shooting them at the corner near the ceiling, one after another. He stared upward and flopped his hair off his forehead by tossing his head back. He looked flushed. Frances didn't see a baby wasp. The wads of newspaper were falling onto the floor in the middle of the room. Simon was standing behind his father in the doorway.

"Pick those up, will you?" Mike called, gesturing with his head, then looking over his shoulder for a second so Simon would know he meant him. Simon knelt on one knee and swept the wads of paper into his hand. He dropped them onto the daybed where his father was sitting. Then he sat down, at a little distance from Mike. Frances's father was coming in from the kitchen. He was drinking a glass of orange juice.

"Simon," he said, "can I offer you some juice?"

"No, thanks."

"Frances is the lady of the house. She can pour juice for herself," he went on. "One of the ladies of the house. But if she likes, I will pour her some anyway."

He stopped and looked at her inquiringly and Frances shook her head. Then she changed her mind and went to get herself some juice. The sun had dried her so thoroughly she needed something wet. She stood in the doorway and watched Uncle Mike shoot wads of newspaper at the ceiling. She could hear the sound of the shower. Her mother, dressed, came out of the bedroom. "We'll eat soon, Nathan," she said. "Those people are coming in for dessert." She had invited two other couples. Frances thought they would probably bring a guitar or a banjo and sing.

"What are we having for supper?" she said.

"Hamburgers," said her mother. "I have some frozen french fries."

Uncle Mike killed the baby wasp he'd been shooting at. "I think you should be ashamed of yourself," said Simon. He was still sitting on the daybed, his finger keeping his place in his book.

"Ashamed of myself!" Mike had gone into the kitchen for the dustpan and broom, and was sweeping the dead wasp into it. He didn't like to touch them with his hands. He opened the screen door and dumped the wasp outside. He let the door slam.

"I don't care for killing," said Simon.

"*You!* How about all those spiders you made me kill for you? You wouldn't go to sleep until I'd killed all the spiders."

"Dad, I was six years old," Simon said. "I don't mind spiders now."

"Well, *that's* good news."

"I haven't asked you to kill a spider in about ten years."

"So you want me to leave these things to sting everybody?"

"I don't think they sting. I don't think they're baby wasps at all. That's purely hypothetical, that they sting."

"Your cousin Frances dislikes the thought that they might brush up against her," said Nathan. This was true. Frances had screamed and batted wildly at the air the first night when one of the strange, slow, long-legged creatures had floated past her.

"You don't have to kill them," she said. "If you could just make them go outside."

Uncle Mike turned his sharp face toward her. "You want me to give them an engraved invitation?"

She laughed, but she wasn't being teased, she thought; she was being criticized.

"A couple of pacifists we have here," Uncle Mike said to her father.

"It's a time-honored position," his brother said.

"You and your time-honored positions," said Uncle Mike. "Sounds like your buddies or some other fringe group. If you kids remembered Pearl Harbor . . ." His voice became sarcastic. "Pacifists were a *big* help. You would deal with Adolf Hitler without killing? Huh?" He was getting angry quickly.

"I remember Pearl Harbor," said Simon. "I thought someone was trying to hurt Mom, because her name is Pearl. I remember wondering what a harbor was. I remember how upset everyone was—a lot of shouting. When I read about it later, I already knew how people felt."

Frances went into the kitchen to help her mother fix supper. Aunt Pearl had come out of the shower and was getting dressed.

"So, Uncle Nathan," Simon went on, "speaking of current events. Or historical events." Frances thought that Simon liked what he had said about Pearl Harbor, liked saying something like that. Nobody had answered him, but nobody had yelled either. "I've been wanting to ask you. Dad talks all the time about your job. Is there really any danger? I mean, you aren't really a Communist, are you? I know you're not—I'm just asking."

Simon sat down opposite her father. There was more newspaper near him and he put a piece into his book for a bookmark and began to make wads of paper for shooting the wasps, as if he felt that he owed that much to his father. He spread out his knees and looked forward. His father had gone out to the porch and was smoking a cigarette. He stood in the doorway. "Hold it," Mike said. "I never said anything like that. Find out what you're talking about before you start quoting me, son."

Nathan was looking at Frances. She was scraping a carrot but she'd stopped and carried it to the kitchen doorway where she could watch Simon and her father. Now she took it back into the kitchen, where her mother had put a piece of newspaper on the table to catch the peel, and scraped it some more. But she could still hear. Her mother was standing at the stove, patting the chopped meat into hamburgers, patting them back and forth from one hand to the other.

"There's no reason to be concerned about my job," Nathan said. He spoke in a low, urgent whisper. "A few crazy people making everyone act crazy. It can't keep up like this."

"So is anybody after you, exactly, or what?" said Simon.

Frances knew her father had been troubled and that it had to do with his job. He had had to go to the Board of Ed for an interview. She didn't understand, and her mother wouldn't tell her what it had to do with. Simon probably understood better than she did.

"Well, the bastards made me come in and go through the mill, they certainly did that," her father said. "A lot of people have lost their jobs. But I can't believe they're that stupid. I can't believe Jansen is that stupid." Dr. Jansen was the Superintendent of Schools. "It's only a matter of time—McCarthy's fooling a lot of people, but I tell my kids every year, Lincoln said you can fool all of the people some of the time and some of the people all of the time. . . ."

"Nathan, don't give me that crap," said Uncle Mike.

"What crap exactly do you object to?"

"Lincoln is dead," said Mike. "Lincoln is a goddamned dead man. You think he's going to rise up out of the ground and save you, because you think he was such a great guy, but my dear brother, he is *dead*."

"April 14, 1865," said Nathan. "I know Lincoln is dead. John Wilkes Booth shot him."

"Very funny."

"Some people think Lincoln didn't say that," said Simon. "Some people think P. T. Barnum said it. But I don't understand what Lincoln has to do with it." Frances understood. Her father believed that because he was a good person, like Lincoln, Dr. Jansen would stop bothering him. Dr. Jansen was investigating Communists in the school system. Dr. Jansen apparently thought her father was a Communist, and that must be why he had summoned him for an interview. McCarthy was the senator who talked about Communists. She didn't think McCarthy actually knew her father, or personally thought he was a Communist.

She wanted to ask why her father didn't simply explain. Perhaps someone else had the same name. She had known all along that Dr. Jansen was investigating Communists. Now she couldn't remember what it was she hadn't known a moment ago.

"McCarthy is not even fooling all of the people," said Nathan. "He is fooling only some of the people. And he can't fool them all the time."

"McCarthy is an interesting phenomenon," Simon said. "I read a long article the other day." Simon read a lot. "He's going about this improperly, but don't you think it's important, at least his basic goals? I mean, we can't have Communists in sensitive jobs. My history teacher was talking about that one day—"

"Now, Simon, my boy, there are things it's hard for you to understand—" Nathan began, but Uncle Mike interrupted.

"You see?" he said, and it was Nathan he turned on, his eyes flashing. "You see? You expect justice. You goddamned *fool*. You think they're going to *listen* to you, to *realize*"—his voice was heavy with sarcasm—"that they made a little mistake! Here they've gotten even the high school kids talking about it, informing, probably—"

"I think common sense wins in the end," said Nathan calmly. "Yes, I think they will realize they made a little mistake."

"You've always been such a goddamned *fool*," said Uncle Mike, and his voice was high, like a woman's. "Nothing you did ten, fifteen years ago made sense—I told you at the time."

"You certainly did."

"You've never learned to look after yourself, Nathan. You have some responsibility. You have a wife, a child."

"This I know."

"You stick your Jewish nose out, you get punched. Look what happened to the Rosenbergs. You stick with your name. You stick with your crazy ideas, your loyalty long after it makes sense—"

"I'm not sure I understand," said Simon.

"My loyalty," said Nathan, reaching out to pat his nephew's knee. "Let's not start on this. The Rosenbergs—"

But Mike didn't stop. "Now it's perfectly clear what you have to do. You have to stop expecting the world to change. Tell these people what they want to hear and get on with your work."

"Tell them what they want to hear?" Nathan stood up and walked across the room and looked out the window as if Dr. Jansen were waiting on the lawn. "Michael, are you telling me I should *purge* myself, as they put it?"

Frances had scraped three carrots while she listened. Her mother put the hamburgers aside. Aunt Pearl came in. "Do you want me to make dessert?" she said. Frances thought she was talking loudly on purpose.

"I thought I'd make chocolate pudding pie," said Hilda. Chocolate pudding pie was the only fancy dessert Hilda knew. She would put graham crackers into a dish, slice a banana on top, and make chocolate pudding, which she'd pour on top of the banana.

"It might not set in time," said Pearl. "I'll make a peach cobbler. We bought Reddi Wip."

"I don't have any flour."

"We'll use Bisquick."

In the other room, there was silence and moving around. She knew her father was angry. Her mother got out the package of chocolate pudding, even if it wasn't going to set in time, and opened it into a saucepan. Frances finished the carrots and slipped back into the living room. Her father looked quickly at her. His face was dark. His hair was pale gray, a little wavy, and it was strange for his face to be darker than his hair. His eyebrows were raised as if he expected her to say something that would upset him too.

When he spoke, his voice was choked. "You might as well face it, Mike. I'm not going down to Livingston Street and telling Dr. Jansen I was a Communist and I'm sorry. I can't think of anything worse than that."

"So you'll lose your job, is that what you want?" said Mike.

"But you weren't a Communist," Simon said. "Were you? Why should you have to tell Dr. Jansen you were a Communist when you weren't?"

Nathan sat back in his chair. Mike picked up the slingshot and a wad of newspaper and shot at something out on the porch. "What is a Communist, Simon?" said Nathan, as if he were in class, Frances thought, as if he were teaching. "What is a Communist? Do you know what a Communist is?"

"Well, I don't know a lot about it," said Simon quickly, "but I know it's someone who advocates the overthrow of the government by force and violence."

20

"Force and violence," said Nathan, as if he'd never heard the words before. "Force and violence."

But now Mike walked back into the living room. He had the slingshot in his hand, and his arm was taut, as if he were holding himself back. "You snotty kid," he said, his eyes flashing more than ever. "You goddamn snotty kid!"

"Mike!" said Nathan, standing, his voice full of pain. "Leave the boy alone, Mike!" But Simon had rushed from the cabin. Frances could hear his feet pounding as he ran down the road. Her mother and Aunt Pearl came in from the kitchen.

"What is it, Mike?" her mother said.

Uncle Mike shook his head. "Nathan, I've never agreed with you," he said, "but I didn't teach him this stuff. I don't know where he gets this stuff."

"What does he know? It doesn't matter. I'll explain to him." Nathan ran his hands over his face, as if to wipe away the dark color.

"I'm making supper," said Hilda. "Is Simon coming back?"

"Oh, he'll come back," Mike said. "He gets hungry too, even if he's too good for the rest of us. Even *he* needs to eat."

Aunt Pearl looked at Uncle Mike and then hurried to the porch. "Simon!" she called sharply. "Simon!" Then she said, "I don't see him, Hilda. I'm going to look for him," and left the cabin.

Hilda took off the apron she always wore for cooking, even in the country. Both men were standing up, looking at her. But then she put her apron back on. "Frances, set the table," she said.

Frances set the table in the kitchen. There wasn't really enough room in there for six people, but she didn't want to ask her father and uncle to pull the table out to the porch.

The frying pan was sizzling. Hilda stood at the stove, her back to Frances, cooking the hamburgers.

"Do you think Daddy is going to lose his job?" Frances said.

Hilda looked over her shoulder and then back at the stove. "No," she said.

"Well, if he has to go and answer questions . . ." said Frances uncertainly. She still didn't know exactly what her father had to do.

"He already answered questions," said her mother.

"So is it all over?"

"Look, honey," Hilda said, "if there's something you have to know, I'll tell you. I wish Mike could put it out of his mind."

"Why does it make Mike angry?" said Frances.

"Oh, he never liked the Teachers Union, or any of your father's friends from the old days," her mother said. Now she seemed more willing to talk. "Mike thought meetings were boring. He'd go to some of them to take down the speeches when he was learning stenography. Your father's friends thought he was some kind of spy. It was silly."

Uncle Mike was a court stenographer. He would have preferred to play the saxophone all day, but he worked in the court, wearing a brown suit. Frances had seen him coming home; he always changed his clothes before he'd been in the house for ten minutes. In court he took down what was said on a stenotype machine, and a couple of times he'd let Frances fool with it and type on it. It was frustrating—it made letters, not words. The letters came down in groups. It was in code, he explained. No wonder people had thought he was a spy.

Her mother put the tray of frozen french fries into the oven. Frances opened a package of hamburger buns. Aunt Pearl came in. "Did you see him?" said Mike

"No."

"He'll come back."

She came into the kitchen. She was flushed from hurrying in the heat. "I don't know what to do, Hilda," she said.

"He probably just went for a walk by the lake," said Hilda.

"But he's upset."

"He'll calm down," Hilda said. "He'll come in while we're eating. It's better than making a fuss."

"I don't know how to get him to stop," Pearl said in a low voice. She moved one shoulder and Frances knew she meant Uncle Mike. Her mother looked quickly toward the living room. "I know," she said quietly, then, in a louder voice, "It's hot in here."

"Stuffy," said Nathan, coming in.

They ate quickly. Simon didn't come in. Mike talked about the slingshot. He thought it might work better with small blocks of wood.

"You need width," he said. "Pebbles wouldn't work. The bugs have to be squashed."

"Mike, forget it, we'll take our quinine and not worry about the insects," Nathan said.

"Mosquitoes cause malaria," said Frances. "Anopheles mosquitoes. These insects are wasps."

"Now you sound like *my* kid," said Mike, but he said it with some warmth, as if being like his kid was not the worst possible thing.

"I don't know if wasps cause diseases," Frances said.

"Well, you wouldn't want to find out," said Aunt Pearl. She stood up to help Hilda clear.

"Frances will do it," said Hilda. Frances was not finished eating. She wanted more potatoes, but there were only a few in the bowl, thin dark brown ones, almost burned. They had not left any for Simon. She began carrying the plates to the sink. When she got there she turned on the cold water and splashed her face.

While she was washing she thought of something. "Daddy," she said, "does McCarthy know about you personally? I mean, does he *personally* want you to lose your job?" She knew McCarthy was a senator, and her father worked for the city of New York, not for the federal government.

"No," said her father.

Her mother turned around. "Frances," she said.

"No," said her father, "I don't believe that the senator from Wisconsin has anything against me personally."

"Well, that's *good*," Frances said. It did seem good. Her mother turned around again.

Uncle Mike said, "He doesn't need to think about the small fry like your daddy. He's got loyal followers to do that."

"Now, Mike," said Nathan. "Let's not get started again."

"Get started? Me? *Moi?*"

Nathan began to carry the juice and the butter to the refrigerator. "What I cannot believe," he said after a while, first talking quietly, as if to himself, and then more loudly, "what I cannot believe is some of my fellow teachers. One of them purged himself in Jansen's office.

This I cannot believe. And the paper goes on about how they can't decide whether it *counts*. The man *vomits* in the superintendent's office—I'm sorry, ladies, that's what I always picture. The man throws up his guts in the superintendent's office, and then, at the hearing, they bicker about whether that's *enough*. Whether he has to do it *again*."

"I know, it's hideous," said Hilda.

"I know, I know."

Mike started to stand up. "You can't think that way," he said, talking fast again. "You can't just— You have to think about survival. It's like a man in a grocery store, and his wife and kids are starving—"

Hilda was wrapping the leftover hamburgers in waxed paper. "Mike, that's enough," she said suddenly.

"I'm not—"

"I know," she said. "I know. But that's enough. I want you to go into the other room and read a book. I've got a book you might like—one of Edna Ferber's books. It's probably on the little table, under my knitting."

Mike, like a boy, watched her for a moment and went into the other room. Nathan looked at Hilda. "He doesn't understand," he said.

"I know," said Hilda.

"I know how you feel, Nathan," Pearl said.

"I remember some of those first meetings," he said. "How I felt then. I felt as if things were actually going to be different—that someone had thought of a way to end suffering. It's like the first girl who turns your head—you may decide later you don't care for her, even that she's not a nice girl, after all. But you don't forget—and when they come to throw stones, you don't pick up a stone."

"Very nice, Nathan," called Mike from the other room. "Very pretty."

"Michael," cried Pearl, but she was laughing. "Michael, you will *never learn*."

"I think I'd better go look for Simon," said Frances. She wasn't sure anyone heard her. She stepped out of the cabin. It was getting dark.

Frances walked down the road she had taken before, but now she was wearing her sneakers. She walked all the way to the lake. There was no one on the beach. The Adirondack chairs were dark spaces against the sand. She sat down and looked out at the lake. Simon might have drowned himself, and she tried to think how he'd manage to do that. She started to smile at the thought of Simon, who would not even take off his shoes and wade, drowning himself. She was pretty sure he could swim. He had gone to camp when he was younger. It wouldn't work for him just to walk into the water. Besides, she thought that even people who couldn't swim couldn't drown themselves that way. The body resisted it. She had heard that you couldn't help thrashing about and trying to save yourself.

Simon would have to take a boat out to the deep part and weight his pants pockets with stones and then jump in. She counted the boats. Six. She thought maybe there were supposed to be seven, but she wasn't sure. In truth, she had never counted them. They bumped softly against one another in the dark, near the swimming area, straining a little on their ropes. She thought she could check to see whether there were footprints near the boats, but instead of standing up she continued to sit in the Adirondack chair, looking at the lake. A mountain just across it was a dark, curved shape, but the sky around it was still gray, not black. The lake was very dark. She liked the sound it made. It might wash up Simon's body, slowly, first his arm and then more of him, until she could make out his entire, somewhat pathetic shape. She'd have to tell. She wasn't sure whether she'd wait while the lake brought up Simon's body or whether, as soon as she saw any of it, she'd go to tell her family. It would be too late for artificial respiration. She could drag the body onto the sand, but she didn't think she'd want to touch it.

When she pictured Simon's body lying on the sand, his mouth in the sand, tiny waves touching it and pulling away, his shoes soaked —for it seemed he had drowned himself fully dressed, as he had been since he'd come—she remembered her new knowledge that she herself would die someday. It was oddly pleasant to move straight to that certainty. It had passed through her mind before, too, when Uncle Mike mentioned the Rosenbergs. It scared her to think about the Rosenbergs. She didn't understand what they had done. Two years before, a girl in Frances's class was named Rosenberg. Probably she was not related to the Rosenbergs who died in the electric chair, but maybe. Even if Nathan was a Communist, he was not a spy, she was sure about that. But Frances and her family were Jewish. Frances was almost like Ethel Rosenberg, except that Ethel Rosenberg, who had looked a little like Hilda, was grown up. Ethel Rosenberg also knew she was going to die, but she knew as she was walking to the electric chair.

Then Frances thought that something else was dead, and she remembered her mother's miscarriage. If her mother had already been fat, Frances thought she must have been almost ready to have the baby. Frances was surprised that her mother didn't see that what she had said was illogical. She shouldn't have expected Frances to accept her explanation.

Frances went to examine the sand near the boats. It was quite dark now, and even though she squatted, she couldn't tell whether there were any footprints. Sometimes the manager of the cottages raked the beach. If it had just been raked, Frances would have been able to see any new footprints near the boats.

She walked back to the cottage, and when she reached it she could hear that the other couples had arrived. There was laughter, and she heard her mother's company voice, pitched a little lower and louder than usual. Her mother would be serving the chocolate pudding pie and the peach cobbler. Frances could hear the voice of a woman who was staying in a cottage in the back row, a thin, nervous woman who had a little boy. She was saying, ". . . care about us, or anything like that."

Frances thought she was talking about whether anyone had cared about her when she came to stay at the cottages that summer, but she heard her mother say, "That's the way it is these days. That's the way it is," and her mother sounded so sad, she couldn't mean summer at the lake.

"Harry, take out your instrument," she heard her father say. Harry was the woman's husband, and he played the banjo. It took him a long time to be persuaded to take it out and tune it up. Frances sat on the steps and listened, slapping at mosquitoes. Nobody seemed to hear her, or to wonder where she and Simon were. At last Harry began to sing. He sang "Joe Hill," a song Frances had known all her life. She knew it was a union song. He sang it distinctly and with interesting pauses, as if he was pretending that his hearers didn't know the words and would be surprised and pleased by them. Her parents joined in. "Says I, 'But Joe, you're ten years dead,'" they sang, and then, after a second of hush for the surprise, "'I never died,' says he. 'I never died,' says he."

2 ❧

THE PRESIDENT OF THE SHORTHAND REPORTERS' ASSOCIA-
tion was an old woman, a pen writer, but Uncle Mike was about to
become the new president, and he used a stenotype machine. Whoever
was the secretary became the treasurer the following year, the vice-
president the year after that, and the president next, so Uncle Mike
had known for a while that one day he would be president. He would
be the first who was not a pen writer. He was to be inducted at a
banquet, and all of them were going.

Uncle Mike had started out writing with a pen when he first
learned shorthand during the Depression. He had taken down
speeches at meetings and lectures and if it was crowded he'd stood
and leaned on the wall. Frances's mother had said he'd gone wherever

someone might be talking. He was proud that he could take down long, strange words.

Later he'd gotten hold of a stenotype machine, and now most of the younger stenographers used them. Uncle Mike could write as fast as people could speak. Once he recited back to Frances a conversation she'd just had with Aunt Pearl about Simon, when Frances hadn't even known he was in the apartment. He'd been in the next room with his machine, taking everything down.

Frances found it somewhat disturbing to watch Uncle Mike using the machine. It was like a small, narrow typewriter on a tripod. It was low, and he pulled it close to his knees. When she'd once walked in on him as he took down a speech on the radio—his hands poised, fingers descending over and over, but with a restraint that seemed unlike him—she'd backed away as if she'd walked in on him in the bedroom or the bathroom.

The machine's touch was soft, and it made hardly any sound, only a swish as dense fabric cushioned the blow of the keys. Sometimes more than one key went down at a time. The keys were not marked. There were not many keys, and they were not all the same size or shape. Quickly, they caused a narrow strip of paper to fill with scattered letters. Though paper moved steadily through the machine and dropped back in folds to resettle as a thick, narrow packet (fold upon fold sinking into a box at the machine's back) there was nothing to read, for Frances didn't know the code. Stenotypy recorded what was said, Uncle Mike told her, syllable by syllable, one at a time. The groups of letters stood for different syllables.

Uncle Mike made Frances test him whenever she was at his house.

Simon wouldn't do it. Frances would read a paragraph aloud from a book or a newspaper, and Uncle Mike would write it down, pausing when she paused, touching several keys at once with his fingertips for each sound. This time, a couple of days before the banquet, when her mother had sent her over with a pair of shoes to ask Aunt Pearl whether they would do, Frances recited, "By the shores of Gitche Gumee. . . ." He could write down "Hiawatha" too.

Some of the stenotype writers believed in using "short forms," Uncle Mike often said, but he did not, and Frances had heard him shout at Nathan about it, as if Nathan, who said he didn't care whether Mike used short forms or not, was in league with the people who favored them. As far as Frances could tell, short forms were abbreviations. Someone had figured out a code within the code, a greater secret. Frances thought this sounded exciting. A whole phrase, Uncle Mike had explained, would be written not with just a few strokes—but *one* stroke.

" 'By the shores of Gitche Gumee'?" she asked now.

"No, nothing like that. Something like 'by order of the court' or 'the State of New York.' "

"I think it would be nice to say something so long with just one little—" she demonstrated "—*poosh.*" She thrust out several fingers as her uncle did.

"For crying out loud!" Uncle Mike said, hitting the table. "Is that what you think is the way to do things—shortcuts?" He didn't shout quite the way he did at Simon, but he looked at her as if he was deciding he disapproved of her. "You want everything made easy for you?"

"I don't take shortcuts," Frances said.

The banquet was in October, a few months after Simon had run away at the lake. He had *not* run away, he had said, when she finally asked him about it.

"You stayed out all night."

"I did not." It was true: Simon had been on his cot on the porch, in his clothes, in the morning. Nobody had said anything.

"But where were you all that time?"

"In the woods," he had said, "thinking."

"Weren't you hungry?"

"No."

"Your mother cried," she had said. After she was in bed that night, after the other couples had returned to their cottages, she'd heard Aunt Pearl crying.

"She loves me too much," said Simon.

The night of the banquet Frances's mother wore a rust-colored dress that made noise when she walked. The neckline was square and there was ruching at the neck, Hilda said. The cloth was bunched there, and gave off a different sheen from that of the rest of the dress. Her shoes were almost the same color as her dress. Frances's dress was wool and didn't shine. Her father wore a suit. They met Uncle Mike and Aunt Pearl and Simon outside their apartment house, a few blocks from where Frances and her parents lived, so they could travel together on the subway.

Aunt Pearl, wearing a blue dress with her coat open over it, came to meet them and threaded her arm under Frances's mother's arm, around her back and out the other side, so Aunt Pearl's fingers reached Hilda's other arm. Frances moved close to Aunt Pearl to see if she'd do the same thing to Frances with her other arm, but Aunt

Pearl put her other hand into her pocket—and then the first hand, too; she'd held on to Hilda for only a moment. They walked in a group toward the subway station. Frances ran her finger down the sleeve of Aunt Pearl's coat, but lightly, so her aunt didn't notice.

Her mother was urging everyone along, trying to get them to walk a little faster. Uncle Mike was walking ahead. It was Hilda's hand, moving as if through water in the air behind Pearl's back, that made her the leader. She seemed to encourage Pearl as much as to hurry her. Aunt Pearl walked with a long stride, in low heels. She always wore low heels because of her height. Her hands pulled at her pockets.

Simon walked by himself, wearing a suit like his father's. Simon's hair was dark. He wore glasses and he never spoke in a loud voice. Frances knew he was smart, and she always expected to hear that he had the highest marks in his school, but Aunt Pearl said he was a sloppy student. Just before they reached the subway, her father began to walk with Simon, asking him questions about school. Uncle Mike put his arm around Aunt Pearl, and Hilda moved over to Frances and brushed her fingers over Frances's hair as if there were specks on her.

In the subway Simon sat by himself. Hilda's dress puffed up through the opening in her coat when she sat down. It might have been nice, Frances thought, to rest her head on her mother's satiny dress and to smell her perfume. She had brought a book, and she read all the way into New York.

When they came out of the subway it was drizzling, and the cars driving by sounded unhappy, their tailfins large and rain-spattered, looking indeed like something from the sea. But the banquet was in a hotel close by, and they hardly got wet.

They hung up their coats in the hotel cloakroom and went into the ballroom, where round white-covered tables were set for ten, and there was a lectern at the front of the room for speeches. The outgoing president, Ellie Potter, a woman in a black silk suit, came to greet them. She laughed like a man. "You brought the whole crowd, I see," she said, shaking hands with Uncle Mike and patting his shoulder at the same time. And when Frances looked around, she saw only one other child, a girl a little older than she was. Hilda and Pearl talked to each other, as usual, and Frances stood near them. Simon backed away and stood by himself, watching his father, who was shaking hands and greeting people, introducing his family to some of them. "My brother," he'd say, and Nathan would shake hands with the person. Then he'd gesture in their direction. "My wife. My brother's wife."

Then Uncle Mike got into an argument with another man. Uncle Mike chopped at the air with the side of his hand again and again, as if what the man thought was a piece of meat and Mike was chopping it with a big knife into smaller and smaller pieces. They were arguing about short forms. The man said, "But it's so easy. It's so fast. You can't imagine—"

It was time to sit down. The man and his wife were seated at their table. The meal began with fruit cup, and Simon didn't eat his. He reached into the center of the table and took a roll from the plate there. "Don't fill up on bread," his father said. Aunt Pearl and Frances's mother didn't notice. They were talking with the wife of the short forms man. Frances ate her fruit cup.

Mike had to lean across the table to argue now. "*My* notes—" he said, his mouth full, and then paused to swallow. "Anybody who can read stenotype can read my notes. I get hit by a truck tomorrow, you can read the transcript. You with your abbreviations—everyone has a private system."

"None of us sticks to the book exactly," said the man.

"Well, I don't know about you," said Mike, "but *I* stick to the book."

"I guess I don't expect to be run over by a truck," the man said. He was smiling.

"I have nothing to hide," Uncle Mike said again. "Anybody who wants to see my notes is welcome."

"How about the pen writers?" said the man. "What sense would they make of your notes? How about Ellie Potter?"

Uncle Mike waved his hand. "Those people are living in the Stone Age. But that's different. This business of hiding things—secrets—"

Waiters took away the empty bowls and Simon's full bowl, and brought plates of roast beef, potatoes, and peas. "Well, the Stone Age!" said the man. "Artie over there was saying *we're* living in the Stone Age, using stenotype machines, not getting ready to switch to tape recorders. That's the future, he says. People won't need to use stenotype machines at all. They'll just record everything by pushing a button."

Now Uncle Mike became extremely angry. He could not keep his voice down as he explained to the man what would be wrong with tape recorders—how they could not distinguish between street noise and the noise of voices, how they could not signal the judge to stop the proceedings if something was inaudible. "Chaos, you're talking about. That's what you want?"

At this point Simon spoke for the first time since they had sat down. "I don't know," he said slowly, and both Uncle Mike and the man turned to listen to him. Even the women turned. "I bet they could make a tape recorder work. And with what they'd save on your salaries, there could be two or three of them. If one didn't pick up the words, the other would."

"That's ridiculous!" said Mike. "Utterly infantile." At that point, though, Ellie Potter got up at the lectern to speak, and the conversation was interrupted.

The presentation and induction of officers took some time and was not interesting. Frances played with the remaining food on her plate. After a while it was carried away and cake with white icing was brought. When it was Uncle Mike's turn to be inducted, they all clapped, and then Ellie Potter gestured in their direction and said, "Mike Lewis's proud family" and Pearl and her mother, and then her father, stood up while the whole room applauded. Frances started to get up but it took her a moment to understand, and by that time almost everyone else was ready to sit down. Simon didn't stand up.

After the inductions came the introduction of the keynote speaker, a judge, by Uncle Mike. This was the reason he had wanted everyone to come. He had to make a real speech, Hilda had explained. Frances had thought he would just stand up and say the judge's name, but her mother said that was not the way it was done.

Uncle Mike talked about how much this judge had done for court reporters, how he had always understood that his reporters were human beings, how he had been willing to take a break if the reporter was tired. "You may think this simply proves that Judge Akers is a nice guy," he said. "You may think this has nothing to do with justice.

But if you do—you're mistaken!" And Uncle Mike glared around the banquet hall.

He had a card with notes on it, and every now and then he looked at it, but Frances could see that on the whole he was making up what he said as he talked, and he was talking very much the way he did when he came to their house and talked to her father on Sundays.

"Why, it's the essence of justice," he said, sounding angry, though he was praising Judge Akers. "It's justice not only to the poor wretch who's taking down verbatim what's being said at maybe two hundred words a minute when people get mad and talk fast"—here there was a little laughter—"but it's justice to the plaintiff and the defendant as well. Because Judge Akers knows that if the transcript isn't accurate, there may not *be* much justice, and he knows we're human. And you know what?" he said, and here he looked carefully around the room. "Being human may mean needing a break every now and then. It may mean having to go to the john every now and then." More laughter. "Which, I admit, is not true of these tape recorders some people want to replace us with." He looked around shrewdly. "I have never heard of a tape recorder that needed to visit the john."

Frances thought it was taking him awfully long, and the audience looked uncomfortable, too. "You have to realize," Uncle Mike was saying, "that it takes a human being to get things right. A machine doesn't know—" and here his voice, which had softened slightly, got louder and harsher, even sarcastic, and he seemed to be looking at Simon. "A machine doesn't know when someone is mumbling. A machine doesn't know when to call in an interpreter, because the witness has just lapsed into a foreign language. There's a lot a machine doesn't know—but people around here, who should know better—

why, even members of my own family—you'd think your own family could comprehend—"

The sentence got lost. He couldn't seem to remember how it had begun, and it ended with a mumble. Frances was embarrassed and looked at her plate. In a moment something happened—some gesture, and then Judge Akers was advancing to the microphone, flushed and nodding in many directions—a small, dapper man—as if *nothing* had happened, and perhaps nothing had happened, maybe only Frances thought something had happened.

Simon stood up and walked out of the room. She supposed he was going to the bathroom, and she thought that if she had had to go, no matter how badly, she would have waited, rather than stand up just as the judge was being introduced, and rather than go to the bathroom just after Uncle Mike had said all that about going to the bathroom, which Frances wished he had skipped anyway. She didn't listen to the judge's speech. She was restless. Next to her, Uncle Mike, who had come back to their table as Simon walked away, looked hot and red.

Simon did not come back. By the time the judge finished talking, Aunt Pearl was whispering to Hilda, and then she sent Uncle Mike to look in the men's room. Uncle Mike left, looking irritated, but he came running back a few minutes later. Now people were drinking coffee or moving around and talking. Music was playing and a few couples were dancing. Miss Potter was talking heartily to Judge Akers. They both glanced at Uncle Mike when he came running, but he ignored them. "He's not there," he said to Aunt Pearl. Aunt Pearl said, "Did you really check?"

But Mike just said, "I'm going to look around the building."

Hilda pulled on Nathan's sleeve. "Mike's worried, go with him," she said, but Frances's father was talking to someone and it took him a moment to understand. By that time Uncle Mike had rushed out of the room again. Hilda explained once more, and Nathan followed Mike.

Time passed and the ballroom began to empty. Ellie Potter, looking worried, came over to talk to Frances's mother. A man came in and spoke to both of them. Frances heard him say he was the hotel manager. Uncle Mike had gone into the kitchens and had a fight with a cook. Hilda left the room with the manager. Now nobody was in the ballroom but Aunt Pearl—who said they should wait in case Simon came back—Frances, and Ellie Potter. Aunt Pearl held Frances's hand as if Frances were three years old, or as if the room were dark and they might lose each other. The room did seem larger than it had before, and their feet made loud sounds on the wooden floor when they moved. "My husband doesn't realize—" Aunt Pearl said to Ellie Potter.

"Of course not," said Miss Potter, but Frances could tell that she didn't know what Aunt Pearl was talking about. She thought of telling Miss Potter that Simon had run away at the lake and no harm had come to him. She could remind her aunt that this had happened. But there, they'd been in a little town of identical cabins, where if you went anywhere among them, or in the scraps of woods surrounding them, you were in your own yard, you had not *left*. This ballroom was not theirs, and the hotel was even less theirs. She didn't like to think that Simon might be outside in the city.

Finally they left the ballroom. Ellie Potter seemed to want to go home, but she went with them as far as the lobby and stood with them some more. They put on their coats. At last the manager came to the lobby with Hilda, Mike, and Nathan. The manager was reassuring Hilda, and she was impatient with him. "You certainly *don't* know he's all right," she was saying. Nathan looked so sad Frances wanted to put her arms around him. She wondered whether he had somehow learned bad news and was trying to think how to break it to them. The manager had called the police, and now a detective arrived and began to talk to the adults. Frances hoped he would talk to her but he didn't. Finally the detective urged them to go home. The police would search. He was pretty sure Simon was not in the hotel. "Why should he hang around here?" the detective said. "Kid wants to run away, he runs *away*."

At last Ellie Potter went off to the subway, and then Frances and Aunt Pearl and Hilda left too. The men had persuaded them to go. Nathan and Mike were going to keep looking. Frances wanted to stay and help them, but of course no one would listen to her. It was very late. Aunt Pearl took Frances's hand again as they left the building. Frances pulled it away, but although Aunt Pearl didn't look down or say anything, she kept closing her hand on air like someone looking for a light-pull in the dark, and so Frances held her hand out and her aunt took it again.

Frances fell asleep on the subway. When she woke up, the rough material on the subway seat was pressing into her cheek. She remembered her book, a library book, and she was afraid she had left it in the cloakroom of the hotel, but her mother had it on her lap. Now her mother was holding Aunt Pearl by the hand, and both of them were crying.

The next day was Saturday and Frances slept late. When she woke up she remembered that there was something she'd rather not think about, then what it was. If Simon never came back she would have to make them all happy, her parents and her aunt and uncle. She would certainly fail, and that would be the end of all of them.

The apartment was quiet. She wondered if her parents had left her alone, but her mother was in the living room with a magazine in her lap, wearing her bathrobe as if she were sick. She looked up at Frances and her face seemed flattened, stretched out, with large white areas around her eyes.

"Is Daddy here?" Frances said.

"He came home and slept, then he went out again. He left early this morning."

"What time is it?"

"About ten. Go eat breakfast."

Frances ate a bowl of Rice Krispies. She ate quickly. Then she went to her room and got dressed and made her bed. After that she didn't know what to do. On Saturday mornings her mother sometimes did the shopping, and Frances went along. Sometimes they went shopping for clothes. She thought it would be all right to read, and she went back to the living room to see what her mother was doing. Her mother had gone into the bathroom. The bathroom door was closed and Frances heard the sound of the shower.

Frances went into her parents' bedroom, looking for her library book. Her mother had had it on her lap in the subway, and she must have brought it home. Maybe she carried it into her bedroom and put it down on her dresser. The bed was unmade, and on the chair were her mother's clothes from the night before, the dress and slip and underwear. Her mother's dress-up shoes were near the chair. Frances didn't see the book. She could still hear the shower. She opened the door of the closet, though there was no reason for her mother to have put the library book into the closet. On the closet floor were shoes. Her father's black shoes had not been put back on their shoe trees. The shoe trees were on the floor of the closet, but his shoes were not. He'd worn his black shoes the night before, and they were on the bedroom floor. He must have put on his brown shoes this morning.

Probably it would be all right if Frances put her father's shoes back on the shoe trees. She liked the shoe trees, which had heavy, solid wooden feet—half feet. Once they were inside the shoes, a shiny steel bar slid satisfyingly into place. After she'd put the shoes away, she thought her mother might mind her being in the bedroom, so she took them out again and put them back where they had been.

She opened the top drawer of her mother's dresser. The drawer was heavy but moved more easily than her own drawers, which stuck. She felt the pile of underwear in the drawer, as if the book might be under it. Then she closed this drawer and opened the bottom one, which was filled with old things, old sweaters and blouses. The drawer might contain some clue her mother had forgotten. She would take the clue out and show it to her mother, and her mother would suddenly understand where Simon would go when he was upset.

Under the sweaters, in the back, was an old white paper bag that was too big for what was inside it and was rolled around it. Frances thought she had better take it to her own room. Her mother was coming out of the bathroom when Frances passed with the bag in her hand, and she held it close to her body, on the side away from her mother, as they passed in the hall. They looked at each other but didn't speak. Frances almost said hello.

She went into her room and sat down on the bed. She heard her mother go into her own bedroom. Someone had written on the white bag in pencil—it was her mother's writing. It was hard to read. "Racket." It looked like the word *racket*. Inside was a pair of baby's shoes.

The shoes were white. They must have been her own. They would have come up on her ankles. They had white shoelaces. Frances turned the shoes over and over again. She didn't see how the shoes could help find Simon, and she didn't think she ought to ask her mother about them. She put the shoes back into the bag. They would be one of Frances's treasures. She didn't have other treasures that she could recall, but there were probably some things. She put the bag under her pillow. She felt as if a great deal of time had passed, but when she went back to the living room, it was only twenty to eleven. She saw her library book on the sofa along with her mother's coat. Of course that was where her mother would leave it. She could take the book and read. Maybe she should offer to go to the store for her mother. Her mother hardly ever sent her to the store. It seemed like something someone in a book might do, someone who had had a tragedy.

She sat down and began to read. When her mother came out of the bedroom, she did offer to go to the store and her mother accepted. "I don't want to go out in case of the phone," her mother said.

She asked Frances to get a few things—bread and canned soup—

and gave her the money. Frances took her coat and went down to the street. It was drizzling. She had a kerchief in her pocket and she tied it over her head. On the way to the store, she looked at everyone she passed, looking for Simon or for her father coming home with news. She wondered whether people passing knew about Simon. Maybe this was important news that had been on the radio or in the newspaper.

She didn't know why Simon had run away, if that was what had happened—if he had not been murdered in the men's room, for example. She didn't know exactly why, that is, but she thought running away would be cool and fresh and delicious, and as she walked, she raised both arms, her hand closed around the money, as if a breeze might lift her up. It would be a relief to run away. That was why Simon had done it. If a reporter asked, that was what she'd say. When she reached the candy store at the corner she looked at the papers, but of course none of the headlines was about Simon.

At home her mother had washed the breakfast dishes. There seemed to be nothing to do. Frances couldn't remember what she or her mother ordinarily did on Saturdays if they didn't go shopping. She could do her homework, but she usually waited until Sunday afternoon.

"I want to go look for Simon," she said.

"I don't think that's a good idea," said her mother.

She did some of her homework and asked her mother if she could go over to her friend Lydia's house, and her mother, who sounded tired, said that would be fine. It might be interesting to show the baby shoes to Lydia, and she went to her room, took them out of the paper bag, wrapped them in her kerchief, and put them into her coat pocket. On her way out of the building she saw that there was mail in their box in the lobby, and she returned to their apartment for the mailbox key. It felt useful to bring in the mail, even though there couldn't be anything about Simon's disappearance. The other day when she had brought the mail up for her mother, there had been a letter to her father from the Board of Education. Her mother had said, "I hope this isn't what I think."

"What do you think?" Frances said. Her father often got letters from the Board of Education.

Her mother had opened it. "Yes," she said.

"What is it?"

Her mother didn't answer and turned away, then turned back and said, "They've set a date for—well, it's like a hearing."

"What kind of hearing?"

"You remember," said her mother. "I told you." Frances didn't remember, and then she did.

"Well, he'll just explain to them, won't he?" she said.

"I suppose so," said her mother.

Today the mail was of no interest. Frances remained standing in her coat while her mother opened the letters, and then she finally did leave, walking down the steps and through the lobby. The banisters became larger on the way down to the first floor. At the bottom of the stairs, the banister was quite large and made of marble, with a big marble newel post. Frances always ran her hand over the banister and then up the newel post.

The lobby floor was tiled in a pattern. Sometimes, to leave the building, Frances walked entirely on dark tiles, first diagonally, then straight, then diagonally again, ending near the mat in front of the door, but today she just crossed the floor and went out.

Lydia lived three blocks away. "She's in her room," Lydia's mother said. She didn't say hello. Frances's mother, who didn't like Lydia's family, would have greeted a visiting child.

Lydia was sitting on her bedroom floor in front of her dresser. The bottom drawer was open and everything she owned seemed to have been dumped out. She looked up. She was sitting cross-legged and she looked to Frances like a pixie. She was skinny, and all she needed was a pointed cap.

"What are you doing?" Frances asked.

"Greetings, noble friend," said Lydia. Her voice always squeaked a little. She made Frances feel large. Frances took off her coat and sat down on the floor. "I'm folding these things. Everything is a mess."

"Can I help?"

"If you want." Lydia was making piles. Some of her clothes no longer fit, but she wanted to keep them. Her mother wanted her to clean out her drawers, which were so full it was impossible to find anything. "She threatened me," Lydia said solemnly. But everything Lydia said was a bit of a joke.

When Frances talked to Lydia she found that she too talked in small jokes. She wasn't sure how it happened. "There's been a disappearance," she said now, thinking that she would regret her tone if Simon turned out to be dead.

"A mystery. Speak."

"My beloved cousin," said Frances.

"Simon the Great. Not again," Lydia said. She had heard about Simon's night out during the summer. She had speculated on where he had gone and what he might have done. Lydia thought Simon had probably been conducting a black mass, sacrificing animals he caught in the woods. "Was there a full moon?" she'd asked.

Now Frances told her about Simon's disappearance from Uncle Mike's banquet, and Lydia was so interested she forgot to fold underwear. She lay down on her back on top of her clothes. Frances lay down next to her. She was lying on sweaters and underpants, with socks mixed in, looking at the ceiling.

"Do you think he was kidnapped?" Lydia asked. She mentioned the Lindbergh baby and other kidnappings. One of them, she said, involved a Jewish child. "And you're Jewish," she concluded.

"Why would someone kidnap Simon?" Frances asked. They were not rich. Her uncle would have trouble paying a ransom.

"Blackmail," said Lydia. "Maybe it's to get your father to confess."

"Confess what?"

"Nothing."

"What did you mean, though? What would he confess?" She wondered if Lydia could know about the notice from the Board of Education, but there was no way she could know.

"I didn't mean anything."

"You must have meant *something*." Frances was upset now, but Lydia's voice changed when she spoke again.

"Maybe your father is a *spy*," she said, drawing out her words, whispering. Of course it was all a joke. "Maybe in his youth, he was—"

"A pirate," said Frances. She didn't want to think about spies—like the Rosenbergs—even if it was a joke.

"A pirate. Precisely. No, a gangster."

Frances folded her hands behind her head. "I don't think he'll talk," she said, tentatively enjoying herself again.

"He'll have to," said Lydia. "They'll begin sending Simon's fingers and toes, one by one. Little packages," she said. "Little bloody packages."

Frances didn't love Simon much but she didn't think she should let Lydia go this far. The little packages reminded her of the wrapped-up shoes. "Do you want to see something I found?" she said.

"What?" Lydia sat up.

"You won't tell?"

"Hope to die."

Frances explained that she had been looking for clues to Simon's disappearance in her mother's drawers. Lydia nodded. Frances took the little parcel from her coat pocket. It looked sweet, wrapped in her green and orange kerchief, and for a moment she was sorry she was going to show the shoes to Lydia. Then she carefully unwrapped the kerchief.

"Baby shoes," said Lydia. She seemed disappointed.

"The mystery is," said Frances, "why would my mother keep my old baby shoes in a paper bag under her sweaters? And—get this—it said 'Racket' on it."

"Racket?"

"That's right."

"That doesn't make sense."

"Precisely."

"They weren't yours, dummy," said Lydia. "They belonged to a murdered child. Racketeers got him."

"But who?" said Frances, considering whether this idea had potential. She wasn't sure what racketeers were.

"We must find out. It will be our task," Lydia said. "These will be the Official Shoes. Whoever has them must find out the murderer. Probably the same person has murdered Simon."

"Do you think so?" said Frances in an ordinary voice.

Lydia spoke slightly more artificially than usual, as if to make a point. "There is, my dear, no telling."

"You are right," said Frances, joking again, so Lydia would know she understood.

"Where shall we keep the shoes?" said Lydia.

"I'm keeping them under my pillow."

"Foolish. They'll be found. Hurry, there's no time to lose." She stuffed the clothes back into the drawers while Frances watched. Then they left the bedroom and Lydia went for her coat. "Where are you going?" came her mother's voice.

"Out to play."

"What do you mean? It's raining. And you didn't straighten up your dresser."

"I'm almost done," said Lydia, winking at Frances.

"You better be."

"I will be beaten," said Lydia to Frances in a low voice, "but we must do our duty at any cost."

"She won't really beat you, will she?" said Frances, as they left.

"She'll slap my face," said Lydia, demonstrating on herself. "But we must find a proper place for these sacred shoes."

They left the house and began to walk toward Prospect Park. Now it was really raining. They kept their hands in their pockets and their heads down. Frances clutched the shoes inside her coat pocket. "Conceal the evidence at all costs," said Lydia when a man passed them.

In the park they took quite some time deciding what to do. No one was there; the rain was steady. A woman with a dog walked along the path near the lake. They followed her at a distance and observed her, but she was nondescript. Finally Lydia drew Frances into a small grove. Some of the tree roots came above the ground. At the back of one tree, two roots ran along the ground a few inches apart. They emerged from a bulbous knob and disappeared into the earth after a couple of yards. "This is the place," Lydia said. They found a stick and took turns digging a hole right at the fork below the knob. Frances insisted that they make it deeper than was necessary. She hated to give up the kerchief, which she often wore. Finally Lydia suggested a sock, and Frances sat down on the wet ground, took off one shoe and her sock, and put the baby shoes into the sock. They stuffed the little package into the hole as far as it would go and covered it with dirt. Frances's foot was cold without a sock. Her shoe was wet. Lydia sprinkled dead leaves over the roots and they walked away. No one was nearby.

"We will meet at the root of the Great Tree in a week, precisely at midnight," said Lydia. "Then we can dig up the shoes and decide whether to take action." Frances knew she didn't really mean midnight. She didn't know what action they could take, but something would occur to them. They walked to Frances's house together. Frances wanted to go in and put on dry socks. Lydia went home alone. "I don't think my mother would like it if I had company," Frances said.

Her father had come home. He was drinking a cup of coffee and talking to her mother. "Did you find Simon?" Frances said, opening the apartment door.

"How can we find him?" he said. "A boy in New York! There are a million boys in New York." He wiped his lips and looked at her mother. "I can't tell you how many times I *saw* him—thought I saw him."

"You walked around near the hotel?" Hilda said.

"We did that at first. Then we came here and walked around here. We searched the schoolyard and talked to every kid we saw. We rang doorbells, but Mike doesn't really know who his friends are."

"Pearl won't come here."

"I know."

"And she won't let me call her. She says when the phone rings, she thinks it's Simon, and she can't bear it when it's only me."

"Why didn't you go there?" Nathan said.

Her mother looked at Frances. "I could stay here by myself," Frances said. "In case the phone rings. *I* won't run away." She ought to have thought of that . . . she shouldn't have been sneaking around in the park while her mother was worrying alone.

"Maybe tomorrow," said her mother. "If he doesn't come home. Frances, are you wearing only one sock?"

"The other got wet," she said, "so I took it off." She hurried into her bedroom.

The next day, Uncle Mike came to the house to call for Nathan. "Where are you going to look today?" said Frances.

Mike just looked at her. "Try the Forty-second Street library," she said, but not in a loud voice, and she was pretty sure he didn't hear her. Once she had gone to the library on a class trip, and she'd wanted to run away from the class and stay there.

Her father was shaving. Uncle Mike would not sit down. He barely spoke to her mother. When her father came out of the bathroom, she saw Uncle Mike look at him and she knew how Mike must have looked when he was a little boy.

It had stopped raining. Her father put on his coat. "Pearl says, if you'd come—" said Mike to her mother.

"Of course," said her mother, and her cheeks reddened. "Frances can stay here. Frances can answer the phone if it rings."

She knew her father was uneasy about leaving her alone. Maybe he thought she would be kidnapped, too. The men left. Her mother was still in her bathrobe, and now she went to get dressed. Frances followed her into the bedroom. Her mother put on her panties under her nightgown and worked her girdle on, but then she took her nightgown off and Frances could see her breasts. "Did you want two children?" she said.

"What?"

"Two children. Did you want two children?"

Her mother had turned to put on her brassiere, and now she reached behind herself to fasten it. "I love children," she said, not harshly. Frances was surprised that her mother said that, although she thought it was true that her mother liked children. Her mother was nicer to Lydia than Lydia's mother was to her.

"You stopped with me," said Frances.

"That's right," said her mother. Frances couldn't think what to say next.

Her mother put on her slip, and then sat down on the bed. She put on her stockings. She rolled each of them carefully, then unrolled it up her leg, smoothing it, holding her fingernails out of the way just as if Simon were not lost. She pulled up her slip and stood for a moment to fasten the garters in the tops of the stockings. She looked over each shoulder to check the seams. Then she sat down again instead of walking over to put on her blouse. She was wearing only her slip, and Frances looked at her mother's heavy arms, which looked girlish even though they were fat. The wrists and hands were small.

"Frances, you know there was another baby, don't you?" her mother said. Her voice was low and Frances thought she should not have asked her mother about children. Frances wanted the conversation to be over.

"Yes," she said, though she didn't really know. She remembered that her mother had said she'd gotten fat when she was pregnant the first time, so there had to be a second time.

"Girls your age know everything," said her mother. "I knew you knew." She was speaking very quietly.

"I don't know everything," said Frances.

"It's all right," her mother said. "It's not a secret." She stood up and put on her blouse and skirt. Frances was afraid she wasn't going to speak again. "So," she said, more brightly, "I once had another baby. She was born a long time before I had you, but she died."

Frances wanted to know how the baby had died, but she didn't think she ought to ask. Maybe she would ask another time. This must be the miscarriage Simon had spoken of. Of course her mother had kept the shoes she'd bought for that baby. Maybe she'd bought clothes, too, not just shoes. People did that—they bought things for a baby before it was born.

"Was she born dead?" Frances said.

"Oh, no," said her mother. She must have died in the hospital, then, Frances thought, just after she was born.

Now Hilda was all dressed. "I don't know why I talked about this today," she said. "We have enough trouble to think about. Don't worry about that baby. It was a long time ago."

Frances thought that if she could only ask the right question, she could find out what she needed to know, but she didn't have time to think. She didn't know what it was she needed to know. She could imagine a tiny baby, dressed in white—she'd seen that in a book or someplace. Maybe they had buried her in white. "Simon once told me you had a miscarriage," she said. She was embarrassed, because it was a private thing about her mother, because she wasn't sure how a miscarriage happened, but also because it was the only time she and Simon had ever talked that way.

"No," said her mother. "Did Aunt Pearl tell him that?"

"I don't know."

"He picks up all sorts of things. You never know what's coming next," her mother said affectionately, as if Simon had not done what he had done that weekend, as if the things he did weren't important.

"Maybe I forgot what he said," Frances said.

Her mother turned and looked at her, her hand resting on her dresser. "Do you and Simon talk a lot?" she said.

"No."

"I mean, he never said anything about running away, or where he'd go?"

"No," said Frances, and at once she thought, for the second time, that it was bad for all of them that Simon had run away. She had been a little proud of him, a little excited. She had been wondering whether her classmates would know on Monday what had happened, whether the teachers would ask her questions, or whether she might have to stay home, as if it were a Jewish holiday. But her mother turned and looked at her as she left the room, and suddenly Frances almost *was* her mother and knew how it would be to be looking at herself, a girl, to be wearing nylon stockings, facing the window, not the door, and feeling gray and terrible about Simon, tattered and frightened.

Soon her mother left. Frances promised to stay indoors and not to open the door to anybody. "What will you do?" her mother asked.

"I have homework."

Frances was alone for many hours. She had never been alone for so long before. When her parents had left her previously, they'd always returned before she finished whatever it was she was doing when they left. Now she had time to think. The apartment felt different, empty of her parents. When her mother left, she walked through all the rooms and looked in the closets. She looked behind the shower curtain into the bathtub. For a second she thought she might find Simon lying in the tub, laughing at her for taking so long to find him—or drowned.

She turned on the radio and then the television, but was unable to find a program she liked. Finally she took out her homework and began to work at the kitchen table. It didn't take long, even though she did it slowly.

For lunch she made herself a sandwich. She found some tuna fish salad in the refrigerator and toasted the bread, but she burned it and had to scrape off the black parts. She was confused. She thought she'd done it just the way her mother did, on Medium Dark, but it was burned. She found herself crying as she scraped the bread with a knife, getting black crumbs all over the tablecloth. It was bad that she could cry over burning the bread but not about Simon. She didn't like toast that had been burned. The sandwich didn't taste good, even though she scraped for a long time.

After lunch, time went even more slowly. She cleaned up the kitchen to give herself something to do and to keep her parents from knowing that she'd burned the toast. She had a glass of milk and some cookies. After a while she sat in the living room, but she had finished her library book and she didn't know what to read. It was the last of the books she'd taken out that week.

She went into her room, then into her parents' bedroom, and lay down on their bed. She was cold, so she pulled the bedspread around her on both sides like a blanket. She knew she should take off her shoes, but she didn't; she just held her feet upright so the soles didn't touch the bed. She thought that Simon could have spent Saturday in a library, but that libraries were closed on Sunday. It was not raining. He could be outdoors somewhere, but she didn't know where he could have gone at night. She wondered whether you could sneak into a department store and sleep in the beds at night. Maybe they had night watchmen who would discover you and have you arrested. Probably they did. Frances was thinking about that when she heard voices and she saw her father and Uncle Mike standing near the bed looking down at her. She realized that she had fallen asleep, because now she remembered dreaming that she was at school. Someone—the teacher or the principal—told her that her mother had come for her, and Frances had searched the school in increasing anxiety, looking for her mother. Finally she saw her mother through a glass panel in a classroom door. It was the kindergarten room, and some small kindergarten chairs had been arranged in a row for several mothers, who sat and watched the children. The children held hands and walked in a circle. It was like Open School Week, but Frances's mother was watching the kindergarten children. Frances was unable to get her mother's attention through the glass, and the door was locked. She knocked on the glass, but the teacher just looked up and frowned at her, and shook her head no.

Her father and Uncle Mike were standing near the bed and looking at her, and they were both smiling just a little. She had never noticed how alike their smiles were. Both their mouths stretched sideways when they smiled, but did not turn up. "Did you find Simon?" she said.

"No," said her father, and he looked sad again. Uncle Mike shook his head. Yet she felt that they had found something. They had found her, and that seemed to please them, but only a little—their smiles were tiny smiles. It was not that they had stopped caring about Simon. They reminded her of her mother and Aunt Pearl, and so she knew that they had not been fighting. She imagined them walking the streets, over and over again, searching, growing tired, falling against each other and leaning on each other's shoulders.

They were standing close together, that was it. And now her father put his hand on his brother's shoulder. Then the phone rang. Frances got off the bed. The dark pink bedspread, quilted satin, was rumpled, and she tried to straighten it. Her father and uncle had gone to the phone, and she heard her father's voice say, "Hello?" and then, "He is? He's there? Mike, he's there. Thank God, thank God. Is he all right? You're sure? Here, Pearl, talk to Michael," and when she hurried into the living room, her father was sobbing and he took both her hands in his. "He's all right, baby," he said.

"A friend?" Uncle Mike was saying. "Sammy? He never mentioned a Sammy. Who knew there was a Sammy? This Sammy, did he talk him into this? No, no, don't worry." He was shaking his head, denying what Pearl was saying. "I'm not going to do a thing, Pearlie, of course I wouldn't hurt him. I just got him back. You think I'm going to do something to him? I'll be right there. I'll be home right away."

He hung up the phone and turned to Frances and her father, who were standing together. Nathan had his arm around Frances's shoulders. "I can't believe this," Mike said. Frances thought he was going to give her father a hug and a kiss, because he stepped forward and raised his arms. But he just touched the sides of their heads, both at the same time, her father's and hers. He hadn't taken his coat off. It hung open as he touched their hair, just above their ears, and Frances felt his fingers shake. Buttoning his coat awkwardly—Frances thought he might have buttoned it wrong—Mike turned and let himself out of the apartment.

3 &

PEARL SUTTER TOOK A SUMMER JOB AT A DILAPIDATED HOTEL
in the Adirondacks where a cousin used to work. Her cousin said
she'd have to answer the phone and take reservations. Pearl was also
supposed to keep track of the band that played on weekends and
communicate with the cab service that brought guests from the bus
station. Pearl knew nothing of the hotel business. Twice she forgot
to arrange for guests to be picked up, but it didn't matter. It was
1935 and there were few guests at all. She knew she was incompetent,
and she didn't complain when the manager, red-faced, told her that
business was so poor he'd have to cut her pay.

Pearl didn't mind the hotel, which was simple and quiet, on the
edge of a lake in pine woods. Her cousin and the cousin's new
husband had driven her there in June and she didn't know where she

was. She liked being on her own. Up to now she'd lived at home and worked in her father's candy store, part-time when she was a girl, full-time after she dropped out of Hunter College in her sophomore year. Now her younger brother was working in the store, and he'd taken to it as Pearl never had, rearranging the candy counter and ordering more magazines. Her father didn't need her, and Pearl, who tried not to think about the end of the summer, preferred being incompetent in the hotel to being incompetent in the store. Other than not knowing what she'd do in September, her main problem was hairpins. She'd forgotten to bring any.

Pearl was a blonde, and she hadn't bobbed her hair but wore it in a thick braid which she twisted into a crown at the back of her head. It had given her a certain distinction in college, where everyone else was determined to be modern. Pearl liked feeling queenly, though she knew it put people off. Here at the hotel, she didn't make friends with the girls who cleaned the rooms and waited on tables, though they were about her age and her sort. She didn't think she was better than they were, but she knew she looked as if she thought that.

It took twenty gold-colored hairpins to secure the braid properly, and Pearl had learned to do it swiftly—her left hand supporting the braid while her right hand poked pins around it at even intervals—generally working by feel because she couldn't see the back of her head unless she had two mirrors. Of course, occasionally a hairpin fell out and got lost. At home she had a good supply, but when she'd come to the hotel, she'd forgotten her little tin box, and had only the twenty hairpins she wore the day of the trip. One must have been lost in her cousin's car: even the next morning, there were only nineteen. She'd written to her mother, but no hairpins had arrived.

Now, after three and a half weeks, having taken meticulous care, Pearl had fifteen hairpins. She didn't see how she could get through the summer this way. She had Thursday afternoons off, and she could have bought more, but she had no way to get to town. Sometimes the chambermaids got rides with friends, but she didn't know any of them well and hated to ask. One afternoon she walked to a store at a crossroads, but couldn't find hairpins in the small stock, mostly bread and milk.

Now she was at the hotel desk on a hot Wednesday afternoon when nobody was likely to come through and need anything. She was reading aloud from a newspaper that was several days old to Mike Lewis, the saxophonist in the band. She was reading an account of a baseball game and Mike was taking down what she said in shorthand, writing rapidly in a notebook. He said he needed all the practice he could get because he was hoping to qualify for a job as a shorthand reporter for the Manhattan district attorney's office. At present he worked in a music store when he wasn't here and wasn't taking college courses at night.

"What made you take up shorthand?" Pearl asked.

"I can't make a living playing the saxophone, can I?" said Mike. The band was now playing for room and board. They were students at City College, glad to be out of the city for the summer. Mike's father was dead and he lived with his mother, and Pearl thought maybe he didn't get along with her.

"You're good at shorthand," she said, looking at his notes, which were unintelligible to her but looked impressive.

"No, I'm not good yet."

The small lobby with its knotty pine walls was hot, and Pearl went out from behind the desk to open the door. She propped it open with a rock that was kept just outside for this purpose. She could smell the pine trees when the door was open.

"You dropped something," said Mike.

Pearl felt herself blush and looked where he pointed. Of course it was a hairpin. She bent down for it, wiped it on a scrap of paper, and stuck it back into her hair. The trouble was that fifteen hairpins weren't enough to hold the weight of the braid, and as it pulled away from her head, it loosened them.

"They must not pay you much," said Mike, "if you have to scrape those things off the floor."

"They *don't* pay me much," said Pearl. She thought that was rude of him, although she didn't mind. But of course she could afford hairpins. "There's no place to buy them," she said.

"I thought girls were born with a lifetime supply."

"At home I have an oak chest with forty thousand," said Pearl, "but I forgot it. I could buy some, but I never get to town."

"I go to town," said Mike. "Come with me. When's your day off?"

"Tomorrow," said Pearl. She thought she'd like to go to town with Mike. He was good-looking—young, slouchy, always with a cigarette in his fingers or something else: his pencil for taking down shorthand, a leaf, a twig. His hair fell into his eyes and he had a habit of blowing hard upward, as if he thought that would be the same as combing it. She'd been aware of him. He looked like the least friendly of the band members, but he was the only one who talked to her. He was abrupt, that was all. The other two stood if she entered a room— Mike didn't—but they had nothing to say. "I didn't know you had a car," she said.

"I don't. We'll hitchhike." She was a little alarmed but tried to act nonchalant, and then one of the guests came in wanting the canoe paddles, which were kept behind the desk. Mike stood to the side while she handed them over, and she found herself glancing to see if he noticed when she ran her hand over her hair, checking, after she bent down. He was looking at her, not smiling, and she couldn't tell what he was thinking.

The next afternoon Mike said it would be easier to get a ride if the drivers didn't know he was there. "A girl alone," he said. He waited behind a bush, and with some embarrassment she stuck her thumb out. The first car slowed for her, and Mike jumped out from behind the bush and got into the back seat. "Well, I didn't see *you,* young man," said the driver, an older man, but Pearl thought he'd probably have stopped no matter who was waiting. He talked all the way into town. He was the owner of a dry goods store in Glens Falls. "Now, that's a nice piece of goods, that skirt you're wearing," he said to Pearl. "I can see quality." It was a narrow gored skirt in dark green and Pearl wondered whether Mike had noticed it.

The man dropped them off at a drugstore in town ("My girl has to pick up some hairpins," said Mike), but it carried hairpins only in black. "They'd look like ants in my hair, going around my braid," Pearl said. Mike laughed at her but accompanied her down Main Street until they found a second drugstore, and there hairpins came in gold as well as black. "Fourteen carat," said Mike. "No doubt about it."

She liked being teased. "I'll buy you an ice cream cone," he said then, and they walked back to the first drugstore, which had a fountain. He paid for the cones and then, without talking about whether

64

they were going to do it, they walked all the way back to the hotel, scuffing their feet in the brown pine needles at the edge of the road, or walking on the road itself when the brush came right down to it. A few cars passed them, but they didn't try to flag them down. After his cone was gone, Mike smoked, or he broke off a twig and peeled it as he walked.

That night Pearl had a blister and her feet ached. She soaked them in Epsom salts, which she found in the bathroom she shared with the manager and his wife and the chambermaids. She sat on her bed with her feet in an enamel basin, looking out the window and watching the light sift away from the trees and from the lake, which she could just glimpse from her room. She took down her hair, putting her hairpins one by one into an ashtray on her dresser—still careful, though now she had plenty, as though the hairpins were small souvenirs of the day.

Mike liked to take walks, and he began to show up when Pearl was just ready to leave the desk at night. They'd walk partway to town, slapping at mosquitoes. As the summer progressed it began to be dark by the time they'd gone a little way, but they walked a bit anyway, facing traffic, turning their faces away from the headlights when, every once in a while, a car came along. Or they went down to the lake. He stood with his arm around her, not saying much. Then he walked her to the main building of the hotel, where she lived. The band lived in a cottage on the grounds. He walked her home three times before he ever kissed her, but once he began, he kissed her every night.

On weekends she'd sit alone at a table in the lounge, listening to the band. She'd never paid attention to jazz before and at first she didn't like it. It seemed disreputable: it made her sad in a way that scared her. Mike said he didn't know what she meant, jazz was beautiful, and after a while she began to pick out songs she liked, at first those that seemed most like what she called "just plain songs." Gradually she began to like others, the songs with low, wailing notes. It surprised her when Mike played these songs. It was like hearing him speak in a foreign language, and sometimes she imagined that if she could read his shorthand notes, they would also sound like great cries and strange muted calls.

At the end of the summer Mike said they should get married. "What else will you do?" he asked bluntly, when she claimed to be astonished, although she'd had the same idea herself.

"I could go home and look for a job," she said. "We can't afford to get married."

"You don't want to go home."

"No." Her father would make her work in the candy store, and make her brother, who belonged there, look for a job. Pearl thrust her feet out in front of her and noticed how the sun made patterns on her open-toed shoes. She and Mike were sitting on the wooden steps of the cottage where he'd been living all summer with the other musicians. They'd been talking in low voices because the other two men were asleep.

"*You'll* be fine in September, whatever we do," said Pearl. The owner of the music store had said he might give Mike a full-time job in September. And maybe he'd get the stenography job. As she spoke she heard one of the other musicians walking around, and then the pianist came out, carrying a towel. He was on his way to the showers, which were in a small wooden building closer to the main house.

"Somebody else is going to grab you," Mike said gruffly. It was the nearest he'd come to a declaration of love. "Some guy will come along." As she watched the pianist, whose name was Moe, walk up the hill to the showers, Pearl wondered if Mike had expected her to have other admirers, and she wondered whether Moe, who was stiffly polite with her, liked her at all. Once she'd been identified as Mike's girl, other people at the hotel had pulled back even more noticeably. The chambermaids were a tiny bit friendlier, and Pearl thought maybe they were afraid of Mike and admired her for being comfortable with him.

"Where would we live?" she said.

"We'd live with my brother and his wife until we found an apartment. You could look for a job, but meanwhile we'd have what I make."

"Your brother wouldn't mind?"

"He won't mind. We'll give him some money. You'll like his wife. You'll get along with her."

Pearl thought of the candy store. It had just one light bulb. The windows were crowded with signs sent by companies that sold syrup and malted mix. When Pearl stood at the marble counter of the soda fountain, near the cash register, she couldn't see out into the street; a large cutout blocked her way. From behind, it was just gray cardboard; in front it was the fading picture of a smiling girl and boy drinking with two straws out of the same soda. She remembered how much it irritated her that she couldn't see out the window.

"All right," she said.

On the Thursday before Labor Day, they borrowed a car and drove to New York for a marriage license. They drove all day, and then, going back, all night, because Mike had to play on Friday. The car broke down. Mike played without sleep Friday night. Labor Day weekend was the busiest time at the hotel all summer, and Pearl took it in confusedly, through tiredness and excitement. They told no one but the band members that they were going to be married. The day after Labor Day, they took the bus to New York, and then Pearl told her family. She'd mentioned Mike in her letters, but she hadn't said much. Her mother cried and tried to talk her out of it.

Pearl stayed with her family that night and the next, and they were married on Thursday, in a rabbi's study, with her parents and brother and Mike's brother and sister-in-law in attendance. Mike said it would be better to tell his mother about it after it was a done thing. Pearl's mother, though she had cried, bought food from a delicatessen and invited everyone to their apartment over the candy store after the wedding. Mike's brother, Nathan, and his wife came along, and Pearl kept her eyes on Hilda, who seemed to be looking everything over, gazing with composure at Pearl's mother and father, her brother, and the small living room with its heavy mahogany furniture.

Pearl thought it would be a privilege to live with Hilda, even for just a few weeks. Hilda was wearing a gray dress and hat, quite plain. Her hair was short, and it was arranged in dark curls around her face. She moved her head slowly, calmly, when she talked to one member of the family or another. She and Nathan were still there when Pearl and Mike left—in the rain—on their honeymoon.

They took the subway to New York and spent two nights in a

hotel. Pearl was a virgin, and she was surprised by sex. She'd imagined something more headlong: a moist, yielding sort of dissolution. This ritual felt a little violent and a little silly, both drier and, somehow, wetter than she had expected. But she liked sleeping in bed with her new husband. She woke in the night and kissed his shoulder and arm gently, careful not to waken him. She kissed him over and over again. Asleep, curled away from her, he looked like a boy.

The next day Mike took Pearl to the Central Park Zoo, even though it was still raining. There was a hurricane in Florida, and everyone was talking about how much it had rained. Later they went to the movies, to see *Anna Karenina* with Greta Garbo, and to a jazz club.

"Did you change your name?" Pearl asked Mike, on the way to Hilda and Nathan's Saturday morning. It fascinated her that her last name was now Lewis, but she'd noticed that Hilda and Nathan's name was Levenson.

"I'm not hiding the fact that I'm Jewish," Mike said. "I'll tell anybody I'm Jewish. But I don't see why I have to advertise it." So her name might have been Levenson. She wasn't sure which she liked better.

Hilda and Nathan lived in a one-bedroom apartment on Bedford Avenue in Flatbush. They had a couch in the living room that was really a single bed, and Hilda had said that if Mike and Pearl could get hold of another single bed, they could push the two together and have a double bed to sleep on. Pearl's parents said they could take the bed from Pearl's room.

As soon as Pearl and Mike arrived at the Levensons' after their two-night honeymoon, Mike and Nathan took the trolley to the

Sutters' apartment and got the bed, which they brought back on the roof of a taxi. Meanwhile Hilda made Pearl a cup of coffee and Pearl sat in the kitchen drinking it, while Hilda cleared away the breakfast things. Pearl offered to help, but Hilda shook her head. Still wearing her jacket and hat, Pearl watched her new sister-in-law. Her suitcase was in the hall, and there was a box of clothes at her parents' apartment that she had to bring sooner or later. Hilda and Nathan's apartment was small.

"You must be sorry you said we could do this," she said.

"Why should I be sorry?" said Hilda firmly.

"You're crowded already."

"I like having people around," said Hilda. "Sometimes Nathan's quiet."

"I'm not quiet," said Pearl. "I'm warning you."

"Well, neither am I," Hilda said. "I'll say when I'm sick of you."

"That's fine." Pearl even tossed her chin, as if she were bouncing a ball off it toward Hilda at the sink, as if she was sure Hilda was joking. "I'm helpful," she said. "I'll clean the bathroom. I'm not a good cook, but I'll try."

"We can clean the bathroom together," said Hilda. She poured herself a cup of coffee and sat down opposite Pearl to drink it.

"You don't take milk?" said Pearl.

"No, I like it black."

"No sugar either?"

"No."

"Oh—" said Pearl, and she laid her hands flat on the table, palms up, open. "You know what?" she said, before she knew what she was going to say, but wanting it to be pretty spectacular. "I *always wanted* a friend who drank black coffee. I never knew people like that. In high school, I wanted to know the girls like that."

Hilda looked annoyed, as if she didn't know what Pearl meant and didn't want to know, but Pearl said, "Don't worry, I'm nice, even if I talk funny." She was scared, despite this brave speech, because Hilda looked irritated. But Hilda didn't say anything and now Pearl thought that maybe she wasn't angry. Hilda was looking at her with her eyes wide and interested, very black. She was shorter than Pearl but several years older, and Pearl felt childish near her, maybe because Hilda's clothes and gestures were so simple.

"It's a nice apartment," said Pearl.

"Thank you." They stood up and toured it, and figured out where there was room for a new chest of drawers. Pearl and Mike could afford one piece of furniture. If they bought it now, they'd have something when they found their new place. It could go in an alcove in the living room—a room Pearl liked, with a dark maroon rug and checked drapes in maroon and tan. There were two easy chairs and between them was a radio. Pearl looked out the window, but the view was just the courtyard in the center of the building.

"The quiet side of the building," she said, though she was disappointed. She'd have preferred to look out at the street.

When Nathan and Mike arrived, carrying the mattress and then the box spring, Hilda and Pearl made the two beds in the living room with one sheet over them, but that night Pearl's bed moved whenever Mike turned over. Mike wanted to make love, but she was afraid Hilda and Nathan could hear them from their bedroom.

"We're *married*," Mike whispered.

She was sore after the two nights in the hotel. "Tomorrow," she whispered back. Mike tried to take her in his arms, just to hold her, but his bed shifted and the crack between the beds opened into an abyss with the sheet stretched over it. He got out and pushed the beds back together, but then he came around to her side. She giggled and claimed she was going to fall into the space, but he just said, "Well, hold on tighter, then." It was a long time before she fell asleep.

The next afternoon Nathan asked her if she liked to listen to music. He had a record collection and a good record player, and he played Beethoven's Ninth Symphony for her. Pearl was surprised when a voice began to sing, and then a whole chorus, after Nathan had stood up many times to change the record.

"What does it mean?" she said, and thought of Mike's shorthand.

Nathan shrugged, turning the record over carefully, holding it by its edges. "This is the real Germany," he said. "Better to listen to Beethoven than the bandits in charge now." He had told her he was preparing to become a teacher and he talked like one already. He seemed much older than Mike. He was comfortable with his arms and legs. Like his wife, he could sit still. Mike never could, and was always moving his hands: fiddling with something, ripping something up, lighting a cigarette. Hilda scolded him now for tearing an envelope, ripping it studiously back and forth so it turned into one long crooked strip. "Stop it, Michael," she said. "You're like a little kid." Pearl was fascinated.

Mike laughed at Hilda. "I thought you socialists were liberated from bourgeois notions about neatness. I thought you had higher things to think about."

"Not me," said Hilda. "Maybe your brother. I'm just a housewife."

Nathan frowned at them for talking during the music—now it

was a different symphony—and quietly swept Mike's trash into his hands and carried it off. "There," he said, when the music paused. "Plenty of room for socialism, a clean carpet, and Beethoven too."

Pearl liked the way he talked and she liked the music and the living room. It was starting to get dark outside, but the lamps had been on all afternoon. She felt safe in her big chair. Nathan had brought in a wooden kitchen chair for himself, and Hilda was sitting on the bed, which now took up most of the room. The warm lamplight was on Pearl's arm. She and Hilda had conferred about dinner, and Hilda had started a pot roast. Soon they'd peel the potatoes. Pearl wished she could stay home and keep house for the four of them, but she knew she had to look for a job, and then that they'd have to find an apartment. Her brother-in-law leaned over the stack of records, putting the ones he'd played back into their brown sleeves. They came in a big album that was dark red like so much else in this room.

After Pearl and Mike had been living with Hilda and Nathan for a little more than a week, Hilda said there might be a job in her office for Pearl. Pearl had been reading the want ads in the paper every morning, but she couldn't find anything that looked right. She didn't want to work in a factory, but she thought she might have to. Hilda was the bookkeeper for a small company that made women's blouses, and she said they needed a receptionist. Pearl would have to type a little, too. Pearl had taken an academic course in high school, not a commercial course, but she'd taken one year of typing as an elective. She explained to Hilda what she'd done at the hotel, and realized that she had learned something over the summer. She had learned to write things down in order and keep pieces of paper having to do with the same thing in one place. At the candy store, her father wrote on scraps of paper that he stuck under the corner of the cash register and never saw again. He didn't know how much money he had or what he ordered each time the salesmen came through. Partway through the summer, after the hotel manager had spoken sharply to Pearl for not writing something down, she had suddenly realized that it was possible to keep track of things. She had decided that must be what people learned in the commercial course, and maybe now she knew it. She was sure she could work in Hilda's office.

"There are two bosses," Hilda said. "Mr. Glynnis and Mr. Carmichael. Mr. Glynnis seems nice but I like Mr. Carmichael better, even though he seems strict."

Pearl listened eagerly. "Is Mr. Carmichael older?"

"I guess they're about the same age. Mr. Carmichael might be a few years older." She arranged for Pearl to have an interview.

Pearl had to take the subway alone to Hilda's office in downtown Manhattan because Hilda left for work early in the morning, but the bosses had said Pearl should come in at about eleven. Pearl was nervous. She was home alone for an hour when the others had gone to work. The last person she saw was Nathan, who left a little later than Hilda and Mike. He had worked in a printing plant, he'd told her, but he'd become active in the union, and now he was a full-time union organizer.

"Do you like it?" Pearl said.

"No."

"Why not?"

"I don't want a strike," said Nathan. "I'm afraid of a strike." He wanted to quit and be a teacher, and he had passed his exam and was waiting to be called from the list.

"Do you go around and make speeches?" Pearl said that morning, to keep Nathan a moment.

"No, I leave that to other people," Nathan said. "I write, and I organize meetings. Today I have to make sure the door will be open and the lights will be on for a meeting tonight. Very exciting."

"*I* think it's exciting," said Pearl loyally.

"Maybe it is," said Nathan, and he sighed and looked sorrowful, but she'd noticed that he often looked that way. "Maybe it's a great moment in history."

Pearl followed Hilda's directions and reached the right building twenty minutes early. It was on Nassau Street. She walked two blocks away and back and it was still ten minutes early. Then she crossed the street and counted the items in the window of a stationery store. When she reached one hundred, she shrugged and went across the street and into the building, whether it was early or not. The blouse company, called Bobbie's, was on the second floor, and when she'd climbed the stairs she found herself in a large room where women were sorting and folding blouses. Hilda had explained that the blouses were not made on the premises, but at a factory in Brooklyn. Here, however, they were labeled, folded, and readied for shipment to stores. "In the big season, we all have to pack," she said. "I don't mind. It's fun. Mr. Carmichael brings in delicatessen and we're there late."

At one side of the room were the offices, separated by glass partitions from the floor. The room was noisy. Pearl stood in the door way of the first office until she was noticed. She didn't see Hilda. Finally someone told her where to go, and she found Hilda, too, in an anteroom to Mr. Glynnis's and Mr. Carmichael's offices at the back of the big room. Hilda looked her over and took her in to see Mr. Carmichael. Pearl thought Hilda didn't like something about what she was wearing—or maybe she was sorry she'd suggested the interview.

"Now, can you handle yourself on the phone is the main thing?" said Mr. Carmichael, even before asking her to sit down. "Do you have a Brooklyn accent?" He didn't give Pearl a chance to answer. "Let's say I'm an impatient customer and I call up. What do you say? Ring!"

"Hello?" said Pearl, giggling and putting an imaginary receiver to her face. It was like a game.

"No. Wrong. You say, 'Bobbie's, can I help you?'"

"Bobbie's, can I help you?" said Pearl.

"Much better," said Mr. Glynnis, who had come in behind her. They had only a few more questions. They seemed pleased that she was Hilda's sister-in-law. She got the job. Riding home on the subway, she worried about whether Hilda had disapproved of her dress or her hat—whether Hilda would be ashamed of her.

"You have no idea how lucky you are," Mike said that night, although Pearl wasn't a baby and she knew she was lucky, that jobs were almost impossible to find.

Pearl started to work at Bobbie's, and she and Hilda rode there together every day and rode back home at night. Hilda introduced her to the other women in the office, and one of them showed Pearl what she was supposed to do. Pearl liked being a receptionist. She had some trouble with the switchboard but gradually she caught on.

She spent much of her time filing, which wasn't hard, and sometimes she typed letters. Mike taught her a little shorthand, and she learned to take dictation, although she was faking it, and she hid her notes —a combination of shorthand, abbreviations of her own, spelled-out words, and blanks where she'd have to remember or invent when she typed. Luckily, the letters Mr. Glynnis and Mr. Carmichael dictated were short.

Pearl had more problems at home than at work. Mike said it would be a good idea to stay with the Levensons for a few more weeks and save up some money, and he insisted that he and Nathan had talked it over and Nathan had said it was fine. They needed extra money for furniture, he pointed out. But Pearl wanted to find an apartment and move out. She thought more about not displeasing Hilda than she did about her new husband. They contributed money for food, but Pearl worried that Hilda thought they ate too much. Mike was always looking for snacks, and she thought he ate more than the rest of them put together. And Hilda wouldn't let Pearl cook. "I don't cook," she insisted. "I just put something on the stove. I don't fuss."

It was true that their meals were simple—baked potatoes, canned vegetables, some kind of meat. Sometimes Hilda made a meat loaf. One day she said she'd make beef stew, and then she went out of the room for a little while. She had a headache, she said; she'd just lie down. They'd come home from work a few minutes earlier and Pearl was tired, but she thought she ought to start the beef stew, and she began browning the meat. Hilda came into the kitchen in her bathrobe, her dark eyes flashing. "I *told* you I'd do it," she said.

"Why shouldn't I do it?"

"Look, I'm trying to rest. I have to get rid of this headache. Here

I am jumping up because I can smell the meat browning. Why can't you just leave it alone?"

Pearl was bewildered. "But I don't understand," she said, fighting tears. "Did I use the wrong pan?"

"No, you didn't use the wrong pan," Hilda said, and returned to her bedroom. Pearl turned off the light under the meat and went into the bathroom, where she laid her face on her towel and sobbed. She stayed there as long as she dared—there was no place else in the apartment where she could be alone—and when she came out, pushing the hair that had come loose off her face and trying to get her mussed braid back into place, Hilda, still in her robe, was making the beef stew.

"I'm sorry," Pearl said.

"It's all right," said Hilda. Pearl peeled potatoes and carrots and set the table. That night, in whispers, she tried to explain what had happened.

"She was just tired," Mike said.

"She doesn't like me."

"Why shouldn't she like you?"

"She hates me," Pearl insisted.

Mike was impatient with her, but she thought he was also interested. He wasn't used to people who hated each other. It was like something out of the movies. He said they could start trying to find an apartment, and from then on, they spent their weekends looking. It helped. Hilda seemed friendlier when they came back, even if they hadn't seen anything that would do at all.

Pearl didn't find out whether Hilda disliked the dress or hat she had worn to her job interview, but after a while she didn't think it was her clothes. Hilda couldn't help backing away from her at times the way some people couldn't help from shrinking if a cat brushed against them. "I'm a ninny," Pearl told herself, excusing Hilda. One night the four of them put on jazz records and danced, and when Pearl got excited, and danced fast with Mike until he stumbled away, then danced on her own with an imaginary partner, she caught Hilda looking at her and her look was not hateful or friendly either but eager, as if she wanted to *become* Pearl. Yet that night, too, Hilda grew bitter and tired. "I suppose you know enough to turn the lights out when you go to bed?" she said, going to her bedroom while Pearl was still dancing.

When they found an apartment it was only two blocks from Nathan and Hilda's place. Pearl was afraid they'd mind, but Nathan borrowed a car from a friend to help them move, and Hilda said she'd help Pearl put shelving paper in the kitchen cabinets. The apartment was on the second floor of a building with an elevator. Pearl liked the dim hallway with its armorial ornaments, and liked pushing the large round buttons to make the elevator come. The elevator didn't work until you had closed first the heavy outer door, which had a long handle, and then the inner door, made of metal strips in an accordion pattern that threatened to pinch Pearl's fingers. The first time she took Hilda there, she had to struggle to make it work. Hilda was impatient. "We could take the stairs," she said.

They took the elevator and Pearl showed Hilda the apartment, and then they put on aprons and began cleaning the kitchen cabinets. Hilda stood on the sink to clean them. She insisted it was necessary, though the apartment had just been painted. Pearl cut shelving paper. Hilda didn't look quite as formidable, perched on Pearl's new sink.

"I won't have much to put into the cupboards," Pearl said. Her mother had given her some pots and pans, and she'd received a few wedding presents. She did have *some* things.

"You'll put food up here, won't you?" said Hilda. "I think pots and pans below."

"Oh, that's right." Of course that was right. She'd have to make a shopping list. She'd never bought food herself before, except under her mother's direction—she'd never thought about what was needed.

"You're going to cook a lot," Hilda said. "Mike eats so much."

Pearl laughed and nodded. "They're so different, even though they're brothers."

"Very different."

Pearl was a little afraid of Nathan. He was older than Mike, who was older than she was, and he seemed older yet. He never lost his temper. He knew about music and kept track of world events. He listened to everything Pearl said as if he expected her to be interesting, even though she knew she wasn't. She'd asked him shyly why he was a socialist, and he'd said with a sigh that he couldn't understand why everyone wasn't, that it was only fair. "Go talk to the people in the shantytowns," he said. "Ask them how much good capitalism has done them."

Pearl said she agreed with him, that socialism was much better. Only later did she remember that her father owned a business—he was a capitalist, she supposed. But when she asked Nathan he said no, not really, Mr. Sutter was not the problem. Nathan was starting to get bald, and he combed his hair back so his bare scalp showed. When he stared at Pearl she felt extremely looked at.

Now she watched Hilda competently cleaning cupboards. Like Nathan, she looked as if she knew how things would turn out and had agreed to them. But Pearl still thought Hilda didn't like her.

"Nathan's wise," she said. "I never knew anybody before who was wise."

"No, he's not," Hilda said. "He's just pretending. He can be as dumb as anybody else."

"I'd like to see it." Pearl finished putting the shelving paper down and Hilda cleaned the stove, clucking over its condition. "You can see that they *think* they cleaned it," she said. "Now this is the sort of thing that would upset Mrs. Levenson."

Their mutual mother-in-law now there was a person who made Pearl nervous. They had all gone to see her a few days after the wedding. Mrs. Levenson was a small woman with dark gray hair, not white or black, who hugged herself as if she was cold, or as if she thought somebody wanted to take away her clothes.

"It's open," she called when they rang the doorbell, and they found her sitting in the kitchen, where Nathan and Mike both bent to kiss her. Hilda kissed her too, and Pearl thought maybe she ought to, but they hadn't been introduced yet. The four of them stood around the old lady in the tiny kitchen, where there weren't enough chairs for them. Finally Hilda said, "Mom, come sit in the living room," and urged Mrs. Levenson along.

"There's something to celebrate?" said Mrs. Levenson

"You know there is, Mama," said Nathan quietly. "You know Mike got married. This is Pearl, your new daughter-in-law."

"A hard name to say," said Mrs. Levenson, but then she got up and shuffled once more into the kitchen. She was gone for a long time, but came back with a glass dish of candy and another of dried fruit. "You like prunes?" she said to Pearl.

"A little," said Pearl, who didn't like prunes.

"Very good for you," said the old woman. "Take."

Pearl thought the prune was like the old lady herself, hard and wrinkled. When they left she turned to Hilda for support, but Hilda was saying that her mother-in-law was looking better than the last time they'd been there. Finally Pearl had reached for Mike and leaned on his shoulder and even wept a bit. Mike patted her back. "You did fine," he said.

Now Pearl had decided it would be a good idea to invite Mrs. Levenson for dinner in the new apartment. She was glad Hilda was making the stove acceptable. Sometimes she felt that Hilda was taking her on, the way a weary but conscientious teacher might take on an exasperatingly slow student. Pearl tried to be grateful for Hilda's steady, honest, unimpressed looks in her direction.

They moved a few days later, and suddenly she was alone with Mike in someplace large enough to walk around in. He reacted with exaggerated glee, hiding in the bedroom closet to jump out at her, wrestling her onto the new double bed. They'd used their savings to buy it, and it had been delivered by two men who called Pearl ma'am.

In the new apartment Mike said she could scatter hairpins wherever she liked. At Hilda's she used to find them in a clean ashtray, all facing the same way. "Wear a magnet on your head," Mike had whispered. Now he played the saxophone into the night, and after a few days someone knocked on the door and asked him to stop. Mike was angry, though he put the instrument away, but Pearl was embarrassed.

As soon as they had a table and chairs, Pearl made good on her plan to invite Mrs. Levenson—who had paid for the table. She and Mike had visited her a second time, and it had gone better. "A sweet girl," Mrs. Levenson said to Mike when they left. She pressed some bills into Pearl's hand. "A nice table you should buy." Pearl invited her mother-in-law to dinner, and of course Nathan and Hilda as well. Her guests were coming on Friday night, and Pearl asked Mike whether Mrs. Levenson would be offended that she didn't light candles for *shabbos*. They hadn't done it in Pearl's house when she was growing up. His mother did, Mike said, but only when she thought the neighbors might come in and notice. He insisted she wouldn't care. Pearl called up her mother and got directions for making a potato kugel, but in the end she decided it was too much trouble to grate the potatoes, so she made mashed potatoes. She bought a chicken and roasted it in the oven. She boiled carrots and peas. For dessert there was a cake she'd bought at the bakery.

The dinner was on a cold day in December. Mike went out to wait for his mother at the trolley stop. Pearl set the table with her mother's old dishes. Then she decided she had time to take down her hair and braid it again. She was already dressed; she'd changed to a fresh blouse when she came home from work. Pearl pulled out her hairpins and let her pale braid fall. She always loved the weight of it hitting her back. She unraveled it with her fingers and ran them through her hair. Her scalp prickled with freedom. She brushed her hair. As she was about to braid it again, the doorbell rang. Pearl went to the door as she was. There were Nathan and Hilda. When they saw her, Nathan blushed a little and Hilda looked away.

"Mike went to meet his mother. Your mother," Pearl said. "Come in. I'm sorry about my hair—I was setting the table."

"Are you planning to wear it that way?" said Hilda.

"Oh, no."

"Mrs. Levenson would think you were a loose woman," Hilda said. Now she was smiling a little, but Pearl still felt her disapproval.

She went into the bedroom and braided her hair and pinned it up. "Take off your coats," she called. "Pour yourselves a drink."

She'd made a pitcher of Tom Collinses, though the book said it was a summer drink. Mike had assured her that his mother would drink seltzer. She and Mike arrived a few minutes later, just as the three of them were starting their drinks. Mike's cheeks were red from the cold, but his mother was sallow. Sure enough, she said, "Just a glass seltzer," when Pearl offered her a drink. Nathan walked to the window, went back to his chair, sat down, looked at his watch. "Well, I lost my job," he said finally.

Pearl looked up, startled. Of them all, Nathan had seemed the least likely to lose his job.

"What? When?" said Mrs. Levenson. "You lost your job? How come you should lose your job?"

"The union can't afford me, it's as simple as that," said Nathan. "I've seen it coming."

Mrs. Levenson shook her head and rocked back and forth in her chair.

"I thought you weren't going to say anything," said Hilda.

"It's on my mind," Nathan said. When they went into the kitchen for dinner, he seemed to relax a little. "Things aren't what they were a few years ago," he said. "There are possibilities now. I might even be able to teach, who knows?"

Pearl thought the chicken was a little dry, but she had taken white meat. Maybe the dark meat was all right. Mike finished the food on his plate and reached for more without offering the platter to anyone else. Pearl glared at him. "Mrs. Levenson," she said, "would you like more? Hilda?"

"I have plenty," said Hilda. Mrs. Levenson didn't seem to hear her. Now Pearl nodded to Mike to go ahead, but he was already forking chicken onto his plate. Pearl was glad he liked it, but he seemed to like everything she cooked. He didn't mind if it was burned or underdone.

When the bakery cake was served, Mike's mother spoke for the first time in a while. "Expensive," she said.

"It didn't cost much," Pearl said, though it did, but she didn't know how to cook desserts.

"Mike shouldn't lose his job, too," his mother said. "Mike, your job is all right?"

"It's fine, Mom," he said.

"I said to Nathan, you shouldn't get married," Mrs. Levenson said now, and she was speaking to Pearl, of all people.

"Mom, that's enough," Nathan said, but the old woman kept talking.

"Maybe one day she can't work. You know what I mean. I say what I think. When Mike goes to get married, he doesn't tell his mother."

Pearl was coming across the room with two cups of coffee. "I'm sorry," she said, wondering if she was going to drop the cups and saucers. "I'm sorry we didn't tell you."

"He wouldn't listen to me," Mrs. Levenson said. "Nathan didn't listen."

Pearl looked around the table. Both men looked stricken, but Hilda looked angry. "Mom," she said, "stop it. Nathan'll get another job. It's not the end of the world."

"Who said the end of the world?" said Mrs. Levenson.

"You know what I mean. Look," said Hilda, and now her voice was gentle, "you didn't pick me and you didn't pick Pearl. Nathan and Mike picked us, and I'm sorry if you think they should have picked different girls. But honestly, there's nothing wrong with us. We won't bring disgrace on your family. We won't make your boys unhappy. We're nice." Now her voice was pleading, even a little teary. Pearl was afraid to look at her. She felt happier than she had since her wedding day. She sat down at the table and began eating her cake.

But Hilda bent her head and began to cry. Pearl had never seen Hilda cry before. Nobody said anything and after a while Hilda stopped crying and drank her coffee and even ate some of the cake. Everyone acted as if it hadn't happened, but Pearl thought Mrs. Levenson was a little friendlier after that.

Mike took his mother home on the trolley a short while later, and Hilda and Pearl washed the dishes. Nathan went into the other room, and then they heard the sound of an orchestra playing on the radio.

Pearl filled the dishpan and began putting cups and saucers into it, and Hilda scraped plates into the garbage. She leaned over the garbage pail, stooping, while her dress, a warm pumpkin color, drooped gracefully to the floor around her. Suddenly she tottered and dropped a plate and it broke. "I'm so clumsy," she said, and sat back onto the floor. "I'm dizzy."

Pearl leaned over to put her hands under Hilda's elbows. "What's wrong?"

"I'm sorry. Your plate."

"Just Mama's old ones. Are you sick? Did I poison you with my dinner that I cooked?" She helped Hilda, who felt surprisingly solid, to stand up, and then she pulled a chair forward with her foot and eased her sister-in-law into it.

"I'm having a baby," said Hilda, and looked up mischievously, and then they both began to laugh. Pearl knelt in front of her and took Hilda's hands, and Hilda bent her dark head so it touched Pearl's.

"I don't know what's so funny," Hilda said. "The old lady's right. I guess we'll starve."

Pearl pulled a second chair over. "It's wonderful. Nathan will get a job."

"I nearly died when she said what if I couldn't work."

"When is the baby coming?" said Pearl.

"August. I feel pretty good, but I won't be able to show up at the office in a maternity dress."

"When did you find out?" said Pearl. "Why didn't you tell us?" She was jealous of the knowledge, as if Hilda were her best friend.

"A week ago. I was going to tell everybody tonight, but when Nathan came home unemployed, it didn't seem like the best time, with his mother coming."

"She doesn't know?"

"No. Nathan says she'll be happy."

"Of course she will be," said Pearl.

Pearl didn't let Hilda help any more that night. She washed the dishes, looking over her shoulder to ask questions, marveling that she had a secret with Hilda. "It's a good thing we moved out," she said. "You'll need the room!"

"I guess so. It'll be tight in that apartment, even so."

"Babies are little."

"I guess so."

"Hilda's having a baby," she said, first thing, when Mike came back. Then, to Hilda—and to Nathan, who had come toward them from the living room, "Is it all right to tell him?"

"Of course," they both said, and Nathan advanced to receive his brother's handshake.

Mike looked astonished. "What do you know?" he kept saying. "How do you like that?" He clapped Hilda on the back. "Anytime you want," he said, "we'll help with the baby. I'll teach him shorthand."

"Well, that's a relief," said Hilda. She looked back as Nathan almost carried her out the door, his arms supporting both of hers, one around her back. "I had no idea how he'd learn shorthand!"

"Do you want to take the elevator?" Pearl heard Nathan say.

"I hate that thing," said Hilda.

"And the sax!" Mike was calling.

It was a good winter. Mike made Pearl laugh. She couldn't remember laughter in her parents' house, except at something little—a child, or a small dog that belonged to a man in the neighborhood and would sometimes wait for him outside the candy store, gazing at the door, to the amusement of Pearl's mother. In their apartment, which was still somewhat bare but began to fill up, they laughed at radio programs, at Hilda and Nathan, and at Pearl's bosses—Mr. Glynnis, who began each request with "suppose" ("Suppose you file these," he'd say, and Mike explained to Pearl that her predecessor was that well-known file clerk, Suppose Robinson), and Mr. Carmichael, who always sat down when he was asked a question, on his own chair or someone else's, as if there were a button in his backside that had to be pressed before he could answer. When Pearl's parents came to dinner, Mike even made them laugh.

Not everything went well all the time. Nathan was without a job for eight weeks, and he would come to their house, fretting about Hilda and the baby, and then about Spain—the democratic government in Spain was being attacked by rebels he said were supported by Hitler. Pearl was used to hearing President Roosevelt spoken of with near adoration in her parents' house, but Nathan criticized him for insisting the United States would remain neutral about Spain, whatever happened. "I used to have a lot of quarrels with the Communists," he said, "but I have to admit they've been right on target on this issue." The Communists, he explained to Pearl, who vowed to start reading the newspaper every day, were outspoken in their support of the Spanish government. When she did read stories about Spain, she too was upset.

Still, when he was out of work Nathan was friendlier—less austere. He seemed to value her encouragement. Then he found out that he might get work teaching as a substitute in a high school, and then, after some more suspense, the job began. An older teacher had died, and Nathan would have her job for the rest of the year. He was instantly full of stories about the students, the other teachers, the routine, the lunchroom patrol. The students liked him, but he said it helped his cause that their former teacher had been strict and disagreeable. Nathan brought in newspapers and read to them about current events. He found the places on the big maps that were rolled at the sides of the room, which he pulled down. "Clouds of dust billow out when I roll down a map," he said to Pearl. "And those maps are so out of date—the old lady apparently thought the Austro-Hungarian Empire was still going strong."

Hilda felt better as her pregnancy advanced, and Pearl thought she looked lovely when she went into maternity dresses. Hilda stopped working, and Pearl missed her at the office, although she felt freer. Hilda's birthday came in March, and Pearl made another dinner for her and Nathan and Mrs. Levenson. At the dinner, Hilda said she needed a lightweight maternity dress for spring and summer and Pearl offered to go shopping with her, but Hilda said she liked to shop alone. After the night when Hilda told Pearl she was pregnant, Pearl had thought they were going to be friends at last, but Hilda still pulled back from her at times, and Pearl felt clumsy and stupid when that happened. At other times Hilda was friendlier than before. She had gained a lot of weight, and she said she was ashamed of how big she was.

"You're supposed to be big," said Pearl.

"I'm too short to look good pregnant," Hilda said. "You'd look nice. I look like an apple."

"I think you look beautiful," said Pearl.

Mike got the job he wanted in April, taking shorthand in the district attorney's office. He worked for the homicide squad, and it frightened Pearl. "The murder's over by the time we show up," said Mike. "That's the whole idea." The office would call him when someone was going to make a confession, and Mike would take it down. He and Pearl got a telephone, and several times Mike was called out in the middle of the night. Pearl could tell he was fascinated by the policemen and the criminals.

He came back from his first case at three in the morning, and Pearl got up to make him some cocoa. Waiting for the milk to heat up, she turned over the pages of his notebook to see the confession the murderer had dictated. "What did he look like?" she said, studying the loops and lines.

"A sneaky-looking guy," Mike said. "I wouldn't have trusted him, but I wouldn't have thought he'd kill someone."

"Did he stab the guy?"

"Shot him."

"What does this part say?"

He picked up the book and squinted. " 'After McGuire left, I heard the door again,' " he said. " 'It wasn't locked.' "

"Is McGuire the man he killed?"

"No, McGuire was someone else. The guy we took in claims it was self-defense. McGuire and this other guy jumped him."

Pearl waited for him to drink his cocoa, rinsed the cup, and pulled the string to turn off the kitchen light. Mike was restless in bed that night, and she too found it hard to sleep.

In the warm weather there were more homicides. Once there were four in one night, and Mike talked about it for weeks. Now Pearl took the subway herself to Fulton Street and walked to Bobbie's. She liked her job and often congratulated herself on being out of the

candy store. She heard herself sound competent on the phone—
pleasant: friendly but not too friendly. If she were calling Bobbie's,
she'd be sure whatever she wanted would work out fine, hearing from
a receptionist like her.

One day in July Mr. Carmichael approached her as she was getting
ready to leave work at the end of the day. Nobody else was around
and he glanced to one side before he spoke, as if what he was going
to say was a secret. "The fact is, Mrs. Lewis," he said awkwardly,
"Jack and I were thinking about hosting a little dinner." Pearl was
confused, but eventually Mr. Carmichael explained that he and Mr.
Glynnis, whose first name was Jack, were inviting her to a party. A
man he knew had gone into business as a caterer, and because he was
starting out and wanted business, he'd given Mr. Carmichael a discount on a dinner for eight. "My wife's in the country," he said,
"and so is Jack's. But some lady friends of ours said they would come.
We're doing it at my house. They send a butler and a maid. It will be a
treat." He wanted her to bring Mike and Hilda and Nathan.

He was younger than she had thought, Pearl realized. Because he
was the boss, and older than Mr. Glynnis, she had thought of him
as someone her father's age, but he was not more than thirty-five,
she decided now. Pearl took time, putting the cover on her typewriter
and straightening her papers for the next day. She would love to go
to a dinner. She could wear the dress she'd bought almost a year ago
for her wedding, a gray silk. She and her mother had hurried into
New York and bought it the very day before she was married, her
mother grumbling and predicting the worst all the way, though she
was mollified by the dress itself, and grew almost sentimental on the
subway ride home. Pearl would look beautiful in the dress at the

dinner. In her mind, Hilda, Nathan, and Mike stood in front of her typewriter arguing with her, while Mr. Carmichael stood on the other side of it waiting for her to speak.

Hilda would say her maternity dresses weren't fancy enough. Mike hated to dress up and meet strangers. Nathan might not mind, but he'd be on his way to some rally on behalf of the Spanish Loyalists, and if he didn't get there the war would go the wrong way.

"We'd love to come," said Pearl primly. "Thank you for inviting us."

"Next Wednesday, then," said Mr. Carmichael. "I'll tell Jack. I'll give you my address."

Pearl persuaded Nathan that her job might even depend on their showing up for the dinner. "I don't want them to think we're not grateful." That made Nathan agree to go, but he looked at her sadly. "You'd be better off forming a union, if you want to protect your job," he said.

Hilda was glad to go. "I haven't been out of the apartment in months," she said, "except for dinner at Mrs. Levenson's, and everything she puts in front of me, she says, 'This you shouldn't eat.' I don't know what pregnant women did eat in her day."

She didn't care about her dress. "I have that black dress," she said. "Black is always dressy. Besides, they're going to throw me out because I'm not dressed up?" She'd wear the pearls she'd inherited from her mother, she said. That would make it fancy.

Mike was baffled, but he agreed. "If *you* want to go," he said, looking mystified but amused.

The night of the dinner was a warm evening in the middle of July. Nathan and Mike wore suits and white shirts and ties. They took their jackets off on the subway and both shook them out and folded them over their arms. Sitting next to Hilda, Pearl watched them. The men hadn't found seats and were holding the pole in the middle of the car—Nathan's hand on top, as befitted the older brother. She hadn't ever noticed that they looked alike. Mike looked so young, with that hair swept over his forehead, and Nathan so much older, with *his* forehead bare, now gleaming under the yellow subway light. And Mike's eyes were blue while Nathan's were brown. But their noses and mouths looked the same. She wondered if Hilda had ever noticed. Mrs. Levenson had, of course, and had probably been waiting for the two inadequate brides to mention it for months. Years, in Hilda's case.

The men put on their jackets outside Mr. Carmichael's house, a brownstone in the East Thirties. Pearl watched the windows to make sure they weren't being observed. They were admitted by a maid, and there was Mr. Glynnis, smiling and blushing, and two women, both smoking, drinking iced drinks in tall glasses. "This is Jean," Mr. Carmichael said, pointing to the nearer one, who was wearing light blue, "and this is Smokie." He introduced the four of them. "Would you like to freshen up?"

He pointed Hilda and Pearl into the bedroom, which was more lavish than Pearl had expected, with long lace curtains. "Look, that's his wife," she said to Hilda. On the bureau was a photograph of a dark-haired young woman with a round, cheerful face pressed in on each side by a child, a smiling boy with neatly trimmed hair and a baby with her finger in her mouth and her eyes fixed on the camera. Pearl took off her hat and ran her comb through her hair—being careful not to disturb the braid—so it would have a little softness. She checked the hairpins.

"Pretty swanky," said Hilda, tilting her head toward the door. "The one called Jean—did you see her necklace?"

"What, is it real diamonds or something?" Pearl was leaning over to look in the mirror. She didn't think she should sit down in Mrs. Carmichael's vanity chair.

"I don't know," said Hilda absently, as if she'd now lost interest. "I guess their wives are away. . . ." She patted her hair and waited for Pearl, and the two of them went back to the living room. "Are you having scotch?" asked the woman called Smokie as soon as she saw them. "Have scotch and soda."

Pearl asked for a Tom Collins because she had drunk it before. Nathan and Mike had whiskey and Hilda had sherry. "Have you lived here long?" Hilda said to Mr. Carmichael. Pearl knew she did that because Mr. Carmichael was standing, and a question always made him sit down. She wanted to show Nathan and Mike. Sure enough, he seated himself and picked up his glass before he said he'd been there for five years.

The maid offered canapés. Pearl said no, because she was afraid she'd drop something on her dress, but then she was sorry and took something right away when the maid came back. There was something on the tray Pearl thought might be pâté, but you had to spread it yourself on a cracker and she was sure she'd make a mess of it, so she took one of the light brown puffs near it—almost like cream puffs, but with something unusual inside. "Is it caviar?" she whispered to Jean.

"No, honey," said Jean, louder than Pearl would have liked. "You wouldn't put caviar into something like this."

"I hate caviar," said Smokie. "I don't like to put things into my body that look like caviar. I prefer to be kind to my body. Don't you?"

Everyone murmured that they liked being kind to their bodies. "I use enemas occasionally," Smokie said.

Jean turned to Hilda. "I couldn't help noticing that you're expecting," she said. "When is your baby due?"

Mike laughed and stopped himself. Hilda was eight months pregnant and perfectly enormous. "Next month," she said.

"A Leo!" said Smokie. She had lots of reddish brown hair. "Oh, Lord."

"That's superstition," said Mr. Glynnis.

"Oh, really?" Smokie said, shaking her hair. "I can guess your sign of the zodiac just by the way you act."

"Go ahead," said Mr. Glynnis.

Smokie looked him up and down and said he was probably a Virgo. "A virgin! You think I'm a virgin?" said Mr. Glynnis—Jack, he had told them to say.

"No, silly—it's just your sign of the zodiac. Or maybe Scorpio."

"Well, my birthday is September twenty-sixth," he said.

"Twenty-sixth? You're sure? I'm just certain you're a Virgo, but the end of September is generally considered Libra. You don't seem like a Libra to me."

Mr. Carmichael—Lester—said he was sure Smokie had many interesting ideas on this subject, but Smokie was asking Hilda what she was going to name the baby, and Hilda was saying that if it was a boy it would be Samuel, after Nathan's father. If it was a girl, she'd be called Rachel. Her mother had been named Rachel.

"You could vary it," said Smokie. "You could name her Rochelle. A friend of mine has that name. Isn't it nice?"

"I think Rachel," said Hilda.

Pearl had never heard the name Rochelle, or heard anyone talk about signs of the zodiac before. She didn't know what her sign of the zodiac was. When they stood to go into dinner, she saw that Smokie's and Jean's dresses were tight. Their behinds were outlined.

At dinner, a different servant—a man—poured wine in their glasses. Pearl knew she'd be dizzy if she drank it but she was having a good time. Nathan and Mike had hardly spoken in the living room, but now Mr. Glynnis asked them where they had grown up and tried to remember whether or not he had a friend in their neighborhood in Brooklyn. Pearl thought he probably didn't. They talked about subway stops.

The food was served in a new way. The waiter carried a platter around and tilted it next to Pearl, and she was supposed to take some food onto her plate from the platter. Pearl was afraid she'd take too much or too little, and that she'd handle the utensils wrong. Hilda seemed to have no trouble, and looked as if she had always eaten her dinner in this maddening fashion. Jean said it was a pleasure to see a meal served properly, it hardly ever happened nowadays, and Smokie said they should be careful not to eat foods that disagreed with them.

"It isn't worth it," she said with bitter cheer. "It just isn't worth it. Now this potato dish looks delicious," she said, "but I'm sure it would be bad for me. No, thank you."

There was a fish course followed by lamb. Pearl liked the food very much, although she thought the lamb had too much seasoning. "Now a nice piece of lamb, simply prepared," Smokie was saying. "There's no harm there."

Nathan looked at her. "You'd get along with my mother," he said. "Does she like lamb?"

"I'm not sure. But she likes to—well, she's careful about food." Pearl saw that Mike was trying not to laugh again.

Smokie ate the dessert, Pearl noticed, even though she was careful and it was quite rich—a pastry filled with custard and candied fruit. And she seemed to have noticed Nathan for the first time. "Did I hear you're a teacher?" she said.

"History." Nathan had received a permanent appointment for the coming year.

"History!" she said. "You probably know all about world affairs. Now what do you think about Mussolini? Should we be so worried about him? Or is this just something a few nervous Jews are trying to make us worry about?"

Nathan looked at her quietly, then looked sideways at Mike. "I think Mussolini is extremely worrisome," he said.

Mr. Glynnis was talking at the same time. "World affairs, yes, they certainly are getting complicated," he said. "Suppose—"

They didn't find out what Mr. Glynnis was supposing. The waiter began serving coffee, and Nathan, holding out his cup toward the silver coffeepot with its curved spout, must have moved the cup at the wrong moment and with too much force, while he said, "Look, if you think Mussolini's some sort of *joke*—" and the coffee arced gracefully onto his pants. He started and the waiter saw what was happening and tilted the pot up, but everyone had noticed.

"Are you scalded?" Smokie asked, jumping up. Hilda ran into the kitchen and returned with a wet cloth. Nathan said he was all right, he was sorry if it had gone on the rug, it was entirely his fault. The waiter apologized, and Nathan clasped him on the shoulder, refusing his apology, insisting he was fine. In the end the waiter led him out to the kitchen. When Nathan came back, Mike stood up. "We have to call it a night," he said. "Awfully nice of you folks." Hilda and Pearl found their handbags and hats and they all thanked Mr. Glynnis and Mr. Carmichael and soon found themselves out on the sidewalk, where, to their surprise, it was almost midnight. A light breeze was blowing; it was cool, and the men took off their jackets and put them around the women's shoulders. Without discussion, they walked past their subway stop and toward the next one. Pearl was pleased —she wanted to keep the evening going.

"You did that on purpose," Hilda said to Nathan then.

"Did what?"

"Spilled the coffee."

"Why would I do that?"

"I don't know—to change the subject, I guess. So they wouldn't talk about Mussolini."

"Change the subject!" Nathan said, and he sounded more excited than usual. "I *wanted* to talk about Mussolini—I wanted to talk about Mussolini a great deal."

"But that would have been worse," Hilda said. "What if they took it out on Pearl?"

"Oh, it wouldn't matter!" Pearl put in quickly.

"Don't be so sure!" said Hilda.

Pearl was startled. She'd thought it was a party—that it didn't matter what they did.

"Nathan was careless with your bosses—with your job," Hilda was saying angrily.

Now Nathan sounded angry as well. "I hope you don't feel that way, Pearl," he said, and his quiet, low voice made her cold. "I don't have much respect for those two, and I don't care to hide my opinions from people like that. That waiter—when I got him in the kitchen I asked him some questions. He's been unemployed for two years. They're paying him almost nothing tonight."

They were still walking. The night was quiet and chilly, and Pearl felt accused, pulling Mike's jacket closer to her body.

"And those women!" said Hilda, but now she sounded amused, not angry after all. "Those women. They were call girls. That's what they *were*—it's that simple."

"Do you think so?" Pearl hadn't been sure.

"Of course! Didn't you see their jewelry? And their dresses?"

"They had nice backsides," said Mike.

"You could certainly discover *that* without trouble," Hilda said.

"Their poor wives," said Pearl, thinking of the round-faced woman in the picture on the dresser. "Do you think they suspect?"

"Women can sense that kind of thing," said Hilda.

"How do they bear it?"

"Maybe it's different for people like that," said Hilda. "People with money." When they came to the next subway station, they went down. They got home late, not talking on the walk to their houses, and just waved good night when they separated. "I'm going to take off my shoes," Hilda called, "and stick my feet in a pail of cold water."

Hilda gave birth to a daughter, Rachel, on August seventeenth, after a long labor preceded by a four-day hot spell that made her jumpy and uncomfortable. Pearl had brought a couple of meals over and Hilda had barely been civil. She insisted it was too hot to eat anyway. She didn't know why Nathan persisted in eating. It nauseated her to watch him.

The day Hilda gave birth was a little cooler. Pearl walked home from the subway station feeling a slight breeze ruffle her dress, enjoying the air after the subway's stuffiness. When she passed Hilda's building, she hesitated. Then she saw Nathan hurry out. He told her he'd just come back for a shower and a nap. He'd brought Hilda to the hospital in a taxi at midnight and she'd had the baby at eleven in the morning. "It was hard," he said. "They didn't let me stay with her. She was in pain." He paused. "I thought it would be different."

But Pearl could hardly listen. She felt her face breaking into a grin. "What does she look like?" she said. "Does she have hair?"

"The baby?" said Nathan. "I had to look through a window. I didn't realize what it would be like. She's cute—she's skinny, though. She was wrapped up, but she looked skinny. I think she has brown hair." He looked at her tiredly. "Maybe later I can see her better."

"What does she weigh?"

"I think about six pounds."

"I guess that's pretty little." Pearl stood up on her toes to give him a kiss on his cheek. His cheek felt like Mike's but a little different. She could feel the stubble on his face and it seemed a little softer than Mike's. He had his own smell. She was embarrassed, as if she might have done something wrong. "Can we visit her?"

"Tomorrow or the next day," Nathan said. "Hilda's pretty knocked out."

"Okay, tomorrow," said Pearl. "Congratulations, Daddy."

Nathan grinned at her as she continued walking. She was oddly self-conscious, thinking of him watching her, watching the way the wind picked up the hem of her dress, a lightweight blue-and-white print, and jumbled it around her legs. But when she glanced over her shoulder he was gone.

4 ⤰

FRANCES WAS SORRY SHE'D SHOWN LYDIA THE BABY SHOES. She'd liked burying them in the park, and in a way her secret had been enhanced, but in another sense it was smaller. And she was afraid Lydia would tell someone about them. Several weeks passed, and Lydia didn't mention the shoes. Frances had trouble bringing up the subject. Then Lydia told their teacher about another secret of theirs.

One afternoon, before Simon ran away and Frances and Lydia buried the shoes, they'd been playing at Frances's house, and had started sorting Frances's doll clothes. Neither of them played with dolls anymore, but they had kept them, and Frances had been meaning to go through their clothes and organize them. But one of the dolls was dressed in a nurse's uniform, and without thinking about what they were doing they began a game having to do with a nurse and her boyfriend and the hospital where they worked. After a while they took the nurse doll to Lydia's house because Lydia had a boy doll who could be the boyfriend.

Lydia's mother was surprised when they got the dolls out. "It's for school," Lydia said. "We're making up a story about nurses for school, and we're using the dolls to help us make up the story." As far as Frances knew, Lydia was not planning to make up a story until she said that, but now Frances said it would be easy to write a story about the dolls—about nurses and their boyfriends, that is—and they began planning the story as well as playing the game. Before they separated, they wrote about a page, mostly taking turns making up sentences, but after that, though they sometimes said, "This would be good for the story," they didn't write down anything more. By the time they buried the shoes, Frances had almost forgotten about the story and the nurses.

Then one day—a week or two after the burial of the shoes— Mrs. Reilly, their teacher, called them over and asked them how their story was coming along, and Frances realized that Lydia had told her about it. Frances didn't really like Mrs. Reilly, who was asking them to show her what they were writing, saying she could mimeograph it and distribute it through the school. They could include illustrations.

"Now we have to write that story," Frances said to Lydia when they left.

"I can't today," said Lydia. "I have to go to the store for my mother."

"Do you want me to come?"

"I don't think she'd like it."

Frances started for home by herself. She wouldn't be able to work on the story alone because the page they'd written was at Lydia's house. It was a cold, windy day but Frances circled past her own block and went to Prospect Park instead of going home. She was still carrying her books. She went to the big oak where they had buried the shoes, but when she came to it, even though she saw no one coming along in either direction, she passed the tree and pretended to be curious about the lake. She went down to the edge of the lake and stood there counting ducks. She even pretended to write down the number of ducks she'd counted in her notebook. Then she went back to the tree. She remembered just where they had hidden the shoes, at a place where a root came out of the ground, and she took a stick and dug in the ground until she felt the sock. She started as if it were alive or as if she hadn't expected it to be there. She didn't want to dig up the shoes without Lydia, though. She put the dirt back and covered the ground with dead leaves.

On her way home she met a neighbor who asked her why she was walking this way when the school was that way. "You still go to the same school, don't you?" she said. Frances said she'd walked a friend home.

"I have checked on the shoes," she said boldly to Lydia the next day.

Lately whenever Frances had acted as if she were starting a game, Lydia had shrugged and turned away, but this time she answered with the same kind of voice that Frances had used, as if they were already pretending something. "The guilty shoes," said Lydia. "Were they satisfactory?"

105

"Without question," said Frances. Then, forgetting to change her voice, "They're right there."

"I hope you took precautions."

"Of course." Frances was pleased and Lydia was even willing to play the nurse game that day for the first time in a long while. A week later they spent an afternoon at Frances's house working on the story, not even using the dolls. The story didn't really have much to do with the doll game. The game was mostly about clothes; the nurses were always changing, either for dates or to disguise themselves (first to hide from their boyfriends, but lately—this was an invention of Lydia's—because a criminal wanted to harm a patient in the hospital and the nurses had to be unrecognizable so as to hunt him).

In the story they wrote, the nurses first had to meet boyfriends, but it took a long time to write that. At the end of the afternoon they spent writing, one nurse had met a boy named Elliott, but the other hadn't even met her boyfriend yet. The part with the criminal was far off, and Frances wasn't sure they should use it, although Lydia was firm. Now Frances was full of plans, but the next day Lydia had lost interest again, and hurried home alone.

Frances's mother had taken a part-time job doing bookkeeping for a shoe company. She said she'd done similar work when she and Frances's father were first married. Several afternoons a week, now, she was out until after five. She liked Frances to be home when she was at work. "Especially because of the park," she said. "I don't want you wandering in the park by yourself. It gets dark so early now."

"I'm with Lydia," said Frances.

"Even with Lydia. I'm sure her mother doesn't like it either."

"She doesn't care."

"Well, I care. This is a difficult time for us, Frances," her mother said, with a frightening catch in her voice. "Don't make it harder."

The next day when they were leaving school, Lydia said, "I think we should check on the shoes again."

"I checked on them," said Frances. She didn't want to disobey her mother, but she didn't want Lydia to think she was a baby with lots of rules.

"That was a long time ago," Lydia said. "Who knows what might have happened?"

"I promised my mother I'd be home," said Frances.

"She won't know. She's at work."

"She calls." It made her feel a little better to say that, because it wasn't true.

"They're stupid, anyway, those baby shoes," said Lydia. "We should dig them up and throw them away."

A few days later they were together in the park after all. Frances's mother was home, and Frances had dropped off her schoolbooks and told her mother she was going to the library with Lydia. They needed books for book reports. Before going home, they detoured through the park. It was Frances's idea; she wanted to check on the shoes again, maybe to dig them up, but she said it was because she'd seen something mysterious the time before and she wanted to show it to Lydia. Once again, it was hard to tell Lydia she was thinking about the shoes, as if Lydia might make fun of her for wanting to go back to that game. Yet Frances didn't want to play a game about the shoes anymore, she just wanted them.

It was a gray day. Leaves blew in their faces, and the leaves' sharp edges and veins—all that was left of them—stung Frances's cheeks.

Lydia didn't even want to walk in the direction of the tree, but Frances, after going the other way for a while, away from the wind, said the mysterious thing was back this way.

"What is it?" said Lydia.

"Wait," said Frances, hoping she'd think of something. "Just keep quiet and come this way. It has to do with ducks. The number of ducks." Sometimes, in the past, this would have been all that was required to start Lydia on a wonderful theory about strange aberrations in the number of ducks, requiring that they hide behind trees and spy on passersby, studying them for proof that they'd committed some fantastic, indistinct crime.

But this time she only said, "Ducks? Oh, for heaven's sake," and trudged resentfully next to Frances. After a while she turned away from the wind to talk. "I don't see anything unusual about the ducks," she said.

"Well, let's dig up the shoes, then," said Frances, risking everything.

"No, let's not."

"Why not?"

"None of your business."

"What do you mean, none of my business?" said Frances. "They're my shoes."

"They're not yours," said Lydia, surprisingly—yet Frances was not surprised. "You stole them from your mother."

"I didn't steal them!"

"I don't know what else to call it."

"Tell me why not, anyway," said Frances.

"You tell me what's mysterious about the ducks," said Lydia. "I think you just made that up. You lied. There was nothing mysterious."

"Yes, there was," said Frances, but she still couldn't think of anything.

In the end they went home, and Frances kept talking, uneasily, about other things. A few days later the teacher asked them again about the story. Lydia said they were going to work on it that afternoon after school. The first pages were at Lydia's house, and when Lydia suggested that Frances come home with her, Frances was so pleased that she disobeyed her mother and went.

"We have to work on our story," Lydia told her mother.

"You mean doll clothes all over the place again."

"No, we're writing a book. I told you."

"All I know is, whatever you do, there's a mess," said her mother.

"We're just *writing*." They went into Lydia's room, which had obviously been cleaned up by her mother. The bed was made and the dolls were stacked on a shelf like bodies, not sitting up, some dressed and some naked. Lydia got the story out. There wasn't much written.

"Dawn should meet her boyfriend now," said Frances. Dawn was one of the nurses.

"Wait. Just before she meets him, she sees a shrunken skull on the porch of a house."

One of Lydia's dolls was larger than the others, a big baby doll named Dawn who had no hair, just curls molded on her plastic head. She had been an awkward participant in the nurses' game because she was so big and her clothes were all baby clothes, but she could drink and wet and Lydia said that trait might come in handy. "The nurses aren't going to wet their pants," Frances had said, but Lydia had liked using Dawn. They had used the dolls like puppets. Becky, the other nurse, was Frances's doll. Now, sitting on Lydia's bed while Lydia sat on the floor biting her pencil, Frances found her eyes picking out Dawn in the stack of dolls dumped unceremoniously on the shelf. She was at the bottom and she didn't have any clothes on, but she had shoes. Frances was thinking about whether there should be a shrunken skull on a porch, but part of her mind stayed with the shoes, white shoes such as a baby might wear. Frances began to feel frightened even before she'd had the next thought. The doll's shoes were the ones she and Lydia had buried in Prospect Park.

"Lydia," she said.

"What?"

"Did you dig up the shoes?"

"No, of course not, silly, why would I do that?"

"What are those shoes Dawn is wearing?"

Lydia turned around and looked over the stack of dolls. "I found them," she said. "I found them a long time ago. I've always had them."

"No, you haven't."

"Of course I have. You played with them yourself. We put them on her one time when she was being the nurse."

It wasn't true. "You dug them up," Frances said. She pulled Dawn out from under the stack of dolls, and the others fell to the floor.

"Look what you're doing," said Lydia. "You're dumping everything out. Why are you so interested in dolls, anyway? Aren't you ever going to grow up?"

Frances sat down on the floor where she was, crying, and took the shoes off Dawn's feet, but Lydia grabbed her hands and peeled her fingers away easily, her nails digging into Frances's hands. "Do you want me to tell your mother?" Lydia said.

"Tell her what?"

"Tell her you stole the shoes from the drawer."

"You wouldn't."

"Maybe I would."

"Well, if these aren't them," said Frances, "let's go to the park and dig up the real ones."

"I can't. My mother says I can't go to the park. I saw a man peeing there. My mother says the park is full of perverts. She says your parents don't care about things like that, but she does."

"My parents do too care," said Frances. "Anyway, I'm going."

"What do I care?" said Lydia. They had not worked on the story, but Frances put on her coat and left. Lydia's mother was in the kitchen, and she turned as Frances passed her. "Waltzing out already," she said.

Frances walked straight from Lydia's house to the park, a long walk. It was starting to get dark when she got there. She crossed the bridle path and stepped onto a path darkened by trees on either side. She hurried to their tree and picked up a stick. She dug for a long time and found nothing. It was difficult—the stick broke and she had to find another one. She wished she had a shovel. The ground was hard. By now it was dark, and Frances was not sure she was digging in the right spot. She couldn't persuade herself to leave, even though she was terribly cold. She kept widening the hole, squatting beside it. She longed to sit or kneel, but she didn't want to be questioned about dirt on her clothes or knees. She kept hoping that at any moment her stick would meet the softness of the sock. Someone walked by, a man alone. Frances stood and hid herself against the trunk of the tree, squeezing her face into the rough bark. Her thighs ached.

The man went down to the edge of the lake and stood there for a long time. Finally he walked away. When he was gone, Frances, whose heart was beating hard, walked as quickly as she could along the open path between her and the park entrance. She was sure she heard someone following her, and ran until she was out of breath and in pain. Crossing the soft soil of the bridle path, she couldn't go fast, and after that she had to walk. Her apartment house was two blocks from the park. When she passed a store and caught sight of a clock inside, she was surprised that it was only 5:25. She had thought it would be late at night, that her parents and the police might be searching for her as they had looked for Simon. She hurried to her own block and her own house. There was a light in their apartment window—third floor, third window from the end—so she knew her mother was home, but probably her father was not home yet. He went to meetings after school and was the faculty advisor of the current events club. Today was Wednesday, current events day.

Her mother heard her at the door and came to meet her. "I called Lydia," she said. "You left a long time ago."

"Not so long," Frances said.

"Where were you?"

"I was coming home."

"You must have gone someplace else," her mother said.

"No, I was coming home," said Frances. There was dirt on her shoes, but her mother didn't notice. In her room, she scraped the dirt off and tried to gather it into a piece of paper which she folded and threw away. She had not considered telling her mother the truth. She could never tell her mother about the shoes, would never mention the shoes. Yet sometimes she imagined a conversation in which her mother asked about them. She might have checked the drawer and found them missing. Frances would deny knowing anything about them, but if such a conversation happened, maybe her mother would go on to talk about the baby who had died, about how she had died.

In a book, the girl who had taken the shoes would tell her mother, and in the end, she and the mother would be closer because of it. The mother would draw the girl up against her, on her lap or next to her if the girl was big, and tell her the whole story. Maybe they would cry together. All this might be preceded by anger. Maybe the girl would be punished for taking the shoes. Frances knew that her mother would not punish her. She might even want to sit and draw Frances close to her without being angry, but Frances could not let that happen. When she imagined it, it was as if she were a baby. She was small enough to sit on her mother's lap. She was both entranced and disgusted, in her imagination, by her mother's smell and the softness of her body. Her mother would cry, thinking once more about the baby who had died. It would be Frances's fault that she was reminded.

Probably, Frances thought, the baby had died suddenly in the hospital and a nurse had told her mother. The baby might have choked on her pillow. Hilda must have fed the baby. Then the nurse took her to the nursery. Hilda was in her hospital bed, reading a magazine. Suddenly she heard nurses calling to one another and to the doctor. She ignored them, thinking the confusion had nothing to do with her, and went on reading. At last a nurse came into the room and sat on the edge of Hilda's bed. Frances found she was imagining Becky, the nurse played by her own doll in the story she and Lydia had been making up. "Mrs. Levenson," Becky would say, "I have to tell you very sad news." She would take Hilda's hand and then Hilda would guess.

A few days later, Lydia brought their story to school and showed it to Mrs. Reilly. She didn't say anything to Frances, who watched from her seat. Later the teacher called Frances over and asked Lydia whether they hadn't written it together. Lydia said both of them had written the beginning, but she had finished it. Frances waited until school was over. She asked the teacher if she could look at the story, which the teacher had put into a folder.

"Why didn't you keep working on it with Lydia?" the teacher asked.

"I didn't want to," said Frances. She took the story and read it, sitting at her desk, while the teacher went around the room watering plants. In the story, Dawn and Becky and their boyfriends saw a series of shrunken skulls in their neighborhood. As they walked past a broken-down, abandoned house, they found a pair of baby shoes on the sidewalk. Then Dawn heard a baby's cry. The two nurses and their boyfriends opened a window and went into the house, where they found two men about to murder a baby with knives. The nurses were able to call the police and stop the men, who had kidnapped the baby.

Frances returned the story to the teacher and went home. The next day she saw Lydia showing something to another girl, and when she got closer she saw that it was the pair of baby shoes. She approached

Lydia as soon as she could be alone with her. "Would you *please* give me the shoes?" she said.

"They are magic shoes. I will not part with them. You have not shown yourself worthy to possess them," said Lydia in her make-believe voice.

"It's not funny," said Frances.

"These aren't *those* shoes, stupid," said Lydia. "I found these."

"But somebody dug up the shoes we hid," said Frances. "I looked in the park. They're not there."

"Well, it wasn't me," said Lydia.

The next day Frances saw her show the shoes to Mrs. Reilly. "The real shoes?" said Mrs. Reilly. "The shoes in the story?"

"Sort of," said Lydia.

"You can read the story in assembly," said Mrs. Reilly. "Then when you're done, pull out the shoes. What do you think of that suggestion?" Each class had a turn being in charge of an assembly and their turn was coming in a few weeks. Most classes put on a play about a holiday, but Mrs. Reilly had said they should have a talent show. Someone was going to play the piano, someone else would sing, and so on. "Maybe Frances will read the part she worked on," she continued. "Or maybe you'd like to write a different story, Frances."

Frances said she would do something else. Parents came to assemblies, and her mother might even take time off from work if Frances were in the talent show. Frances and a group of girls had planned to sing. If she were one of a large group, maybe her mother wouldn't come.

She considered telling Mrs. Reilly that Lydia had taken shoes that belonged to her, but she was afraid that if she seemed upset, Mrs. Reilly would tell her mother. Or Mrs. Reilly might think she was jealous of Lydia. Lydia didn't claim that she herself had burst in on robbers who had kidnapped a baby, but Frances found that when she pictured the events of Lydia's story, it was Lydia who climbed through that window, wearing a nurse's uniform that was more like a Halloween costume.

Frances sat in the kitchen at home, watching her mother cook dinner. Hilda moved around the small kitchen as if she knew the pots and knives she wanted would come to meet her, rising slightly from the table or sink when she reached for them. Frances thought that her mother must sometimes think about the baby who had died. Maybe she had loved that baby more than she had ever loved Frances and was always a little disappointed in what she had gotten instead. She had scarcely known that baby. How much love could you have for someone who was only a few days old? Yet right at this moment, Frances thought, her mother might be thinking about that baby. "What are you thinking about?" she said.

"Why?" said her mother. She was breading veal cutlets, patting them between her hands so the crumbs would stick.

"You looked as if you were thinking about something." This was not true. Hilda often looked thoughtful but now she didn't. She was wearing a red-and-white cobbler's apron over her dress. Frances liked to look at that apron. Sometimes the pattern looked like white diamonds on red, sometimes like red diamonds on white. There was a moment when it changed. Under the apron her mother had on a brown woolen dress which she always wore with a copper pin on the shoulder. Now the pin had caught in the edge of the apron and made her mother look rumpled. Her mother was a little fat, and her hair, which was getting gray, waved around her face.

"I was thinking about Daddy," she said.

"What about him?"

"Well, I was wishing for his happiness. For things to work out."

"What things?"

"Oh, you know what things."

"The trial?" Frances remembered the hearing. She'd heard her father call it a trial. She was always remembering and forgetting. Sometimes she heard her parents talking about it in the living room after Frances was in bed. She knew she could learn more about it, but she didn't ask. Her father was not a criminal, and they had assured her it was not that kind of trial. No matter what happened, they said smiling, he wouldn't go to jail. Yet Frances had already known that. Surely she had known it.

"Will it take a long time?" she said now.

"I think just one day."

"What do you think will happen?"

"I don't know." If they were people in a book, Frances would have suggested that they pray, but she had never heard anyone in her family pray and wasn't sure how to go about it. "Please, God, let the trial turn out okay," thought Frances experimentally, but was unable to say that.

"Maybe it will turn out okay," she said.

"Maybe," said her mother, and looked grateful. Maybe her mother was thinking about praying.

Especially with this trouble happening, Frances couldn't tell her mother about Lydia and the shoes, even if she could bring herself to confess the search in her mother's drawers and the burial of the shoes in the park, which her mother would think was childish and silly.

Then she had an idea. Maybe it would be possible to discuss this problem with Lydia's mother. Lydia's mother could take the shoes from Lydia and give them to Frances, and Frances could sneak them back into her mother's drawer—or even keep them. She just had to stop Lydia from carrying them around and showing them to people.

Lydia's mother smoked lots of cigarettes and there were always full ashtrays in the house. She usually seemed to be cleaning, but the apartment wasn't clean. Frances didn't like the way she spoke. "I don't know what's wrong with his aim," Mrs. Howard had said once, coming out of the bathroom carrying cleaning supplies. "Why can't he get it inside the bowl?"

Still, in some ways Mrs. Howard was easier to talk to than her own mother. Mrs. Howard complained to the girls if she gained weight and her clothes were tight, or she asked them whether she looked fatter or thinner. She was strict with Lydia, but only when she was in a bad mood. Lydia joked about being beaten, and Frances had seen Mrs. Howard slap her, but it was more like a bigger kid bullying a smaller one than a parent punishing a child. It made her feel that Mrs. Howard wasn't quite an adult. Frances hoped that Lydia's mother wouldn't hit Lydia for taking the shoes, though the idea gave her satisfaction, too.

Lydia would say that Frances was a tattletale and she would be right. Frances wished she had said the same thing to Lydia when Lydia had threatened to talk to Frances's mother. Surely that would be tattling too. It seemed that there was a kind of telling that wasn't tattling, and Lydia had been implying that she had that kind in mind.

It took Frances several days to think through this idea. Meanwhile she was feeling steadily worse. Lydia had entirely stopped being friendly. She was definitely going to read the story at assembly, which was coming up soon. When the class had a rehearsal, Lydia read her story and then flourished imaginary shoes, which Frances could see as clearly as if they'd been there, dangling and swaying as Lydia held the laces with her fingertips.

Mrs. Howard had known about their game all along, and she might even have wondered how Lydia suddenly acquired those shoes. In some ways she was the kind of mother who could see a kid's viewpoint. Once she had dressed a doll, searching among the doll clothes for the right thing. She had slumped on the bed—something Hilda didn't do—and she made the doll jump along the bed and spoke in the doll's voice.

If Frances could approach Mrs. Howard out of concern for Lydia, it wouldn't be tattling. Lydia had misbehaved and no reasonable adult would approve. Frances didn't want revenge, she just wanted her shoes back. The conversation she imagined was full of courtesies. Frances would not hold a grudge. Mrs. Howard would explain gently to Lydia and Lydia would understand that Frances was just *upset*. After all, it had to do with her dead sister. There had been a death in Frances's family, and people should treat Frances kindly as a result. This was all she had that had belonged to her baby sister—who would have been her older sister, come to think of it, if she had lived, but that wasn't the point.

It would be difficult to catch Mrs. Howard alone. Frances would have to wait for a time when she saw Lydia leave. For several school days Frances went home, dropped off her books, and—risking her mother's disapproval—went back to a corner from which she could see the front door of Lydia's apartment house. It was cold. One day it was raining. Frances acted as if she were waiting for someone, consulting an imaginary watch and looking down the street away from Lydia's house, then stealing glances at the door again. She was too cold and bored to do this for long—and too worried that her mother might find out. After an hour or so, she'd go home, wishing she could just ring Lydia's doorbell and play with her again.

She began her vigil on Monday, and on Thursday she saw Lydia come out. Frances was so relieved that she considered abandoning her plan, catching up to Lydia, and simply trying to explain how she felt. But she had waited so long. When Lydia turned the corner, she went to the house and rang the doorbell. The apartment house had a buzzer, but Mrs. Howard just buzzed everyone in. Frances started up the stairs to the apartment.

"You forgot your key again?" said Mrs. Howard, coming to the door.

"It's me," said Frances.

"Lydia went to the store for me," said her mother.

"Could I talk to you a minute anyway?"

"Suit yourself." She backed away from the door, and Frances went into the foyer and stood there, unbuttoning and rebuttoning her coat. She was wearing a long scarf around her head and shoulders; a bit of fluff from the scarf had gotten into her mouth. She kept trying to get rid of it without attracting attention to it. Her scarf was made of dark pink angora, and Frances had felt beautiful when she got it, but now she was breathing fluff and it distracted her when she needed to think.

"Lydia and I have a problem," Frances began.

"What's up?"

Mrs. Howard seemed younger than Frances's mother or even Aunt Pearl, but more tired. Frances couldn't stop noticing Mrs. Howard's slacks, which were black and green with a large, sloppy design. Somehow she knew that a person who could understand what she was going to say would not have chosen those slacks, but she tried to put aside this idea and concentrate. She found herself telling the story from the beginning: how she had found the shoes, which had probably belonged to her little sister, who had died when she was just a few days old, and how she and Lydia had buried them in Prospect Park.

"You dug a hole and buried them?" said Mrs. Howard.

"Yes."

"Who'd you think was going to take them?"

"Nobody," said Frances. "We did it—well, it just seemed like a good idea."

"If you say so," said Mrs. Howard.

Now Frances had to explain about the nurses' game and the story. This was difficult, because the game was and in a way was not the story, and she and Lydia were and in a way were not Becky and Dawn. Even the dolls were and in a way were not Becky and Dawn. She got interested in the explanation and forgot to consider whether it could make sense to Mrs. Howard.

When she came to the part about the missing shoes, Mrs. Howard interrupted her. "Look, honey, Lydia *found* those shoes. She didn't dig up your shoes."

"But *where* did she find them?"

"How should I know where she found them? You got carried away with that imagination of yours. Those shoes aren't anything special. She found them in the street, probably. Somebody threw them away because they were too small for the baby."

"But they're mine," said Frances. "They belonged to my sister. She lived only a few days."

"I told you, honey, those aren't your shoes. Lydia's always coming home with junk she finds—I don't know why she does it."

"But don't you see that doesn't make sense? Why would there be two pairs of baby shoes?"

"Honey, there are *thousands* of pairs of baby shoes."

"I know that." Frances was close to tears. "But don't you see that it's a little strange that Lydia found some baby shoes just when I lost some? Don't you see that they're probably the same shoes?"

"I don't have time for this," said Mrs. Howard. She led the way into Lydia's room. The stack of dolls was on the shelf, and Frances could see right away that Dawn wasn't wearing the shoes.

"I don't see them," said Mrs. Howard. "She probably threw them away."

"No, she didn't," said Frances. "She's going to show them at assembly when she reads the story."

"Don't be silly," said Mrs. Howard. "Look, if I saw them here, I'd give them to you, even though I'm sure Lydia found them in the street, but I don't see them. What do you want me to do?"

"Could you ask Lydia about them?" said Frances. "Could you ask her where they are when she comes home?" The shoes were probably in Lydia's schoolbag. Or maybe she had them with her in her coat pocket.

Just then she heard a key in the lock. "Here's Lydia," said Mrs. Howard. Frances waited uneasily.

"Mom?" called Lydia.

"In here," said her mother, and Lydia came into the bedroom.

"What are you doing here?" she said to Frances.

"It's those shoes," said her mother. "She thinks they're hers."

"So you go tattling to my mother?" said Lydia. She started to cry, which startled Frances. "You want the stupid shoes, you can have them," she said. She opened her desk drawer and took them out. She threw them on the floor and stamped out of the room.

Frances stooped for the shoes. As soon as she touched them, she knew they were the ones she had hidden under the dirt. Mrs. Howard took one out of her hand. "Look, honey," she said. "I know you don't mean to tell lies. I can't imagine what they teach you at home. But you can see these aren't shoes for a new baby. These are for a baby a year old, maybe older. Look, they've been walked in. The soles are dirty."

"That's because Lydia's been carrying them around," said Frances. "And the doll wore them."

"You don't think I'm going to believe *that*, do you?" said Mrs. Howard. She had a nasty tone now. She looked at Frances as if nothing Frances said or did could be trusted. Lydia had come back and was standing in the bedroom doorway between Frances and the door. Mrs. Howard was still holding one shoe, pointing to the sole, where Frances could see perfectly well that what she said was true. Frances had not noticed. And the side of the shoe was creased and had been polished. Where the chalky white polish was flaking, she could see leather underneath, and it was slightly discolored. She grabbed at the shoe and started to cry.

"You're a past master at this, aren't you?" said Mrs. Howard, and now she was speaking too crisply, with her mouth too small. "You're responsible for some of these ideas Lydia comes home with," she said. "I told her to keep away from you. Look, your father—I wasn't going to hold that against you, but—here he's been fired, teaching God knows what. He should go live in Russia, he likes it so much."

"My father's been fired?" said Frances. "What do you mean?"

"It's in the paper," said Mrs. Howard. "Somebody told me and I said it couldn't be true, but it's in today's paper."

Frances clutched the shoes and ran. She had to push Lydia aside, and Lydia felt light and scared and bony as Frances pushed against her. "I don't mean you're a liar," Mrs. Howard was saying, "just because of your father. That's not what I meant."

Frances ran down the stairs so fast she fell down the last three. No one was there, and she sat on the floor and cried. She had scraped her knee and hurt her elbow. After a few moments she picked up the shoes and ran home.

Frances had been intending to find out about her father's trial, to ask him exactly what it was about and when it was going to happen, and she hadn't done it. Any other girl her age would have found out everything. After a block she slowed down and walked, still clutching the shoes, her coat unbuttoned. She couldn't believe that this important event could have gone by without her noticing. It was Thursday. She couldn't remember if she'd ever known when the trial was supposed to take place. Her father had not left at the usual time one morning this week, she remembered now. She had been upset, worrying about speaking to Mrs. Howard, and she hadn't paid attention. There were days when her father had a different schedule for one reason or another, days when he had to attend meetings, days when high school students had exams.

It was getting dark when she got home. There was a light in their window, and she hurried up the stairs. She didn't know what she was going to say to her mother, but when she put her key in the lock, she heard her father's step coming toward the door. He opened it as she did and looked down at her with some surprise, as if he'd forgotten that doors opened. He was wearing an apron.

"Where were you?" he said.

"I was at Lydia's house," said Frances.

"Oh, Lydia's house," he said. He turned and went back into the kitchen. Frances could hear him moving around, and she could smell something cooking. She took off her coat and put it on her bed. The shoes were in the pocket. Then she went to the kitchen. Her father was wearing a blue-and-white bib apron of her mother's. The bib was folded inside and the apron was tied around her father's waist. It was toast Frances had smelled.

"Isn't Mommy going to make supper?" she said.

"I haven't eaten all day," he said. "I couldn't wait."

"Where were you?"

"I was at the union." The union meant the Teachers Union.

"Couldn't you go out and have lunch?" It was true, then. Her father had not gone to work.

"I guess I could have, but I didn't." He had put some butter in a small frying pan and it was sizzling. He was making scrambled eggs. He'd broken the eggs into a bowl, and now he added some milk and beat the eggs with a fork.

"Do you want me to do that?" said Frances. He shouldn't have to do it for himself.

"No, thanks, I can do it," he said. "I have a headache. I'm going to eat some scrambled eggs and go to bed."

"That's a good idea," said Frances. She sat at her place at the table, from which she often watched her mother cook. Then she thought to get up and take a plate out of the cupboard and put it on the table for her father. She folded a paper napkin and put it under a fork. She put out a knife and a spoon, too. Then she took the two slices of toast, which had popped up, and put them on the plate. She put the butter dish next to her father's place. Then she sat down again and watched him. He poured the eggs into the pan and stood with his back to her, stirring them with the fork.

"Now, you understand what's happened, don't you?" he asked gruffly after a few moments.

"I don't know," said Frances.

"I've lost my job," he said, "but you don't have to worry. Your mother is working, and we have savings. And of course I'll find something else."

"But it isn't fair," said Frances.

"Well, of course it isn't fair," he said, looking over his shoulder at her.

"You're a good teacher," she said.

"A very good teacher," he said sadly. He was turning off the burner and scraping his scrambled eggs onto his plate with the fork. He sat down and buttered his toast and began to eat hungrily. He looked at her as if he expected her to speak.

"I've been wondering," she said, and he looked interested, the way he might have looked in the classroom if a student began to ask a question: welcoming the question. Yet he also did not look exactly that way. He looked as if he was afraid of being hurt even more. She didn't want to ask a question that would make things worse. She had been going to ask exactly what had happened at the trial. She shouldn't ask that—but now she had said she was going to ask him something. She had to change the subject.

"Daddy," she said, "that baby who died before I was born—you know, that baby?"

He looked startled, but a little relieved—pleased to be reminded that there were other subjects in the world. "Rachel," he said.

"Rachel?" She had not known the baby's name. Something inside her began to flutter, and she felt tension rise in her throat. "Was her name Rachel?"

"Yes, you didn't know that? Of course her name was Rachel."

"Daddy, how old was she when she died?" Frances said.

"How old? I know exactly how old," he said. "She was fifteen months."

She wanted to go and look at the shoes. "Could she walk?" said Frances.

"Oh, yes, she walked early," he said. "Earlier than you. She could walk easily."

"How did she die? Was she sick?"

He put down his fork. "It was an accident," he said. "It was a terrible accident. I don't want you thinking—"

"What?" She could see that he didn't want to talk about this, but now she didn't care how he felt. She needed to know. It was as if the accident were still about to happen—to her little sister, not her big one, and she could prevent it if only she could understand.

"She climbed out of the stroller," he said, and his voice was low and cold, almost a mumble. "Your mother had gone into a store."

"Do you mean Rachel got lost?" said Frances.

Her father shook his head. He had finished his food, and he was picking up the plate and putting it into the sink. Then he put the silverware into the sink and put the butter dish back in the refrigerator. The carton of eggs was on the work table next to the stove, and he put that away too. "A car," he said then, in a low voice.

"Oh," said Frances. She sat perfectly still. She would not be able to help this baby, no matter what she did, and she might not be able to help her father either. She was making him feel worse after all. Her father stood in the middle of the kitchen, taking off his apron and looking around him as if he were in a circle of accusers and knew that whatever he said, they would not understand.

Her mother was at the door, turning her key in the lock. She came in holding a bag of groceries. She stood in the doorway, glanced at Frances, looked at Nathan. Her arm in its black sleeve moved to point to a newspaper that was sticking out of the bag of groceries. "It's in the paper," she said.

"I know," he said. "I saw it."

5 ❧

"MIKE WANTS TO BUY A CAR," PEARL SAID TO HILDA. SHE thought Hilda might be able to reply to that remark without sounding angry. Pearl knew—for once—that Hilda was not angry with her for any particular reason, or with any of them, but she sounded angry all the time.

Mostly, though, people talked to Hilda only about Rachel. "Did the baby sleep better last night?" Pearl herself had said when she arrived, after promising inwardly not to start by mentioning the baby, and Hilda had responded, "Better than what? Better than me?" Just at that moment Rachel had been waking up in her bassinet, which stood near the living room couch where Hilda was stretched out reading the newspaper. Pearl had been given a key, and she'd let herself in.

129

The baby lay on her stomach in her white sacque, which had worked itself up to her armpits. Her legs looked surprisingly long and thin to Pearl, pulled up as a frog's might be, with her heels near her crotch. Her dark, angry face—Rachel looked as angry as her mother—was turned to the left, and she had stuffed her left fist into her mouth and was gnawing at it, making little grunts of effort and frustration.

The first surprise, a few weeks ago now, was that Rachel looked like *Rachel*, not just like "a baby." The second surprise was this anger of Hilda's, the third that Pearl, who had spent a year waiting for Hilda to speak to her in a friendly way, now didn't care. It was as if Hilda *were* being friendly. Today, after Hilda's answer to her question, Pearl had gone to warm up Rachel's bottle without another word. When it was ready, Hilda had sat up and given Rachel the bottle, whispering intently to her as if she had something to say that she preferred to keep private.

Pearl thought Hilda might be interested in the car, and she was. Pearl had to talk fast. She'd found that if she dropped in at Hilda and Nathan's on her way home from work, she could help out for an hour without getting too tired and hungry, then go home and cook dinner. Nathan was sometimes there, sometimes not. Today Pearl knew Nathan wouldn't be there. Mike had gone to a meeting with him—union people planning protests against the fascist rebellion in Spain. Mike said he wanted to listen because the speeches gave him good shorthand practice. He took down what he heard. Pearl thought maybe he liked the meetings for themselves as well; she wasn't sure.

"He's buying it from the clarinet player," she said. Mike was still in the band, and it had been playing on weekends at a few hotels in the Catskills, sometimes at the one in the Adirondacks where they'd met. The band would drive up together in the clarinet player's old black car, which smelled of cigarettes. Now the clarinet player had a new job and he was leaving the band and even buying a new car.

"A car would be nice," said Hilda.

"We could all four go places," Pearl said. "All five. We could have a picnic."

"Maybe," said Hilda. She was wearing a dark red bathrobe pulled tight around her waist. Her hair hadn't been trimmed for a long time, and Pearl liked the way it tumbled onto her shoulders. Hilda's hair was naturally wavy. She'd gained weight and it made her face look younger and softer. The angry tone was surprising each time.

"I guess Nathan will be home soon," Pearl said. Rachel was awake now, lying on her back on the couch at Hilda's side. She waved her legs in the air. Now and then Hilda gave her a finger to chew. "She likes to suck my wedding ring," she said.

"She's a good kid," said Pearl.

"He's on his way to Spain, I suppose," said Hilda.

"What?"

"Nathan."

"Oh. Right." Pearl glanced at the newspaper Hilda had been reading. It had slipped to the floor. She couldn't see the main headline. Lately the headlines had been mostly about Spain. The rebels were taking over cities and towns, the Loyalists struggling.

"I'm serious," said Hilda.

Pearl was startled. "You don't mean Nathan is actually on his way to Spain?"

"No, Pearlie, I don't. I'm exaggerating for effect. But I think if it weren't for Rachel, he'd volunteer. A friend of his is talking about volunteering—several friends from the union."

"It's hard to imagine, going off to fight in a strange country," said Pearl respectfully.

"It's hard for our country to imagine that it may be necessary," Hilda said firmly, as if she had to speak for Nathan in his absence. "It's hard for our government to take off the blinders. This is Hitler's war. The rebels are fascists, just like the Nazis."

"Well, I know," said Pearl.

"I wish I could go to some of these meetings," said Hilda.

"I didn't know you wanted to."

"Well, I do." She picked up Rachel and held her on her lap so the baby could suck her fingers more easily. Hilda wasn't good at holding a baby yet, and Rachel's legs were in the wrong place, stretching off Hilda's lap. Yet Rachel was barely a handful. Changing her diaper, Pearl liked to fit her hand over Rachel's hard little backside. "Having a baby is great," said Hilda now, as if she had been asked a question, "but there are lots of things you have to give up."

Hilda didn't say anything else for a long time, and Pearl couldn't see her face. She was leaning over Rachel, looking down at her. Both of them looked disheveled. Rachel's sacque was open and so was Hilda's robe. Under it, she was wearing a slip, not a nightgown. She was half dressed.

Then Hilda looked up. "Pearlie," she said quietly, with a catch in her voice.

"What is it?" Pearl moved to the couch and made room for herself. She scooped Rachel up and held her. Rachel felt damp.

Hilda leaned against her. "You smell of the outdoors," she said. "And the office. I smell typewriter, and office floor, and Mr. Glynnis. What is it he smells like? Does he use cologne? Have you been kissing him?"

"No," said Pearl laughing. "Certainly not." She stood and carried Rachel into the bedroom. "I'm going to change my niece and go home," she called.

"Thanks. You really don't have to treat me like a convalescent anymore," said Hilda, straightening her bathrobe as she followed Pearl.

"I like changing her." Rachel was so small that it was hard to pin the diapers tightly enough—they had to be folded so many times that the pins wouldn't go through all the thicknesses of cloth. Pearl worked at it, holding her finger under the point as she'd learned to do when she was a teenager, baby-sitting her cousins. Rachel was cooing and half crying, but she didn't seem to mind being changed. She batted at the air, at Pearl's face. Pearl had to stoop over her. This changing table would work for Hilda, but Pearl was taller.

"Let us know if you get the car," Hilda said when Pearl left. "It might be nice, having a car."

And it was. Mike came home with the car two days later, and the following Sunday Pearl persuaded both Mike and Hilda that a picnic was a good idea, and even Nathan came along. They brought a blanket to sit on. Pearl made roast beef sandwiches and hard-boiled eggs and brought celery sticks and cookies. She thought Hilda needed building up. Mike got directions from the former owner of the car to a park in Queens. It was a bright fall day.

At the last minute Hilda was grumpy and uncertain. "We can't put the carriage in the car. What are we going to do with her when we get there?"

"We'll put her on the blanket," said Mike. "Or we'll take turns holding her." He had told Pearl he liked to hold the baby.

"I'll walk her," said Nathan.

The food was already in the car, and Hilda and Nathan were standing on the sidewalk in front of their house, where Mike and Pearl had come to get them. Now Hilda said nothing more, and Nathan took Rachel from her while Mike helped her into the back seat and put the baby into her arms again.

Pearl found she was keeping track of Hilda the way a nursemaid might study the appetite of a sick child. Yet she was also a little annoyed. Hilda was silent for many blocks. Then she said, "The leaves are turning."

Pearl twisted around to agree.

"I've been in the house so much," said Hilda.

She was edgy with all of them. She told Mike she thought he drove too fast, and when Nathan disagreed she said, "Since when do you know anything about it?" When Pearl chattered she seemed disgusted. Nathan, next to Hilda with Rachel's pink diaper bag on his lap, looked conscientious and a little scared when Pearl turned around from the front seat to watch them.

Rachel started to cry long before they reached the park. They couldn't figure out what was wrong. She'd just eaten. "Maybe there's a pin stuck in her rear end," said Mike.

"Don't be silly," said Pearl. Hilda would feel accused. Hilda didn't seem surprised by Rachel's crying and made no effort to stop her, but Pearl turned around and patted the baby tentatively, and Nathan felt the pins through Rachel's clothes to make sure they were closed.

At the park, Pearl tried patting the baby's back and walking with Rachel against her shoulder, while the others unloaded the picnic supplies and looked for a good spot. It was a moist, hazy day, with yellow leaves in abundance. It all made her feel sad. This baby wailing and wailing—her body jumping with sobs—seemed to know bad news. Pearl was unsure of herself as a singer but she tried singing in a low voice as she walked Rachel up and down. "Rock-a-bye baby," she tried, then, "Night and day, you are the one. . . ." Singing, she was moved, as though she were singing to someone else, an adult, not just Rachel.

Nathan came up behind her and when he touched her shoulder she jumped. "I'm sorry," he said. "Don't drop my daughter."

"I won't," said Pearl. She felt awkward because he'd heard her sing. She had no idea how to make Rachel stop crying. With her hands free as Nathan took the baby, she brushed aside the hair that had come loose from her braid and blown into her eyes. Nathan patted the baby, looking grim. Together they walked back to Mike and Hilda, who had spread a blanket on the ground. Hilda was taking food out of the basket. Mike was stretched out watching her. "Didn't work, did it?" he said. "You're sure she's not hungry?"

"I'm sure," said Hilda, sounding annoyed, but she offered Rachel a bottle. Rachel turned away and cried harder.

"Maybe her stomach hurts," said Pearl.

"Maybe." Hilda laid Rachel on the blanket. Her cries sounded tired to Pearl, cantankerous and complainy, and sure enough, after a while she fell asleep. All four adults had been sitting and watching her, just watching her.

"I guess she was tired," said Nathan. He reached for a sandwich and they all followed suit. "Oh!" he said then, pointing a finger in Mike's direction. They all waited and Nathan swallowed. "Did you take down Garber's speech the other night?"

"Garber?" said Mike.

"The tall man with the long neck," said Nathan. "He spoke next to last."

"Yeah, I got him. Why?" said Mike.

"They said you did. I thought you'd stopped," Nathan said. "I told them you only took down the first two or three."

"I got bored, but then I got even more bored doing nothing, so I started taking them down again," Mike said.

"What did you do with your notes?" said Nathan.

"What difference does it make? Does somebody want a copy of the speech?" Mike said. "For a fee . . ." He was smiling, leaning back on one arm.

"Not exactly," Nathan said. "They were somewhat peeved with me for bringing you, but I assured them you weren't some sort of spy."

"Spy for who?"

Nathan unwrapped another sandwich and shrugged. "I don't know. The list of dissatisfied former comrades is long."

"I don't recall that the speech was particularly interesting," Mike said.

"I know, I know," said Nathan. "Some of them have lively imaginations. They'd like to have your notes."

"Well, they can go to hell," said Mike amiably. He was peeling a hard-boiled egg. "Is there salt, Pearl?" he said. Pearl had brought a twist of salt in waxed paper and she handed it to him. She had not been interested when this conversation began, but she thought Nathan was more concerned than Mike realized.

"You don't need the notes," she said to Mike. "It was just for practice, wasn't it? You usually throw them out." She shrugged and smiled at Nathan. He looked back at her, looked as if she made him think of something different and important, looked for a moment as if he had something to say, so that Pearl said, "What?" and Hilda, who had eaten only a quarter of a sandwich and was lying on the blanket near the baby, playing with the blades of grass next to the blanket, her back to the rest of them, glanced over her shoulder at Pearl. But Nathan shook his head and turned back to Mike.

"That's not the point," Mike was saying, angry with Pearl now. "It's not the point whether I throw them out. What right do they have to ask me for my notes? What the hell do they think I'm going to do with them?" His voice was raised.

"Take it easy," said Nathan.

"I don't know why you put up with that crowd," Mike said. "They think they're so important? They think I've got nothing better to do than convince the *Herald Tribune* to run their silly speech? I'm tempted, but it's too dull. *Nobody* would run it."

"Forget it," said Nathan.

"It's not *like* you," Mike said. "Why do you care about these people?"

"Look, I said forget it," Nathan said.

"It's not that simple," said Mike.

"All right," Nathan said. "I care about these people because they are keeping their eyes open and looking at Spain, looking at Germany. You think Hitler is some sort of joke? You think if you don't look at Spain it will go away?"

Pearl thought about Hitler. She'd seen newsreels. The marching soldiers were frightening. She knew that as Jews they would have been in trouble if they had happened to be born in Germany instead of New York. Her parents were upset about Hitler, too, though they didn't talk much about Spain.

"I thought I'd go to the rally next week," she said to Nathan. She hadn't known until this moment that she was actually planning to go. It was a rally sponsored by several organizations in support of the Spanish Loyalists. She'd seen signs, and a woman in her office had talked to her about it. The woman's boyfriend was thinking about volunteering, about going to Spain as Hilda had said Nathan wanted to do. The rally was to be at Union Square, not too far from where Pearl worked, and it was to start at five o'clock.

"The rally on Thursday in Union Square?" said Nathan. "That's good. We'll go together." As so often, he sounded weary, but pleased with her. She ate her lunch.

"Aren't you hungry?" she said to Hilda.

"Not very," said Hilda. She was leaning on her side, her legs bent, her hips looking heavy and luxurious. The baby was next to her, still asleep on her stomach.

A man and a woman walked past their blanket, then turned back. They came closer—a gray-haired couple, arm in arm, clutching each other as if they were afraid of stumbling in the grass. "That baby's going to smother, lying on the blanket," said the woman in a loud voice. "He shouldn't be on the bare ground on the blanket."

"She isn't on the bare ground," Hilda said, not sitting up, but with new animation in her voice. "That's the point. She's on the *blanket.*"

The woman turned away. "I was only trying to help," she said.

"He looks like a monkey," said the man. He spoke to the woman but they could all hear him. "That baby looks like a monkey."

"Go to hell," called Mike. He looked around the blanket at the rest of them. His eyes were bright and his face was red. He looked as if he was deciding whether to laugh or to be angry. Nathan looked appalled, sitting back as if he'd been hit. But Hilda laughed—a bitter laugh, but a laugh.

Pearl had brought a thermos bottle of coffee and they all had some, though it wasn't terribly hot. They ate cookies from the box she'd brought. Then Hilda lay down on the blanket again.

"Do you want to take a nap?" Nathan asked her.

"The baby will wake up."

"I'll take her for a walk," he said.

"Don't wake her until she wakes up on her own," said Hilda. She curled up and Nathan took off his jacket and spread it over her. Hilda was in open-toed shoes and a cotton summer dress, which she pulled down over her knees. Her calves swelled and tapered.

"Do you mind if I go for a walk *without* the baby?" said Nathan. "I want to stretch my legs."

"Go ahead."

"You can go, too," said Mike to Pearl. "There's something I want to do. If the baby wakes up while Hilda's sleeping, I'll walk her."

Pearl and Nathan set out on a path through a little wood. Nathan was silent for a while. "What does Mike want to do?" he said.

"I don't know," said Pearl. "He didn't bring his saxophone, and he can't take down what anybody's saying if nobody's talking."

"He keeps busy."

"I know it. Sometimes it makes me tired, just watching him." Yet it wasn't as if Mike were indefatigable, like her mother, who really did make Pearl tired, always rushing someplace. She had come to Pearl's house once just to do Pearl's ironing. Mike was usually fidgeting or figuring something out—a new way to wash dishes so they ended up on the left side of the sink, closer to the cupboard where they were going; a way of stacking bills that came in so the one that should be paid first was on top. There were many bills, in fact, and always more than one that should be paid first. Mike was doing all sorts of jobs—working for the district attorney's office, playing the sax, and one day he really had taken down a speech he'd heard and sold it to a newspaper. She wondered whether Nathan knew that. What he was afraid of might happen, not because Mike cared about the speeches he'd taken down, but just because he was happy to be able to get them on paper, eager for people to know about this trick of his.

"He doesn't mean any harm," she said, about the speech.

"I know, but he doesn't think," said Nathan. "He'll show anything to anybody."

"But they can't read his notes, and he's not interested in transcribing them."

Nathan sighed. "I wish I had that speech," he said.

"It's important to you, what the rest of them think of you," she said.

"I guess so."

140

They were walking through a grove. She thought she could see water beyond it. "Hilda says if it wasn't for the baby, you'd go to Spain," she said.

Nathan laughed. "I'd make a great soldier," he said. "The original flabby armchair idealist."

"No," she said. She didn't think Nathan was flabby, she thought he had a nice physique. It wasn't as wiry as Mike's; it was a little softer, a little more mature.

"I'd like to do something," he said. "I care about this very much. Talking and raising money—well, that's all right, but of course it's not actually *doing* anything."

"Don't you think the Loyalists hear about our rallies and feel braver?" she said.

"I don't know, Pearl," said Nathan. "I don't know."

"And then our government will pay attention."

He was silent for a while. "If Franco wins," he said then, "it's such a loss for all of us. Not just the Spaniards . . ." They had reached the edge of the pond, and the path turned and widened. She had been walking a little ahead of him, but now they walked side by side. Nathan moved a few branches aside so they wouldn't snag Pearl's legs. He was quiet for a long time. Then he said, "You're quite surprising." His voice seemed to shake with some kind of feeling, which made her uneasy, but she put the thought aside.

"What do you mean?" she said shyly. She had been thinking he probably thought she was ignorant.

"I don't know what I mean," he said, seeming to rouse himself. "Maybe just that you're thoughtful. You're a thoughtful girl."

"Thank you," she said.

"And you're kind to Hilda," he said.

"I think being a mother is harder than she expected," said Pearl.

"Whatever I do lately," he said, "she makes me feel stupid."

"She doesn't mean to," said Pearl, but he'd spoken with vehemence, and she knew he wasn't going to hear her.

"I don't know," he said again. "I don't know what she means."

She wanted to comfort him, and the thought that came to her was of pulling down his serious face with its balding forehead and kissing the bare place on the top of his skull. She turned and touched his wrist lightly, but that was all. They walked back to the blanket in silence. Hilda was sitting up, giving Rachel a bottle. Mike seemed to be taking a nap. Propped on the picnic basket was a sign constructed out of the cookie box, which he had laboriously torn and flattened. That was what he'd wanted to do. He had a pencil, apparently, and Pearl read aloud what he'd written. "Little Racket," she said. "Little *Racket?*"

"Rachel. Don't you know what an *h* looks like?" Mike said, sitting up.

"It looks like a *k* to me, and if that's not a *t* why is it crossed?"

"*Rachel.*"

"Little Racket," Pearl persisted, teasing. "Your real writing is as hard to read as your shorthand. Little Racket, the Human Monkey. A Nickel a Look."

"Very good," said Nathan. "Any customers?"

"It's been quiet," said Mike.

"We *should* call her Racket," said Hilda. "She makes a racket, all right." She leaned over and pulled the baby toward her and kissed her forehead. "Racket," she said. "Sleepy little Racket. Skinny little rickety Racket." Hilda looked better, Pearl thought. Her nap had done her good. She had color in her cheeks. Pearl began gathering the picnic things, which were still lying on the blanket. Mike had lit a cigarette. "Do you two want to walk around a little?" Pearl said. "I could feed the baby."

"Come on, Hilda," said Mike, pulling her up. "I'll go with you. Or Nathan can take another walk. Good for him."

"No," said Hilda. "I'd rather not."

The day of the rally, Nathan called for Pearl at work. He arrived a few minutes before she was ready to leave, and stood quietly in the midst of departing employees, looking grave, as usual. Pearl felt self-conscious, and as she straightened the papers on her desk and sealed some letters she had written for Mr. Carmichael, she didn't know how to move her hands properly, as if she were trying to play the part of herself on stage. Licking an envelope didn't feel familiar.

At last she pinned on her hat, sticking the hatpin through her braid as she always did, and took her coat, and she began to relax. She was looking forward to being alone with Nathan, though it also felt somewhat alarming. She'd told Mike she'd be home late, but in fact he would be later yet, or he might be out all night. He was on call that night for the homicide squad. She explained it to Nathan as they went downstairs and out into the street.

"Still collaborating with the *gendarmes*," said Nathan.

"He just does shorthand. He just writes down what people say."

"Well, I'm glad he's comfortable," Nathan said. They were walking to the subway station.

"What do you mean?" said Pearl. She didn't like Nathan to disapprove of Mike.

"Don't worry, I don't mean anything," Nathan said. "Mike and I have been arguing about this stuff all our lives. And we always will."

"In a way, you're close," she said.

"In a way," said Nathan, which was not what she expected.

On the subway they had to stand. "How's Hilda?" said Pearl, over the noise of the train. Nathan shrugged.

"And the baby?" Another shrug.

He cheered up when they got out of the subway at Union Square. It was crowded. A woman was speaking, and though she had a megaphone it was hard to hear what she was saying. People pushed closer to hear her. It was getting dark, a cool October evening, and the rally looked the way Pearl imagined an event in Europe might look. Everyone seemed to be wearing dark clothing, and they were pressed together in a quiet, serious crowd. Light shone on some of the up-turned faces. The square was full of people. The woman's speech was interrupted with shouts and applause; then people would listen quietly again. "These suffering people . . ." Pearl heard her say. Then, "the frightened peasants." Apparently she had recently come from Spain. Pearl could hardly make out any of the woman's sentences, but she joined in the applause and cheers. Nathan clapped his big hands slowly together when the woman finished. He led Pearl along the edge of the crowd, trying to find a place where they could hear better. Now a man from the labor unions was speaking. Pearl could hear him, but she wasn't as interested as she had been in the woman. "Our members pledge themselves to stand in solidarity . . ." She cheered him too.

They listened to speaker after speaker. She grew cold. It wasn't a cold night, but she was wearing only a light coat, and the wind cut into her. She didn't want to ask Nathan to leave before it was over. She was hungry.

At last he looked at her. "You're shivering," he said.

"I should have worn a sweater under my coat."

"This is almost over. Let's go to the Automat before it gets crowded." He steered her through the crowd and they walked down the street to the Automat, which was crowded already, but at last they reached the end of the change line and got their nickels, and then they were able to buy food and coffee. Pearl always bought macaroni and cheese at the Automat, and Nathan did what she did. They managed to find a table near the wall. Now she was happy. Maybe people would hear about their rally and do something to help the Loyalists.

"I guess this isn't as good as going to fight in Spain, but I like it," she said.

"No Automats with macaroni and cheese in Spain, I imagine," said Nathan. "I'm not complaining." They ate slowly, talking about the rally, then about other things. Pearl talked about her office, about the two bosses and some of the other workers.

"Hilda misses the office," Nathan said.

"I suppose she does," said Pearl.

"She calls the baby Racket now," said Nathan.

"I think that's cute," Pearl said.

"Pearl—" said Nathan. He stopped. She looked up but he shook his head and said nothing. Then he said, "I'll take you home." On the subway, Pearl was exhausted, as if the rally had lasted hours and hours. She was glad Nathan was taking her home. She was excited under her tiredness, though. She wanted him to stay when he took her home, so she could talk with him for a long time. She felt safe with Nathan, she told herself, and that was surprising. She didn't feel unsafe *without* Nathan.

"I'm very sad," he said suddenly in the street, half a block from Pearl's apartment. She was startled and stopped, turning to face him. They were under a street lamp, and he did look sad, but he always looked sad.

"Why?" she said. "Did I say something wrong?"

"No, you didn't say anything wrong," he said, and she was reminded of something Hilda had said a long time ago, of trying to work out something that had gone wrong between her and Hilda.

"Is it——" She didn't want to ask him whether he too was hurt by Hilda.

"I don't think very well of myself right now," he said. "I don't think I'm a good man. The sort of man I should be."

"Because you can't go to Spain?" she said. But she knew that wasn't what he meant. They had begun walking again.

"It would be good if I could do something like that," he said. "Be a hero. But I'm a lot less than a regular person, a lot less than just somebody who isn't a hero. I'd like to be satisfactory. If I were one of my students, I'd give me a C or a D. I'd like to get a B, even if I'm not an A person."

"What do you mean?" she said. She wasn't cold now. Nathan was talking differently from the way he'd ever talked. It seemed amazing that he might talk that way to her, of all people. She didn't want him to think so badly of himself, but she was happy—she was breathing in so deeply that she was getting light-headed. He hadn't answered what she'd said. She put her hand on his arm and said, "Nathan, can I help?"

He put one hand on her shoulder and she stopped. They were walking beside apartment buildings, and they were passing an alley between buildings. He drew her a step into the alley and tilted her face up toward him with his fingertips, then bent down and kissed her cheek lightly under one eye. It was just a slight, dry kiss, but he kissed her again an inch away and again and yet again. Pearl stood with her hands at her sides. Finally she put her hand on his sleeve again. Nathan kissed her cheeks in many places, and then, finally, her lips, and then he seemed to shudder and began to kiss her lips harder. He stopped and shook his head. "I can't believe I'm doing this, Pearl," he said. "May I go home with you?"

In answer she reached into her bag for her key. They were only half a block from her house, and they hurried there with their heads down. She fumbled with the elevator door and he turned her toward the stairs, as if he wanted to be slowed down, to be made tired, but soon she was opening the door with her key. For a moment she wondered what would happen if Mike were there after all, but he wasn't. She wasn't letting herself think too far. She wanted to comfort Nathan, to kiss away his sadness. She wanted to kiss him back so he wouldn't think she believed he was a bad person for kissing her. Sometimes things like this happened, she explained to herself. She said it again as she took off her coat and hat and took his coat, making it take as long as possible. Sometimes things like this happened. Her surprise reminded her of something and she remembered what it was—the first time she'd started to bleed. "This is something that happens," her mother had said, and Pearl had felt dizzy with suspense about the rest of her life. If girls and women bled this way and she hadn't known it, if she hadn't known about something so significant, so—she couldn't help but feel—*unusual*, then what else might happen?

She and Mike had a one-bedroom apartment. She knew she wasn't taking Nathan into the bedroom, and knowing that made her know she was going to bed with him. In the living room was the single bed she'd had as a girl. It had been part of their bed when they lived at Nathan and Hilda's, and now it was their couch, with a row of pillows on it against the wall. Her mother had made pillow covers for her of flowered fabric. Pearl sat down on the couch and lifted her face to look at Nathan again. He didn't sit with her but sat at her feet on the floor and then pulled her gently down to him and began kissing her once more. But it was different. It was more reckless, less as if he were telling her a secret no one else had ever heard. This was more energetic; he seemed determined to do wrong and get it over with. Yet it was kind. Nathan's hands, touching her, seemed to be asking, not telling her what would happen. Asking whether she too wanted to do this.

After many kisses he brought the pillows down from the couch and helped her off with her dress and underwear and eased her down. There was a pillow under her head and shoulders and one under her backside. Nathan stood and turned away, still without speaking, and took off his own clothes and laid them on the couch. He didn't exactly fold them, Pearl saw, watching him lovingly from the floor, nervous yet proud of her long body, but he smoothed them and placed them respectfully. That was how he touched her: with respect.

"You're the sweetest girl. . . ." he said. She was amazed at what was happening, amazed that it could happen. Her body responded to him with waves of pleasure, as if she'd been waiting for exactly this event to take place. Nathan's shadowed face hovered over hers, and at the climax he sank into her arms as though he would never stand again. He eased out of her carefully and kept his arms around her. She felt that he was the whole world, that Nathan was the oceans and mountains, the Loyalists fighting in Spain and the thousands of people cheering at rallies. "I love you," she whispered into his shoulder, inaudibly. "I love you, I love you, I love you, I love you." Not out loud.

He dressed quickly. She remained lying on the pillows, watching him, noticing the slope of his shoulder as he picked up his undershirt and put it on, the way his chest hairs curled darkly over its edge when he was wearing it, the flare of his nose, seen from below, as he looked to see where to fasten his shirt cuff. Putting on his pants, he looked at her and blushed. He did not turn red, the way Mike did when he blushed. Nathan's face darkened and he looked aside. Pearl stood up and went into her bedroom for her bathrobe.

He kissed her again before he left, two tiny kisses that barely touched her lips but seemed full of messages. She put her arms around him and held him, and then he left. Her bathrobe was loose and she tied the belt again, then picked up the pillows, smoothed their covers, and arranged them on the couch as usual. She felt dazed and she moved slowly. She took the pile of her clothes into the bedroom and put it on the bed. Then she went into the bathroom. The sight of the toilet reminded her that she wanted to urinate and she did, a long stream that eased her. She felt the urine leave her body with rather more attention than usual, as if her mind were stilled of everything else and she had nothing more to think about. She flushed the toilet and began to fill the bathtub. She took a long bath. The water was Nathan, the pitted tub over whose familiar surface she ran her finger was Nathan. The towel with which she dried her whole body, even her toes, was Nathan. Still without thinking, she was asleep before Mike came home.

Pearl never woke easily, but in the morning, this time, she knew she was happy before she knew why. It was sad that Mike couldn't know and of course wouldn't share in this happiness. In a way it was hard to understand, as if Mike too was simply part of Nathan and would rejoice as she did. She had to remind herself firmly that no one would rejoice.

It was Friday. She went to work. She didn't read on the train, she just sat and looked around her. She had never noticed how interesting people were, how you could know things about them if you just looked. An old woman opposite her had her fingers curled through the hemp handles of a shopping bag, and when the woman stood to leave the train at her stop, Pearl discovered that she could feel how the heavy bag settled and how the handles cut into the woman's fingers.

There were children on the train, high school students. The boys almost made her cry. Even when they seemed outwardly tough or cold or stupid, she could suddenly see that their lips and eyes were innocent, a little fearful, full of hope and uncertainty. She caressed them with her eyes and wanted to bless them. She wanted to bless all the people on the subway, to put her fingers on their foreheads in a half-remembered, half-invented holy gesture. Standing and walking among them, getting off at her stop and joining the throng on the platform, where some people were already mounting the stairs and others shuffled behind her, Pearl discovered that she believed in God.

She was sure they'd be happy, she and Nathan. She didn't know how. At work, she let herself think about him only now and then, as a reward for typing a stack of letters, or for approaching Mr. Carmichael with a difficult question. It would be *all right*, she said to herself over and over.

In the late afternoon, as it was growing dark, she was suddenly afraid. A sheet of fear passed over her body the way it might have if she'd looked up to see a masked gunman in the doorway. She pressed her hands into the papers on her desk. "Are you all right?" asked the bookkeeper, Ruby—Hilda's replacement—walking past her.

"I shivered," she said, but Ruby kept walking.

She told herself again that everything would be all right, that Nathan would know what had to happen, that if she just waited patiently it would all become clear. She needed to think, anyway. She didn't want to see Nathan just yet, or even speak to him. She wanted to think of him, to run her fingers over his body in her imagination.

All she cared to do in the next days was sing and listen to the radio. She sang love songs. She'd known them for years but had never paid attention to the words. She'd never known that the people singing *loved* someone.

She still had a good time with Mike. He was funny and he was her husband. She neglected the cooking and cleaning for the next week because she was always staring out the window and doing nothing, but that was not right. When her mother dropped in one after-noon and asked what Pearl was making for supper, Pearl didn't know. The next day she bought a cookbook so she could make better meals for Mike. There was nothing wrong with Mike. When she and Na-than spoke at last, he must not be allowed to say anything bad about his younger brother Mike. He might say she should divorce Mike and he'd divorce Hilda, and they'd get married, but she wouldn't agree, at least not right away. They owed a lot to Hilda and Mike and besides there was the baby. She'd tell Nathan they had to keep silent and wait, and see how they felt about each other over the years. Maybe they'd have to wait until Racket was grown up. That seemed hard but worthwhile. She could picture herself, ennobled by love of Nathan, waiting until they could act on their love without hurting Racket.

Pearl went to see Racket and Hilda one afternoon on the way home from work, as she had at first. Of course she felt strange but she told herself that the world was a strange place, people all over were feeling and doing things that they had never expected. Ruby's boyfriend hadn't expected to become a soldier in Spain—he was a student at City College—but he was talking about going. Pearl hadn't expected to marry Mike and that had happened. Things happened.

"I took her for a walk in the carriage," Hilda said. "I'm glad I got back before you came over." She was peeling potatoes with the play-pen set up next to her, though the kitchen was so small the playpen filled it. Racket was lying in it on her stomach, flailing her arms like a little swimmer.

Pearl picked her up and Racket batted at Pearl's nose. She was a dark-eyed baby, solemn for a moment, but then she laughed. "She laughed with a sound," Pearl said.

"I know. She did that yesterday, too. It's cute, isn't it?" said Hilda.

The baby reminded Pearl of Nathan. She was the first person besides familiar Mike whom Pearl had touched since she'd touched Nathan. Racket seemed sinewy and busy for a baby, twisting in her arms. Pearl lowered her into the playpen again. She was half relieved, half disappointed that Nathan wasn't there, and she hurried home before he could come in.

As the days passed Pearl noticed that Nathan's touch had changed her. Her breasts felt different. She touched them and shaped them with her hands as she was getting dressed in the morning. She thought they were more beautiful than they had been. She'd never thought of herself as having beautiful breasts, as being beautiful at all, except for her hair, but now she stretched to see herself in the mirror over her dresser and liked the long line of her body. She had good feet— she'd never thought of that either. They were narrow and her insteps were high. She would have liked those feet if she'd seen them in a shoe ad in a magazine.

But she was tired. Just thinking about Nathan tired her. She yawned when she was standing in Mr. Carmichael's office while he explained something he wanted her to do. She had to think about climbing the stairs. When it was finally night, she'd lie in bed next to Mike, thinking of Nathan. Sometimes Mike wanted to make love to her, and she complied, but she was so tired she felt almost nothing. "Come on, sweetie," Mike would say, "don't you like this? How about this? Do you like this?"

And he'd fondle her. He too sculpted her breasts with his hands. "Baby, I think you're growing," he said to her one night, a few weeks after her night with Nathan.

"Don't be silly," she said, smiling.

"Your breasties are really something. I never noticed."

"You never looked."

"I looked, I looked, believe me."

Pearl was frightened, as if Mike were about to discover Nathan's fingerprints on her breasts. She stroked him to hurry him. She felt dry inside. She didn't really want to do this, and it wasn't because he was Mike instead of Nathan. Maybe she was getting her period, she thought, although she didn't recall that being about to get her period usually made her feel this way. She began to try to remember when she had last had her period.

She always meant to write it down, but she never did. She'd been caught by surprise at work more than once, and had had to get permission to run out to the drugstore for sanitary pads. She was pretty sure she hadn't had her period when they'd gone on the picnic, and she knew she didn't have it the day of the rally, October eighth. She counted up. The rally—the day she'd slept with Nathan—was more than three weeks ago. She hadn't had her period *between* the picnic and the rally, because then she'd have been thinking about it when they made love, thinking about whether it was really over and whether he'd mind if there was blood. She hadn't thought about it at all.

But this didn't make sense. Pearl was regular—twenty-eight days. She counted back twenty-eight days—she could hear Mike breathing deeply in his sleep now—but that was October 6, the week between the picnic and the rally. Then she remembered her last period. She'd left work early that day to go to the dentist. She'd said something to Ruby about how it wasn't fair, the dentist and the curse in one day.

She couldn't figure out what that date had been, but it felt like a long time ago. And now she knew what she was thinking about. Pearl was going to have a baby. In the morning she checked her calendar. Her dentist appointment had been September twenty-third. Now it was November fourth. She had to be pregnant. That was it. She was pregnant.

She was sure it was Nathan's child. That explained everything—why she had been so happy, why she had not realized for so long. She had kept it a secret from herself.

Then, "Hey, are you pregnant?" said Mike at breakfast.

"What makes you think that?"

"I don't know. I was thinking about your breasties, I guess."

"Would that be bad?" said Pearl, blushing. He didn't use that word except in bed. "If I was pregnant?"

"Of course not," said Mike. "It would be great."

"I'll go to the doctor and find out," said Pearl.

"But do you think you are?" said Mike.

"Well, maybe," said Pearl. "It's too early to tell." But it wasn't too early to tell. She was pregnant with Nathan's baby. Sometimes she and Mike didn't make love for days, especially if he was working at night. Of course it was Nathan's baby.

This changed everything. She and Nathan might have to act now. They had to stop hiding from each other, at least. She had not seen him since the night they had made love, which was unusual for them.

Ordinarily they all visited back and forth. Just before their night together, she had promised Hilda she would pick a day and invite them to dinner. Hilda had said she could bring Racket in the carriage, and take it upstairs in the elevator. Maybe the baby would sleep, and they could talk. Pearl had not thought about inviting them from that day until this.

Now she had to talk to Nathan. She made an appointment with the doctor and she thought about how to talk to Nathan. After a few days she wrote him a note. "Dear Nathan, I have to talk to you about something important." She thought for a long time about how to sign the note. "Love" wasn't enough. She might have written "love" when he was just her brother-in-law. "All my love," she wrote, at last, then crossed it out, threw the note away, started again, and wrote her name without any complimentary close at all. She mailed it to Nathan at Erasmus Hall High School, where he taught.

Two days later she was working alone in her part of the office, retyping a letter on which she had made some mistakes, when she looked up. Later she thought that she must have heard footsteps, but at the time she wasn't aware of them. She knew Nathan was going to be standing there, and so she looked up—but when she saw him, she stared as if she didn't know who he was. He looked exactly the way he had looked the day of the rally, and for a moment she wished it were that day and that the only thing happening was that she and Nathan were going to a rally. Nathan was wearing his dark overcoat, which made him look more old-fashioned than usual. He was not smiling or speaking.

"You came here," she said.

"You said you had to talk to me."

"Here?"

"Can you leave for a while?"

"I'll ask." It was late in the day—after four. She bypassed Mr. Glynnis's office because she knew that Mr. Carmichael, who liked her, would say yes. She told him that her brother-in-law had a problem he needed to discuss with her, and Mr. Carmichael said, "Oh, yes, the fellow with coffee on his trousers." Pearl got her coat and she and Nathan went into the street. They walked until they came to a little luncheonette and went inside. Nathan ordered coffee, but Pearl said she wanted a malted. She needed strength.

"A malted, of course," said Nathan. He crossed his arms on the table and stared at her so hard that Pearl, who had taken off her coat and put it around her shoulders, looked down at her sweater to make sure it was properly buttoned. Or maybe he too had noticed her breasts. "I should have talked to you before," said Nathan.

"It didn't matter," said Pearl. He thought she just wanted to talk about what had happened that night.

"It mattered a lot," said Nathan. "Pearl, I want you to know I have nothing but respect for you. And I always will. I could never explain it except by saying that I think you are a very—a very lovely girl. I've been thinking about it, day after day. I know you are not that sort of person."

"What sort of person?"

"The sort of person who is accustomed to—"

She couldn't understand him. "Accustomed?"

"Pearl, you never did that before. Did you?"

"You mean—make love?" She was so confused she felt shy about saying they'd made love, as if maybe she'd imagined it, and he would be shocked.

"Well, yes."

"With Mike," she said quietly, like a child answering a question in school.

"Yes, of course, with Mike—but not with anybody else. I mean, it's none of my business—"

She thought he wanted to know whether she'd been a virgin when she married. "No, not with anybody else." She thought he wanted to make sure of her.

He accepted his coffee from the waitress and put cream and sugar in and stirred it. "That's what I mean," he said, a little impatiently. "You're not like that. And I hope I don't—"

"I love you," said Pearl simply, in answer. Her malted had come. There was a tall glass and a metal container with more malted in it. She always liked that thought, that there would be more when she finished the first glass. It usually made her feel rich, like someone who didn't have to be careful.

Nathan reddened, glancing out the window, where a man in a shabby coat was walking by with a thin dog on a leash. Nathan stirred his coffee some more. Then he looked at her. His eyes were pleading. "Pearl," he said.

"Nathan, I wouldn't have done it if I hadn't loved you," she said. "Now, I don't know what we should do exactly. And I have something to tell you—the reason I wrote to you. But please—"

"I understand," he said.

"What I wanted to talk about?"

"No—I mean, I don't know."

"Nathan," she said. She wanted him to be a little different, to speak more definitely. She'd imagined this conversation only two ways. One way, he'd say they should run away together. The other way, he'd want to wait. But now that there was this baby, she didn't see how they could wait. She was a little impatient with him. She didn't know why he kept saying he respected her. She didn't care about that. She drank some of her malted while she thought about what to say. It was comforting—it tasted as if she were a child. But she wasn't a child. "I'm having a baby," she said.

"Oh, Pearl, that's good," he said. "Congratulations. I didn't know."

"Nobody knows."

"Mike doesn't know?"

"Mike asked me if I was. I told him it was too early to tell. But it's not too early. I'm sure I'm having a baby."

"Did you go to the doctor?"

"Not yet."

"But you're sure—that's good, Pearl. I'm glad."

"Nathan," she said. It was painful, having to explain so much, so many times. "I'm not sure it's so good. It's your baby."

"What?"

"It's your baby."

"But how do you know?" he said. He looked alarmed. "Haven't you and Mike—"

"Oh, sure," she said. She didn't want him to think she and Mike weren't normal. "But I can tell. A woman can tell."

"You mean you just imagine it's my baby?"

"No, not that, more than that. I mean, I had to get pregnant sometime, right? Well, I remember—"

"You couldn't be sure," he said. "How do you know what day it was? You could have gotten pregnant on lots of days. Don't you know that?"

"No, I don't think that's right," said Pearl, but she wasn't sure, now that he was acting this way, exactly when a woman could become pregnant.

She had had it all worked out. Now she couldn't remember, couldn't explain about having her period the day she'd gone to the dentist but not the week of the rally. He wouldn't believe her.

She drank some more of her malted. It was sweet and rich. "I'm sure," she said again.

"Well, I don't see how you can be," he said, and he sounded like a teacher, as if she'd just explained to a teacher that he'd misunderstood her answer on a test, that she had had the right answer all along.

"But—" she said.

"Look, Pearl," he said. "It happened and I'm not going to deny it. But let's be reasonable here. If you insist you're pregnant with my child, look what's in store for us—for the child, for Hilda, for Rachel, for Mike, for everyone. Mike doesn't know what happened that night, does he?"

"No, of course not," she said.

"Good," he said, nodding briskly. "He doesn't ever have to know. It would only hurt him. I'm sorry it happened, I can't explain it, but I can't change it now. Only if you insist that—"

"It's not that I'm insisting," she said. "It's just the way it is. And I love you. Isn't that important?"

He dropped his balding head into his hands. He had drunk his coffee and pushed away the cup, and his arms were on the table. He looked up at her and said, "Yes, Pearl, it's important. I'm—I'm touched that you say you love me." And he lowered his face to his crossed arms.

"But you don't love *me?*" said Pearl. She had not drunk much of the malted. The second portion, in the container, was still there. She was angry that he wouldn't look at her. She thought he was only pretending to be overcome with emotion. He looked like a child hiding his eyes while he counted in a game, to give everyone a chance to hide. She stood up.

"Good-bye, Nathan," she said. Her coat slipped down when she stood up and she had to reach to the floor for it; then she tripped on it. She stuffed it under her arm and ran outside. Out of the corner of her eye, she saw the waitress, her face alarmed, take a step toward her as she opened the door and the cold air rushed in. She began to walk rapidly, not noticing where she was going. She knew she was hurrying across streets without making sure it was safe, but she did it anyway. It was dark now. People who had come from offices were rushing toward subway stations and disappearing down the stairs into the lighted wells. Pearl ran past them. She was crying, and she bumped into a man when she bent her head and wiped her eyes with her hand. She expected him to be angry, but he put his hands on her shoulders for a second, like someone straightening a wobbly ornament on a mantel, and in a kind way said, "Mind your step, Missy," before he hurried away. He was a white-haired man and Pearl wished she could bring him back and tell him what had gone wrong, why she was crying in the street without a hat or coat. She stopped and put her coat on. She had to figure out where she was and go back to the office. She had not put the cover on her typewriter and straightened things for the end of the day, and she had left her hat there. And there was another reason she had to go back, though she didn't know—didn't quite know—what it was.

She was lost, and she walked two blocks before she saw where she was. She had been going the wrong way. It was a long walk back to the office and she was exhausted, but now she knew what she was going to do there.

When she reached the building she hurried up the stairs. There were a few lights on, but almost everyone had gone. That was good. If the place were altogether empty, it would be even better. Pearl went into her own cubicle, which had no door. She would just take the risk that someone might see her. She took off her coat and hung it up. Then she sat down at her desk. There was the letter that she had been typing. Even the second one was full of mistakes. The sentences seemed like the foolishness of a child. "I remain in hope of your pseedy reply," she had written. Of course she had meant speedy. She had written the letter herself. Mr. Carmichael had told her what he wanted to say—it was to a supplier of buttons—and she had written it.

Glancing at the letter, she pulled the hairpins out of her head with one hand—a practiced gesture, which she could perform in an instant. For the last few, she steadied the braid as usual so it wouldn't pull the final hairpins out as it fell. Then, a handful of hairpins in her right hand, she let go with her left and the braid dropped heavily to her back. She opened her desk drawer. She started to put the hairpins into the tray where she kept paper clips, but then thought better of it and opened her hand over the wastebasket under her desk.

In the drawer was a pair of old scissors with battered black handles. Pearl held the braid back, pulled to the side, with her left hand. With her right hand reaching up behind her, she began to cut. It was hard to do. The scissors were dull and the angle was wrong. It took a long time before she had cut even halfway across the braid. Then she held it with her right hand and tried to cut with her left, but she couldn't manage the scissors left-handed. Finally she put them back in her right hand and tried to hurry, glancing up a few times. Once she thought she heard footsteps. At last it was done. The braid came away in her hand and she shuddered when she saw it lying on the desk on top of the letter. She reached her hand up and felt her bare neck and the rough ends of her hair. She looked around quickly. On the desk was a manila envelope used for interoffice mail. It had a red fastener and red lines across the front. It had gone to three people and their names were written on it. Someone had brought something in it to Pearl without writing her name on the envelope.

She turned it over. On the other side it was blank. She put the braid in, and she had to stuff it to get it all in. When she tried to write on it, her fountain pen punctured the envelope. She had to pull the braid out again and see it once more, and that was the hardest part. Now she wrote Nathan's name and address—his home address—on the envelope. Then she put on stamps from her desk. She stuffed the braid in again and closed the fastener and sealed the flap with tape. Then she put on her coat. Her hat would look terrible.

She had a big square silk scarf, and she tied it over her head. She would have to walk a couple of blocks out of her way to find a mailbox big enough for a package. The one on the corner took only letters.

She put the envelope under her arm and left her cubicle and started down the stairs. Just as she reached the staircase Mr. Glynnis stepped out of the supply room, looking startled. "I didn't know you were still here, Pearl," he said.

"I'm just leaving," she said.

"Good night, Pearl." He stood and watched her as she walked down the stairs, the envelope under one arm, her other hand holding her coat so she didn't trip. Her head was sore. She'd pulled hard to make the hairs tight and easier to cut.

"Good night, Mr. Glynnis," she said.

6 ❧

IT WAS A SATURDAY MORNING. NOTHING LIKE WHAT WAS
going to happen had entered my head. I'm not the sort of woman
who lives life beforehand, imagining it. After breakfast I put the baby
down for a nap. She cried but then she fell asleep. I took a shower
and started to get dressed. I was wearing my slip when I decided to
trim my toenails. I sat on the bed, cutting my toenails with a nail
scissors and holding the parings in my other hand.

Nathan was in the living room. I heard him running the carpet
sweeper with long slow strokes. Then he put it away and went out
of the apartment. I knew he was going down for the mail. I was still
cutting my toenails when I heard him coming back, and I knew
something had happened. His footsteps were too quick and loud, and
without thinking I looked over at the baby. She was in a bassinet in

our bedroom. Maybe I looked at the baby to make sure Nathan's footsteps hadn't awakened her, not to make sure she was all right.

I heard him let himself into the apartment, and then he ran past the bedroom doorway, holding the mail, and into the bathroom, and I heard him vomiting. I went running in my bare feet with toenail parings in my fist. Nathan was leaning over the toilet vomiting. There were letters on the floor—a couple of white envelopes and a big manila envelope. I put my hand on his shoulder and he shook it away. "I'm all right," he managed to say.

"What happened?" I said.

I thought he must have seen something terrible when he went for the mail. I thought of an old woman who lived in the next apartment. But even if Nathan had found Mrs. Moskowitz lying dead in the hall, he would not just come inside and vomit.

"Are you going to throw up any more?" I said.

He shook his head. He was pale. He flushed the toilet and I said, "Go lie down," but he sat down on the white tile floor. I dropped my toenail parings in the wastebasket and went for a washcloth. I wet it with warm water and wrung it out and started to wash Nathan's face with it, but he took it and washed his own face. I left him for a moment to bring a rag to clean the toilet. When I came back, Nathan was still sitting on the floor. His back was against the tub and his head was down, with his hands over his face. "Do you feel faint?" I said.

"I'm all right."

"What happened?" I still thought he'd seen something outside. "Is there something I ought to do?" I suppose I was thinking I might have to call the police or the super.

Nathan gestured toward the little pile of letters on the floor. I thought he meant that some vomit had gotten onto them. It was smelly in the bathroom. I rinsed out the cloth and hung it on the towel rod. I looked at the mail but the letters were clean. I picked them up. There was something from the Board of Education, but Nathan hadn't opened it yet, and there was an advertisement from a store that sold baby furniture. I'd been getting things in the mail since I had the baby. The manila envelope was soft and strange in my hand. It was open, and I looked into it and started. I thought it was a dead animal. But the color was familiar. In a way I knew everything right then.

"I bedded the wench," said Nathan. I didn't know what he was talking about. I picked up the envelope and drew out what was in it, and it was a woman's hair—Pearl's hair, I realized. Her long, beautiful blond braid, cut off. For a second I thought it meant that Pearl was dead. I couldn't imagine any other way for her hair to be in this envelope. I tried to think and think, so as to understand what Nathan had said—to remember it, a moment after he'd said it. I stroked the hair and was angry with him for throwing up at the sight of Pearl's hair.

"It's Pearl's, isn't it?" I said.

"Yes."

"Is she all right? For a moment I thought she was dead."

"She's not dead. She cut it off because she's angry with me."

I didn't know Pearl knew Nathan well enough to be angry with him. "Why is she angry?" I said, and then I remembered what he'd said.

I didn't say anything for a minute. Then I said, "You took Pearl to bed?" I was in my brassiere and girdle and slip, barefoot, and I was cold. I realized that I'd been stroking my body as I spoke, stroking the smooth fabric of the slip. It had lace around the top, and I had always liked the color—a cream color, not white.

I felt as if I were out in the cold air in my slip. For a moment it seemed that I'd feel better if I could only get Nathan off the floor and warm up. "Go sit in the living room," I said, and went into the bedroom and hurriedly put on a skirt and blouse and stockings and shoes and then I added a heavy sweater and buttoned it up to my neck. I already had so much to do, taking care of my difficult baby. She would wake up any minute and I'd wasted her nap wiping vomit when I'd intended to run out to the store while Nathan watched her. Now it seemed I would never be at rest. What had they done, Nathan and Pearl—what had they done to give me more work?

When I came out, Nathan was sitting on the edge of the couch. He looked up when I came in. Nathan had always looked dignified, but now he looked ashamed and foolish. And I didn't know why he had talked that way: he bedded the wench. It was a way he talked when I first met him, with his friends at City College. I never liked it. They'd spend evenings listening to jazz on someone's radio, and then later to symphonies, and he'd take me along. He and his friends would talk about books in that way, or talk about happenings in their lives as if they were in a book, and as if that made them unimportant. When one of his friends asked about my parents, he said, "Hilda is a motherless urchin." I was embarrassed for Nathan. My mother had died years earlier, but the friend might think I was in mourning right then and that Nathan had insulted me. Yet the friend only said, "Ah, an orphan maiden." And it was a terrible thing that my mother was dead. I'd cried for years about it, and worn myself out looking after my father and brother.

I sat down on the chair opposite Nathan and said, "I want to know what happened."

"I was very stupid," he said.

"I see that." But that felt pointless to say. "Don't say that," I said, which contradicted it, and Nathan looked up, confused, and then looked down again, as if he couldn't understand anything that was happening, so it wasn't surprising that he didn't understand this particular thing.

He said, "One night I was with Pearl and—and something came over me."

"What do you mean something came over you?" I said. "You're not like that."

"I know. But this time —" He stopped.

"You mean it had never entered your mind before and all of a sudden you were carried away with passion?" This seemed so silly I couldn't believe it. "When were you even alone with her? Was this at that picnic?"

They'd gone for a walk together at the picnic. I'd been grateful to Pearl for keeping him company when I was busy with his baby.

"No, not then."

"So when was it?" He didn't answer.

"I don't believe you did it," I said.

He looked up at me with dreadful eyes. When he spoke he sounded like someone choking, but he almost screamed. He said, "*I did it.*"

I heard the baby crying. I hadn't even started warming her bottle.

After weeks of screaming baby, I'd finally learned to warm the bottle before she got up—to sense when she was going to wake up, or to keep an eye on the clock. I left him and went to pick up the baby.

Racket was screaming and thrashing her arms and legs, and I picked her up and rocked her, trying to calm her. I tried to guide her arms and legs back in toward her body and to smooth the damp, wrinkled receiving blanket wrapped around her. She was soaked, I discovered when I felt under the blanket. I didn't like to change her when she was hungry. If she wasn't hungry she didn't mind being changed, but would follow my face with her curious, dark, staring eyes. Still, the bottle wasn't warm yet.

"Warm up the bottle, will you?" I called to Nathan, hating to say it, because I knew that once I let him do something for Racket, I wouldn't have a serious fight with him. Yet if I warmed the bottle myself, there would be extra screaming, and the only thing I simply couldn't bear was more screaming.

So I changed her, and it gave me a kind of distant pleasure to take off her damp clothes and soaked diaper, to pat her dry with the puffy cotton balls I kept on the changing table, and then to put a little powder on her skinny, thrusting legs and her bony backside. I put a fresh diaper on her, and fresh clothes, and wrapped her crisply in a clean blanket the way a nurse in the hospital had taught me: I laid Racket on a turned-down corner of the blanket and tucked the other corners tightly around her as if she were the filling in a bit of pastry.

I carried Racket into the kitchen, where Nathan was standing at the stove watching the bottle, which he'd set in a pan of water. I tested the milk on my wrist and sat down right there to feed the baby, instead of going into the living room, where I'd be more comfortable, as I usually did. Nathan continued to look at the pan of water even after the flame had been turned off and the bottle taken out.

"I wish I didn't have to tell you," he said.

"You weren't going to tell me?"

"I didn't want you to know the worst about me."

"Who should know if not me?" I said, not as nicely as the words themselves seem. I wasn't telling him his wife could forgive him anything. I guess I was saying that houses, where people live with the people they live with, are where vomit and infidelity belong. Ugliness belongs at home and a home has ugliness. I didn't know what my own ugliness was, but I knew I had some, and I didn't want Nathan to suggest that I was too pure to know about his dirt.

"Well, there's not much to say," he said.

"I think there's a great deal to say. I think you should sit down at this table and say it." He turned around and sat down. "Pearl is your brother's wife," I said.

"She is."

"How long—"

"Oh, once, once only. Don't think that, Hilda. I only did it once."

"But how long ago did you—"

Nathan looked across the table out the window, though there was nothing to see because the apartment faced the courtyard. Still, he waited, as if he was watching something. Maybe he was watching a bird.

"She's very lovely," he said in a low voice.

"Well, yes."

171

Yet I was surprised. I had grown to like Pearl, but I thought she was mousy, even though she was tall. She was pretty, but always pulling back and blinking and apologizing. But when I said it, I discovered that I thought she was lovely, too. It seemed to me that Nathan and I were two ragged old people, wizened by too much knowledge—too much sense, maybe—while Pearl was young, the kind of person who would always be young and not sensible: someone we should protect and cherish, not push into trouble. It was almost as if I'd taken her to bed myself, the way it went through my mind. In another minute it was something else. I went back to being angry with Nathan—just now because he was taking himself so seriously. He was still going on about it. You could see that he liked thinking of himself in this new way, even though he was ashamed.

"I suppose I hadn't realized how much of an impression she made on me," he was saying. "I don't mean in a permanent, important way. But she was like a flower—and here I was up with the baby nights —and you—"

"I'm not much like a flower these days," I said. It was becoming clear to me that I wasn't going to lose the weight I'd gained when I was pregnant.

"I don't mean that," he said. "I mean you were so serious. You had to be. We both have to be. We're a father and mother."

"And Pearl's a child?"

"She's a girl. She thought I was handsome. I was foolish, Hilda, very foolish."

"Pearl said you were handsome?"

He hesitated. "I can't remember if she said it," he said. "Maybe I just knew she thought it."

I put the bottle on the table and held Racket against my shoulder to burp her. I was still surprised, each time, that when I patted her, my hand covered her back. She belched loudly and Nathan smiled sadly.

"I'm so sorry," he said, close to tears.

I wiped the baby's mouth where she'd spit up a little, and stood to carry her into the living room so I could put her into the playpen. I still didn't know anything. He hadn't told me how it had happened, or when. I wanted to know, even though it seemed as if I shouldn't want to know. I'd gone through all those weeks, not thinking anything like this was happening. I wanted to insert the information into my memory of the day when it happened.

"So when was this?" I said, calling over my shoulder. He followed me.

"A few weeks ago." Finally he told me it happened the night he and Pearl went to a rally for the Spanish Loyalists, and of course I remembered that they had gone to the rally. I had wondered how they'd find enough to talk about for a whole evening, and figured they didn't have to talk much—they could mostly listen to the speeches. I thought I recollected that I was asleep when Nathan came home that night. I realized that I'd never asked him about it—what the rally had been like, or how Pearl had behaved. I'd been surprised that she was interested in a rally at all.

Finally we did sit down in the living room, facing each other, as if we were going to tell each other truths. I discovered that I too had a truth I could tell or not and it was that I liked the power I felt. Nathan had given me power by what he'd done, and I was shocked to realize that I was partly pleased that he had done it—while starting to feel very bad at the same time. But I wasn't going to say that. "Why did she cut off her braid?" I said. Where was it—what had I done with it? I ran and brought it from the bathroom, in that ridiculous manila envelope. It was the kind of envelope with a little red paper disk and a red string that winds around it. I closed the fastener and sat down again with it on my lap. "Why did she cut it off?" I said.

"Pearl's pregnant," said Nathan.

"What?"

"She's pregnant. She thinks it's my child."

I was so startled that I shoved the envelope off my lap. Then I picked it up. "Well, is it?"

"Of course not."

"How do you know?" I said. This scared me. This scared me more than anything else that had happened. "How do you know it's not?"

"Why should it be?" he said. "It was just that one time. She's a married woman. Surely she and Mike—"

"But it could have been any time she went to bed with a man," I said. "It *could* have been that time. Why shouldn't it have been that time?"

"It's not," he said. "Believe me, it's not."

"How can you be so sure? *Pearl* isn't sure, I gather."

"Pearl is hysterical. She cut off her hair—see what a state she's in?"

"Well, we'll have to find out," I said. "We can find out whether it's your baby, Nathan." I don't know what I was thinking. Blood tests, or something.

"Hilda," he said, "we don't want to find out. This is Mike's baby. If God forbid it isn't—if it isn't from Mike's sperm—it's going to be his in every other way and the only reasonable thing is to make up our minds that the subject is closed."

"Does Mike know?" I said.

He stood up. I thought he was going to walk out of the room, but instead he picked up Racket, who had been lying on her back in the playpen, not crying, trying to put her toes into her mouth. When he picked her up I felt uneasy, as if we were in a game in which whoever held the baby got to decide what happened next.

"I don't care whether Mike knows," he said, and then he really did walk into the other room, into our bedroom, carrying Racket. I sat where I was for a time, and then I put on my coat and went out to buy the groceries.

It was a cold day and I wore my gloves and hat, but my ears were cold and I turned up the collar of my coat. I still couldn't warm up. I felt like an old, old woman, someone from another time, from a country in which old women huddled along the street and bought a few potatoes to feed crowds of people. I was still in my twenties, I told myself, but it seemed that women who had babies were old, that women with husbands like Nathan were old. A man looked at my legs and I told myself again that I lived in the twentieth century and was a *young* woman.

I had a chicken at home and I was going to buy soup greens. In the store, the thick carrots and turnip and parsnips and parsley seemed more my friends than Nathan. I couldn't imagine him touching me again as freely as I touched the parsley and carrots. They were mine, I had a right to them if I paid the fruit and vegetable man a little money, but I was afraid Nathan would never again think he had a right to touch me. He had that way of looking at things.

And yet I had no choice. I would have to care for my husband instead of being his lover, and I couldn't leave Pearl alone, mourning her hair and pregnant—pregnant with somebody, no matter whose child it was. And Mike. I couldn't imagine what had happened over there. Now I tried to imagine, and I couldn't. I thought of the shorn-off blond braid, with the ends coming unbraided at the top and bottom—so strange, like an amputated limb—and it did seem that cutting off the braid must have been the end, that Mike might have killed her when he saw what she'd done, because he'd have guessed what had happened if she didn't tell him. That was the only thing I could imagine, Mike stabbing Pearl with a kitchen knife. I took my soup greens and walked to their house.

I always walked up the stairs but this time I took the elevator. I don't know why. When I got out on their floor, I saw Pearl locking her door with her back to me. She had a scarf over her head. I stood there and she turned around. If I'd taken the stairs I'd probably have missed her, because she always took the elevator. When she turned around I was struck by how beautiful she looked in that foolish scarf. The scarf was red and mustard-colored and she looked like someone in a costume, dressed up as a peasant woman in a ballet—dressed as what I felt like. I didn't look like a peasant woman, though I'm short and round. I had on a respectable brown coat and a nice hat with a feather. But Pearl was wearing a plaid jacket that couldn't be warm enough and a skirt in a checked pattern and with all her patterns she looked like a waif, a child without parents.

She stood there with her purse and her key in different hands, looking at me. I said, "I'm sorry about your hair."

She reached up and touched the back of her head quickly, and then smiled slightly, a smile I took to mean that she knew I'd seen the gesture and that it didn't make sense, also that what I'd said wasn't a fraction of what was going on. I could see her realize that I knew what was going on.

"Do you want to come inside?" she said.

"Were you going someplace?"

"To have my hair trimmed," she said. "I still didn't do anything about it. I was home sick yesterday."

"Does it look very bad?" I said.

"Do you want to see?" Pearl glanced to either side but no one was there except me. She took off the scarf and turned around slowly. Her hair was chopped off unevenly. It hung on her neck pathetically in bunches of different lengths.

"Mike wouldn't trim it for you, for a start?"

"He's not here," she said.

I thought for a moment she meant he'd left her. "Where is he?"

"He's been going out a lot. I don't know where. He hasn't touched me. I was afraid he'd hit me."

"You told him the whole thing?"

"I had to," she said. "When I did it, I didn't think about Mike seeing me—or about you, when Nathan got it. Is—is Nathan all right?"

"He'll live," I said.

"I didn't think you'd come here," she said. "I mean ever. I didn't think you'd ever come here."

"I came because I'm upset," I said, but it wasn't just that. I was worried about her, too. I'd come because I was worried. And disgusted. I wanted to say something impossible to her. I didn't want to say "I hate you" or "I'll never forgive you." I wanted to say, "So it happened. My husband put his penis up your vagina, which is not the end of life on the planet. Will you stop taking yourself so seriously?" That felt like the one thing I wasn't allowed to say.

Pearl tied the scarf over her hair again. "Do you want to come in?" she said once more.

"I'll walk you to the beauty parlor," I said.

"All right."

We didn't talk, all the way down the stairs and out into the street. Walking with Pearl, I have always had to hurry to keep up, and it was true that day, too. Her stride couldn't help but be longer than mine.

We didn't say anything for the first block either. Then she said, "You will never forgive me."

"Can we talk about something besides forgiving?" I said.

"If you want to," she said meekly. Then, after a pause, "I'm afraid to go into the beauty parlor."

I thought about that. "They won't know what happened."

"I know," she said. "I thought I could say I got tired of long hair and I just couldn't wait to get over there. They won't know the whole story from looking at me." Then she seemed to remember who I was and how I'd be feeling. "I'm sorry," she said. "I'm even worse than you thought, worrying about the beauty parlor."

"It's not going to make me feel better if you're embarrassed at the beauty parlor," I said. I'd become interested in the problem of what she could say to the woman there, even if it *was* a trivial problem.

"You mean I deserve so much worse. Should I tell the truth?"

"The truth?"

"I like her—I go to Beatrice. Do you go to her?"

"No."

"She'll ask what happened and I'm afraid I'll tell her the whole thing."

"I don't think that's a good idea, Pearl," I said.

"Hilda, you should have nothing to do with me," she said. "I should go away from here. You've been kind and look at what I did. Why are you even walking with me?"

She started to cry, and as we walked she cried harder and harder. We had reached Flatbush Avenue and there were a lot of people, some of them looking at us.

"Pearl," I said, after a while, "I understand you're having a baby."

"I'm sorry, Hilda."

"It's all right to have a baby," I said.

"But—it's Nathan's baby," said Pearl.

I didn't answer, and we didn't talk for two blocks. It was cold. We were behaving like schoolgirls, walking without a purpose; when we passed the beauty parlor we kept going without even mentioning it. We didn't even slow down and glance at it. I wanted to walk until I was tired enough to think. I was still carrying my soup greens. I was hungry. When Nathan told me Pearl said the baby was his, I thought she would know whether it was or wasn't. Now that seemed silly to me.

"You've had relations with Mike?" I said finally.

"Oh—yes."

"So it could be Mike's baby."

"You don't believe me either," she said.

"You *want* it to be Nathan's?"

She'd been crying and stopping and crying and stopping, but now she sat down on the bottom step of a house we were passing, lowered her head, and sobbed.

"You love Nathan," I said.

"Yes."

"Well, you can't have him," I said.

For some reason I didn't wonder whether Nathan would leave me for Pearl. The vomit seemed to establish that he wasn't going to. He would probably think Pearl wouldn't clean up his vomit. Maybe she would, I don't know—this is just what I thought Nathan would think.

I stood looking down at her for a long time while she sobbed. Then I said, "Let's go buy a pair of hair-cutting shears and go to Prospect Park and I'll give you a trim."

"All right," she said, snuffling.

"Did Mike hit you?" I said then, suddenly thinking that something from before wasn't right.

"Yes," she said. "Yes, he did."

"A lot?"

"Not a lot."

"In the face?"

"In the face," she said, and then I put my arm around her.

But that wasn't right either. I stood there, leaning over a little, and it was awkward and of course not honest.

Pearl stood up and we walked back the way we'd come. There

was a five and ten nearby, and when we got there, I said, "Wait here," and went inside. I didn't know why I didn't want her to come in. I found the scissors counter, which held quite an array of scissors in different sizes, all arranged before me in categories: nail scissors, paper-cutting scissors, big shears for cloth. They all looked shiny and sharp. I found the hair-cutting scissors and bought a pair, thinking it was wasteful. Pearl might already have some—the ones she'd used to cut off her braid.

Outside, she stood obediently, looking into the shop window at the dishpans and scrubbing brushes, as if she took an interest in anything like that. I began to walk again and she fell into step. Now the wind was in our faces, and it made my eyes tear. I walked quickly, almost kicking at the pavement, my little parcel containing the scissors tucked under my arm, my soup greens still in my other hand. I felt more like a peasant than ever, an impatient, unfeeling peasant.

I was taking Pearl to the park to cut her hair because it was more or less private there and I could sit her down on a bench. Hurrying her—for once I walked faster—while she hastened meekly and silently at my side, it was as though I were going to drown her in the lake, or to murder her and leave her body under the trees, as though she had been chosen to be sacrificed in some ghastly rite—the young blond virgin, except that Pearl wasn't a virgin. First the girl's hair must be cut off, the ritual would go, and then she would be strangled and thrown into the lake. She would be the most desirable maiden in the village, overwhelmed and terrified by her good fortune, too stupid to understand that after her death she wouldn't be around to see the celebration. In the park she would suddenly panic and scream and fight me, but I would manage her.

When we reached the park, Pearl looked around as if she wasn't sure where she was. We walked along a path near the lake. There were benches, but it was windy and the benches were exposed. Finally we came to one that was set back, with more trees around it. I stopped and patted the bench and Pearl sat down. She took off her scarf. I put down my soup greens and took out the scissors.

I didn't know much about cutting hair. I just held the clumps of blond hair in my hand and tried to even them. I had to bend over and my back ached. I'd taken off my gloves to work and my hands were cold. Pearl must have been freezing in that light jacket but she didn't complain.

At last, her head still bent, she said, "I'm sorry I love Nathan."

"I don't know why you love him," I said, though in a sense I loved him too. I thought of jabbing the sharp point of the scissors into Pearl's neck—not that I wanted to, exactly, I just found myself worried that I might. I might even do it by mistake. I didn't know how to cut hair safely any more than I knew how to cut it attractively.

"Look, if we can just make you look decent," I said.

"I'm not decent, why should I look decent?"

"I think you're proud of yourself."

"In a way I am," she said. "I really love him. I guess I'd do it again. I'm sorry, Hilda. You must hate me for saying that."

I didn't hate her for saying it. "No," I said, "it seems more sensible than what you said before. I can't stand all the apologizing."

"I don't feel apologetic," she said. "I just love him. And I'm so upset that he doesn't love me, and doesn't love this baby. I'm going to have Nathan's baby, if you and Mike don't kill me."

"I won't kill you, and I don't think Mike will."

"I'm not so sure," she said.

And then I suddenly—wildly—couldn't bear what had happened. Maybe it was because I had just promised not to kill her. I'd let her know I was going to keep on being nice to her, of all things! Maybe I did want to kill her.

I left Pearl sitting there, her head still bent, her neck bare, and I walked to the lake, just below our bench and the path we'd walked on. I stood on the granite rim around the lake. There was a police sawhorse with a sign on it, *No Skating*, and it was half in the lake and half leaning on the bank.

I flung the scissors into the lake, underhand, not knowing I was going to do it—so they didn't go far—and when they fell, I could see them wavering under the water at the bottom of the lake. I'd thrown like a girl, and suddenly I felt like a girl, not a strong woman, not a peasant. I remembered that I was a young mother whose husband had been unfaithful. My throat tensed with knowledge and misery, and I thought I'd feel bad forever. And the only person present was the one least likely to help me, the woman with whom he'd done it. But I had no mother, I'd never made friends easily, and I couldn't think who else I wanted.

I walked back to Pearl and said, "I'm not feeling well. I have to get home to the baby."

"Do you want me to carry the groceries?" I was reaching for them but she took them. She didn't comment on what I'd done with the scissors. Her hair looked a little better. She didn't put the scarf back on but tied it around her neck and tucked the ends into her jacket. I looked up at her as we walked. Her hair blew back and she looked like a boy, an old-fashioned boy with hair down to his neck, a page boy or the king's messenger. Her eyes looked blue; indoors they were darker. If Nathan wanted her—if he wanted someone tall and blond . . . but even then I knew enough not to be worried. Nathan couldn't have Pearl, I thought. And then I thought something that startled me: I needed her for myself.

On the way home I began thinking about Mike. I could believe he'd hit. Nathan would never do that, but Mike could. In his rage, he would hit hard with his eyes closed, not knowing what he was doing. "Will Mike be home when you get there?" I said.

"Probably."

"Are you afraid of him?"

"Sometimes."

"Do you keep fighting?"

"He doesn't talk."

"He hasn't talked at all?" I said.

"Not since that night. I came home. I was crying a lot. He saw my head. He couldn't figure out what was going on. Maybe he thought I'd gone crazy. Then I told him—about the baby, too— and he hit me. He slapped me. No, he ran at me with his arm swinging. It wasn't really a slap. I fell back. He ran out of the room and he ran in and did it again. He kept running, as if he were in the park. As if he were outside."

"And then what?"

"Nothing. He goes in and goes out. He hasn't said anything."

"We have to talk to him," I said. I don't know who I meant by *we*. I felt alone—but there were things I had to do. It was as if there had been a train wreck and I was lying in the wreckage, in pain, and then I saw that I was the only one in the car who could still crawl.

I had to drag these stupid people out of the wreckage. Mike, for example, had to be made to forgive his brother. Now there was a job. I guess I'm just bossy, because I thought it was *my* job.

I had been out for a long time, and as I walked home at last with my soup greens, I thought guiltily of Racket. But Nathan knew how to take care of her, and sometimes he could calm her better than I could. He was walking her when I came in. He had a regular route he'd take through the apartment, from the window at the back of the bedroom through the hall into the living room, through the living room and into the kitchen. Then he'd turn around and start back toward that same bedroom window. He'd always glance out of it when he got there.

Now I wondered whether he thought of Pearl whenever he looked out the window, which faced her house, a couple of blocks away, though of course he couldn't see her building. Our bedroom looked out at the back of the apartment house, and the block behind ours had one-family houses with yards, so there was green to look at, back yards behind a fence.

Nathan always looked sorrowful, like a monk humbly making a pilgrimage, as he made this trek, with Racket propped against his shoulder, wrapped in one of her quickly fading receiving blankets. Now, though, he looked even sadder, or I couldn't help thinking he did. He seemed to be marking the stages of a journey, working out a kind of penance. I hoped Racket had cried a lot while I was gone, not just to make him suffer, but to make him feel he'd been punished, so we could start to get on with things. But no crying in the world was going to make him feel that.

He didn't comment on how long I'd been gone or how for all the length of my outing I had nothing to show for it but soup greens. I took off my coat and got my soup pot out from the cabinet and washed the chicken and cut it up. Nathan followed me into the kitchen. Racket was just falling asleep. She'd drooled all over his shirt. He looked worn out.

"We're going to have to get Mike over here," I said. Now it seems nonsensical that I talked like this. I should have gone to bed and cried for a week, getting up only to polish my nails.

Nathan winced. "Mike," he said.

"I'm going to call them and tell them to come here."

"They won't come."

"I'll make them come. He's been hitting her."

"You saw Pearl?"

"Yes. Mike hit her."

Nathan carried the baby out of the room, and I heard him take her into the bedroom. I thought he was putting her to sleep in her bassinet, but when I got the soup going and went to see, he was lying on our bed with her curled next to him. He was facing her, his knees drawn up, and she was in the curve formed by his body. They were both asleep.

When I wasn't making a plan or giving orders, that week, my insides hurt. It felt as if a tight, rough piece of twine were cutting into me and tying off some part of me deep inside. I couldn't reach it no matter how I might try. So I kept planning. As long as I was organizing something—figuring out when to call Pearl and Mike's house, something like that—the twine loosened a little.

Once I woke in the night and felt like a forsaken wife, someone whose sexual beauty had been denied, as though Nathan had preferred the smell of Pearl's vaginal secretions to mine, or preferred the shape of her breasts. I was devastated. I hadn't known I cared about anything like that. I've always thought my body was all right, wished I were thinner, but you know how it is. I wouldn't have thought I'd mind if Nathan or anyone else preferred the shape of different breasts. But I did mind. I sobbed silently next to him for a long time, feeling big tears slide one by one down my cheeks and nose. Nathan hadn't made love to me for a long time—not since he'd made love to Pearl, apparently. We'd had sex only once since Racket was born, right after the doctor said it was all right. But I wasn't interested. I was so tired from taking care of Racket, I didn't want to be touched by anyone, and I was angry with everybody then—with Nathan, too.

Now, lying there crying, I wanted him to make love to me. I thought that if I cried louder he might wake up and soothe me, or at least touch me, but he didn't, and after a while Racket woke and I shuffled into the kitchen and began warming the bottle, holding her instead of my husband.

But that was the only time. By morning I didn't want him. I didn't want him to find me beautiful or sexy or attractive, didn't want to *be* beautiful or sexy, simply wanted to make things happen. I read the newspaper—about the battles in Spain—and wondered whether my lust to take action was like what people in those battles felt, or whether they really were fighting for reasons. If I'd been a general there would have been a battle, and hundreds dead.

On Wednesday morning, after Nathan left for school I called

Mike. I knew Pearl would be at work, and I knew he stayed home Wednesday mornings because he worked late on Wednesdays. "Hello," he said.

"Mike, it's Hilda."

"How are you?" he said—without feeling, as if it were a business call.

"Fine, thank you. How are you?"

"Fine."

"Mike," I said, "I want you and Pearl to come here on Sunday afternoon."

"I don't think that's a good idea, Hilda. Nothing personal."

"I don't expect you to think it's a good idea. I think if we don't sit down and have a conversation—all four of us—someday we'll wish we had."

There was a long silence. "I have to deal with this myself. I'm sorry."

"You'll never forgive either of them," I said, though I'd yelled at Pearl for talking about forgiveness.

"And you?" he said, and suddenly he was furious. "You can forget it? Maybe that's easy for you, sister, but not for me."

"It's not easy for me, Mike," I said.

"There's no point in talking about it."

"Mike," I said. I was cheating but it was the only thing I could think of. "What if we can prove it's your baby?"

"There's no way to prove it," he said coldly.

"Maybe that's not true," I said. "Come over Sunday. Anyway, you and Nathan—look, you're brothers."

"Not all brothers get along, Hilda," said Mike.

188

"What about your mother?" I said, trying everything. "Someday she'll die—we're going to go to the funeral and not speak to one another?"

"Now, nobody needs to say anything about this to Mom," he said, as if it fit with what I was saying. "Pearl and I can solve our problems without her."

"For God's sake, I'm not going to tell her," I said, "but sooner or later she'll wonder. She's always asking Nathan how you are."

He was silent for a while.

"What time Sunday?" he said.

"Two o'clock," I said. "Will you tell Pearl?"

"Of course I'll tell Pearl." I hung up. Racket had been crying for a while. I picked her up from her bassinet and lay down on the couch with her, rocking her in my arms and crying over her, then just holding her on my stomach. I lay back and stared at her skinny face with its big dark eyes. "You do look like a monkey," I said. She had no hair then—she'd lost the hair she was born with and had just a dark fuzz on her head. She lay on my stomach clutching the placket of my blouse. As usual, she was damp. Then she smiled. I pulled myself up and began making faces to get her to smile some more. "I'm glad you can't talk," I said to her. "You have a nice idea of the world."

On Sunday I wasn't sure they'd come, but they did. They managed to look as if they had arrived separately, even though of course they came through the door one after the other. I suppose people who are together are usually one step apart and maybe Mike and Pearl were two steps apart, something tiny that you don't see but sense. I had put out a candy dish and a bowl of fruit the way I did whenever company came. I took their coats and carried them into the bedroom. Pearl had had her hair trimmed. She didn't look at Nathan and he had barely spoken when they came in, but stood humble and eager, like an innkeeper welcoming guests when business has been poor.

I sat down on the floor, for some reason. Mike had sat down in the middle of the couch—looking down, not speaking—so there was no room for anybody else. Nathan had been standing in front of one chair, so he sat back down again. That left the other chair, but Pearl sat down on the floor opposite me. There was silence, and for a moment I was afraid I would laugh, the kind of nervous laugh that comes to the lips at the worst time, usually when you have to tell someone about a death. But I also wanted to laugh because they had obeyed me, even though what I'd asked them to do was preposterous.

"Would you like coffee?" I said.

"Don't go to trouble," said Pearl in an extremely low voice, like a child who has been coached by her mother.

Of course that was the signal to go and make coffee but I didn't. I just forgot, then and there, as soon as I'd spoken. When they finally left, later, I went into the kitchen and saw the four cups and saucers laid out, and the percolator with coffee grounds and water already measured.

"Where's Racket?" said Mike gruffly. I was surprised that he spoke and surprised at what he said.

"Asleep," I said. "I hope she'll sleep for a while."

He nodded succinctly, as if it was information he needed for a practical purpose. He was leaning forward, his knees spread.

"I'm afraid you're never going to speak to me again," said Nathan.

He sounded deeply sympathetic and respectful, talking to his brother, but also as if this was a little amusing. After that afternoon, I often noticed that bitter amusement in Nathan's tone. I could never remember whether he'd always had it, or whether it started here. It made a joke of things, but not in the way that sounds. It was as if he was saying that God would be amused at the awkwardness of His creatures. "I mean, Michael, I wouldn't blame you."

Mike shrugged. As we sat there, I was horrified not at what they'd done—Nathan and Pearl—but at what I'd done. In some ways it seemed less allowable, more shocking, to make such people sit in a room together than for them to have sneaked off to bed somewhere in the first place. I felt as nervous as any of them.

"Pearl," I said, "when did you have your friend?"

"My friend?"

"When did you menstruate?"

"I—"

I went into the bedroom and came back with a small calendar. They were all looking at me. "I think we can figure this out," I said. "I'm not saying this was a wonderful thing that happened, but for this baby's sake, this new baby, I think we have to—we have to—" I couldn't explain.

"It's Nathan's," said Pearl quietly, and I saw Mike stir and turn red.

"How do you know?" I said.

Pearl didn't remember when she and Mike had had sex. She was sure she would have remembered if it was soon after October eighth, the day of the rally. "That was the day—" she said.

"I know," I said. "But when was your last period? Maybe you were already pregnant when this—this unfortunate incident—happened."

Pearl was snuffling. "I didn't have it when we went on the picnic," she said. "I had it the day I went to the dentist."

I looked at the calendar, counting and figuring, and I didn't like the way it was coming out. But it was a little calendar, and I was sitting on the floor with it. Nobody could see it but me. Finally it became clear: Pearl had had a period on September twenty-third. I could see that she might perfectly well have gotten pregnant on October eighth, but on the other hand, she might have been pregnant already. That was certainly a possibility.

"I ought to be able to get this straight," I said. "I got a ninety-two on the Biology Regents."

"I don't think they covered this topic," said Nathan.

"Of course they did." I counted once more. I looked around at the three of them, all flushed in different ways, all staring at me, staring *down* at me—Pearl was on the floor like me, but she is so much taller that she also looked down. Mike was gazing intently. I'm not an especially intelligent person, but at that moment I felt intelligent. I knew that whatever I said would go. None of them would ever do the bit of arithmetic I was doing. None of them would check me.

"Well, that settles it, then," I said. "September twenty-third? You're sure? Then it's Mike's baby. No doubt about it."

I really had gotten a 92 on the biology exam, but I had no idea whether anyone on earth could pinpoint a pregnancy as I had just done. But I had done it. The signal was that Mike sat up and took his face out of his hands. I could see the marks of his fingers on his cheeks, he had been pressing so hard. He believed me, at least at that moment.

Somehow, we talked about other things after that, although I don't think Mike spoke much—I don't think anyone spoke much except me. I talked about Spain. Nathan mumbled something about Hitler and Germany, and I suppose it occurred to all of us that this baby Pearl was carrying might have been born in Germany, to a society that would condemn it for its Jewishness, that the least we could do was welcome it. For a moment I was afraid Nathan might ask Mike again about the notes to a speech Mike had taken down, but he didn't.

Pearl spoke only when I made her answer a question, but at one point I mentioned that the son of a neighbor had talked about volunteering to go to Spain, and ritualistically I said I hoped he'd be all right. "I hope so," said Pearl. That was all, but she said it in her regular voice, not this new timid voice she'd adopted since going to bed with Nathan.

And that made me angry with her. Had she forgiven herself so quickly for spoiling my life? For my pain came rushing back to me, and it seemed that she and Nathan had flaunted—were flaunting—their passion, his rejection of me. It had been self-flagellation to bring her there. I scrambled to my feet. "I hear the baby."

Nathan looked up. "I don't," he said.

"Well, I do."

But Pearl stood gracefully and followed me, walking between the two men, not looking at either of them. I let her catch up to me and we went to the bedroom together. Racket was still sleeping, her thumb in her mouth. We both moved over to the crib and looked in. I saw that Pearl was crying and I took out my handkerchief and handed it to her.

"It's clean," I said in a whisper.

"It doesn't matter," she whispered back, and blew her nose and wiped her eyes. We stood there at the crib looking, as though Racket were scheduled to do something unusual.

"Your hair looks good," I whispered, though I was still angry.

"Thank you."

Then I thought of something. "Pearl, do you want the braid? Your hair—do you want it?"

She looked at me as if she didn't know what I meant for a moment. "You have it?"

"I didn't throw it out."

"Nathan gave it to you?"

"It was right there," I said. "I saw it right away. What did you think?"

"I don't know. I thought—maybe he kept it."

I thought of telling her what happened when he saw it but I didn't. I said, "I put it away."

"I don't want it," said Pearl, still whispering.

I was silent for a while. Then I said, "So here we are."

She stared down at Racket and smoothed her blanket. "I hope I die giving birth," she said.

I put my hand on her arm. "Stop it," I said, still in a whisper, as sternly as possible.

"You take the baby," Pearl whispered.

"I'm sorry, Pearl," I said. "You're the mother."

She was quiet for a long time, and now Racket did begin to stir. "Don't be angry with me forever," she said. "I couldn't bear it."

"I'm not angry," I said in my own voice, because now Racket was awake. My voice sounded loud after the whispering. It sounded as if I'd shouted.

7 ❧

"WHY DID YOU CUT YOUR HAIR, PEARLIE?" THEY SAID AT
work, especially Ruby, who sat at the next desk. Mr. Glynnis was
known to call them the Jewels.

"I got tired of long hair," said Pearl.

Everyone accepted that but Ruby. "You always said you'd never
cut your hair," she said. "If I had hair like that, I'd never cut it."

Pearl looked up at her. Ruby was passing her desk and had stopped
to sort papers she was taking to different parts of the building. They
hadn't even been talking about hair. Ruby filed the letters going to
Mr. Glynnis between her first finger and middle finger, the ones for
Mr. Carmichael between her middle finger and ring finger. She had
a system. When she had letters to go downstairs, where the company
now had an accountant working, she put them between her ring finger

and her pinkie. Ruby was short and her fingers were thick and stubby. Pearl had always liked the way she held them out with the letters gripped between them. Now Ruby looked back in a funny way as she left the cubicle. Over the partition Pearl could hear the sounds of the floor, where women packaged blouses and men hauled boxes. Soon Ruby returned, her hand empty, and stopped again at Pearl's desk. "I hope I didn't speak out of turn," she said in a low voice. "I think your hair looks very pretty."

"I didn't mind," said Pearl. She had finally had it trimmed at the beauty parlor. No one there had asked questions after all.

"Long hair must have been a nuisance," Ruby went on.

"My husband liked it better before," Pearl said. If that was true, she didn't know. She and Mike were still barely speaking. The way things were at home reminded Pearl of a time when she'd been in high school. Her father had caught her with a boy he didn't like and had threatened her. They didn't speak for weeks except for things they couldn't help saying: "Come eat." "Mama wants you." Once Pearl watched for ten minutes while he searched for his hat, and didn't tell him she could see it on the floor behind the dining room table, tipped sideways where it had fallen.

"He was angry that you cut it?" said Ruby.

"Yes."

Pearl thought her grief might kill her or kill the baby. She kept imagining herself shrieking. When Mr. Carmichael called her into his office to dictate a letter, Pearl could hardly wait for the moment when she could sit down. His habit was to keep her in the doorway while he explained where the letter was going, as if she might object to writing to a department store in Trenton. After she nodded, he'd clear a place for her to sit, moving papers from one chair to another. Waiting, an hour or so after her conversation with Ruby, Pearl was afraid she would hurl her face against the doorjamb, slamming it into the wood.

"I want to write to Mr. Montgomery," said Mr. Carmichael. "Mr. John Montgomery, is it? James?"

"I'll check," said Pearl. "I think John."

"John, John, yes, certainly John." It took time for Mr. Carmichael to stop circling a letter and *land* on it, Pearl and Ruby used to say —though before, Pearl didn't mind. He was patient with her own inadequate, slow shorthand. Now as she finally sat down, instead of just wishing she were dead or worrying that the baby would shrivel up in her unhappy body, Pearl had a new thought: she could tell Ruby a partial truth.

"I want to tell you something," Pearl said to her later that day. She and Ruby brought sandwiches from home and always ate lunch together in a little room at the back of the floor where cartons were stacked. "Killington," Pearl would read off the cartons over and over again—a supplier of boxes. Now Ruby was sitting between Pearl and the window. The boxes looked dusty in the bright winter light. "I've fallen in love," Pearl said. "I've fallen in love with my brother-in-law."

Pearl thought Ruby might not be too shocked if she didn't say she'd done anything about her love. They could talk. It might help. But Ruby pulled her short body downward as if her stomach hurt.

"I think about him all the time," Pearl said.

"But that's how I feel about Billy," said Ruby. Billy was her boyfriend.

"No, it's different," said Pearl.

"Because you're married?" Ruby looked frightened.

Pearl ignored her. She was sorry she'd mentioned it. It was impossible to say how much she loved Nathan—far more than Ruby could possibly love Billy—how the dusty cartons and the dust in the air itself seemed different once you knew Nathan was in the world. And he didn't love her. It would be unbearable even if she weren't having a baby—yet it was also wonderful. Ruby couldn't understand it.

"I'm sorry, Nathan," Pearl whispered, running down the stairs at five, when it was finally time to go home. She stepped into the damp winter darkness. People were nearby but she could whisper. "I'm sorry, darling," she said. "I'm sorry I told her."

Sometimes Pearl hoped. Maybe, after all, Nathan would come to her late some night when Mike was not home and urge her to run away with him. "You don't really want to," she'd say, avenging herself. For she was furious with him and hated him, even while she loved him.

It wouldn't have been possible for their night together to have taken place if he hadn't loved her. Leaning back in the subway one day, her eyes closed, letting herself be shaken by the sloppy but rhythmic thrusting of the train, Pearl imagined a grain of something shiny in the middle of a dark waste. The shiny spot was the chance that Nathan loved her after all. She couldn't remember now exactly what he had said the day of the malted. She had left so quickly, maybe she hadn't understood.

She would never again speak to Nathan about what had happened, and he might never speak to her, but if she could believe in the shiny spot, she could live.

She had no morning sickness, which made the doctor look sober. "Are you sure?" he repeated.

"Yes. Isn't that good, not to be sick?"

"Sometimes it's better to be a little sick," he said.

That made Pearl think something was wrong with the baby. Surely he couldn't tell what she had done. She remembered that she had offered Hilda the baby. That was shameful. It was her baby. It was all she had. Of course the doctor did not rise from his listening posture to accuse her of bearing a child whose heartbeat revealed the wrong father. Nor could he tell, apparently, that Pearl was in trouble with her husband. He called her Mother, and advised her to eat baked potatoes and not too much salt.

He worried less as she began to grow bigger. "Well, you're a lucky girl," he said finally. "Some mothers never do feel sick."

"I feel fine," said Pearl. Ruby said it was because Pearl was tall and so the baby had room and didn't squeeze her stomach. Ruby was excited that Pearl was having a baby. Pearl had told her about it before she told anyone else in the office, and that secret went over better. It was two weeks after she'd told the first secret, which had not been mentioned again. This time Ruby sat up straighter and grinned. She gave a great sigh, as if she'd been worrying all that time about Pearl's love for Nathan, and now she could cross off that problem.

Pearl thought about Nathan all the time. She could feel his sad stare behind her as if he followed her through her life, drawing his conclusions about what she did. He was always there. One bright day in midwinter, Mr. Glynnis sent Pearl to another office a few blocks away with some papers. Pearl walked slowly, watching as people hurried along the wind-polished pavement, and she thought that they held their hats to their heads like folk dancers, though their clothes were not colorful, like dancing costumes. Suddenly she thought of Nathan, with a rush of pain, and realized that for those moments, watching the people clutch their hats, she had forgotten him. She'd had a moment without him for the first time in weeks and weeks.

She liked that, and shook herself, reaching under her coat to follow the curve of her tummy. So far she could hide it with a sweater at the office, but not much longer. Some day, she thought, picturing herself with a baby in her arms, she would go an entire day without thinking of Nathan. Now he was her first thought each morning, and the shame and sorrow of it fell on her when she opened her eyes.

She felt better as the day went on. Sometimes, though she thought about Nathan, it was perfunctory: she'd drop a stack of papers on the floor and think, Nathan!—as if he might have caught it. It didn't count but it did.

Ruby was having a hard time. Her boyfriend, Billy, was talking about going overseas to fight in the civil war in Spain. Pearl had met him. He was like a boy, a little like Mike but without Mike's cynical shrug. Mike would never voluntarily go to fight in a foreign country for people he didn't know, but Billy seemed to glory in that thought. If someone had told him that people in Spain were even more different from him than he believed, that they carried their young on their backs for three years and set their dead afloat in baskets on rivers, Billy's luminous eyes would have grown even brighter and closer together and he would have been even more determined. It was hard on Ruby, a small woman with freckles who looked about fourteen. Pearl could tell by her wide-open, puffy eyes and fixed look when something had pushed Billy closer to a decision. Once it was a conversation with a friend who was going, another time the departure of the first American volunteers at the end of December.

"My husband thinks the volunteers are crazy," Pearl said one day, as they ate their sandwiches in the little room filled with cartons. She swallowed hard. "But my brother-in-law thinks it's wonderful. He'd go if he didn't have a baby. I went to a rally with him."

It was the closest she'd come to touching on that subject again, but Ruby ignored that part of it. "It's not that I don't think it's important to support the Loyalists," she said seriously.

"Of course," said Pearl.

"But what good will he do anybody if he dies? If he stayed here, if we had children—"

Pearl stood and walked to the window. Her body was beginning to slope outward. She would look better pregnant than poor Hilda had. She knew Ruby was studying her with admiration, as if it were noble just to be pregnant. Pearl looked out the window. "Maybe Billy should talk to Mike," she said. Listen to Mike, she amended it in her mind. Mike had stopped being so angry with her. He had not been able to sustain it for weeks and months, though she knew that he was still unhappy, and they still had not seen Nathan and Hilda, not since the day Hilda had made them come over.

"Oh, that would be so helpful," Ruby was saying. "Maybe I could bring him over some night?"

"Sure," said Pearl. "Whenever you want." Mike would shout about foolishness. Of course Billy wouldn't listen—people like that didn't, and Mike was so loud and argumentative he nourished everyone's spirit of opposition. He was turning Pearl into an arguer despite herself. "College kids," he'd said the other day, talking about the volunteers. "What do they know about war? They'll just be in the way."

"What does anyone know about war?" she had answered. "Soldiers are always kids." She had a stab of fear, then, that her baby would be a boy, and someday he'd go to war.

But for once Mike didn't want to argue. "Where do you get your ideas?" he snarled, leaving the room. Maybe what she had said sounded too much like Nathan.

"My husband isn't always very nice," she said to Ruby.

"I'm sure he's nice underneath," Ruby said.

Pearl snorted inwardly, to think of what Ruby didn't know about her family life. Mostly she was so busy thinking about Nathan and her sorrow that she lived in dazed inattention, but sometimes, when she and Mike were together in the apartment and she was alert, she didn't know how she could keep on as his wife. She could feel his anger, although when he played the saxophone in the other room, she thought it sounded more fearful than angry. She heard the fear of a younger brother whose older brother can take away his treasure because he is bigger. Then she wished heartily that it had never happened—until she remembered the night with Nathan, and the days following it. She would not have been Pearl if it had not happened. She had been an ignorant woman.

Hilda's birthday was coming. When Pearl first remembered it, she almost cried, to her surprise; she wanted to be with Hilda on her birthday. And Mrs. Levenson, her mother-in-law, would assume that the family would gather on this occasion. For days Pearl thought about it. They had to make up for Mrs. Levenson's sake. They had to celebrate Hilda's birthday.

Finally, one night after supper, when she was washing the dishes and Mike was loitering behind her, she said, "I want to invite Hilda and your brother and your mother next Friday."

"How come?"

"It's Hilda's birthday."

"It is?"

"Yes. We did the same thing last year."

"If you say so." Pearl didn't know whether he was agreeing about last year's dinner or this year's, but while Mike was playing the saxophone in the other room, she phoned Hilda.

"This is Pearl," she began.

"Hello," said Hilda.

"How's Racket?"

"She's fine. She's getting big."

"Is she fatter?" said Pearl. It was March—more than four months since they'd seen the baby.

"Longer. Not fatter. She can crawl."

This seemed friendly, so Pearl risked her invitation. Hilda accepted. Pearl found she couldn't say Nathan's name.

"We'll bring Mom," said Hilda.

"That's fine." Pearl would have to see Nathan—she was afraid but also excited. She was grateful to Hilda for being friendly. "Don't forget Racket," she said foolishly.

"Now is that likely?" said Hilda.

"Of course not, of course not," Pearl murmured, overcome. Off the phone, she tried to think about cooking, but it was a difficult week.

Fifteen minutes after her guests arrived the following Friday, Pearl realized that Mrs. Levenson and Racket made anything possible. She and Nathan were unimportant. Mrs. Levenson wanted to hold Racket, who was still bundled up for the cold outside, and who objected to being held and wriggled out of the old woman's arms. Hilda put her on the floor to show off her crawling, but Racket thrashed her arms and legs and tore at her hat. Hilda undressed her and smoothed out her dress, but now Racket wanted to crawl, and she was vaulting out of her mother's arms before Hilda was done with her. Hilda set her on the floor again. "At first," said Nathan— they were the first words he had spoken, "she could only crawl backwards. Her little face would get farther and farther away."

Now Racket crawled expertly to a chair and began to suck on the chair leg. Pearl laughed, but Mrs. Levenson said, "Look, look what she's doing!" and seized the baby.

Again Racket tried to get away from her. "What's the matter, you don't like your bubbi?" said the old woman. She lifted Racket into the air with her short arms, leaning her head back and laughing. She was ugly, and it made her uglier when she threw back her head and held her legs wide apart to steady herself, but Pearl, watching from the doorway, rather liked Mrs. Levenson for the first time. The uglier she was, the less ugly, Pearl thought, and didn't know what that could mean. She ought to go into the kitchen and check on the dinner, but she remained at the edge of the group in the living room and watched Mrs. Levenson try to win over Racket, who cried, but then stopped and reached for her grandmother's teeth. Mrs. Levenson had big false teeth that showed now, as she laughed at the baby. At last Racket settled into the old woman's arms, and then her grandmother—who was something like the baby, Pearl noticed—tired of the game.

"You take her, Michael," she said, thrusting Racket away. "You should learn, a baby coming."

"I know how to hold a baby," said Mike, who had been scowling and watching. He took Racket and she snuggled her head into his neck. Pearl saw the look in Mike's eyes, and she saw Nathan watching. He glanced at her. Nathan would come to hate her, she thought, and rushed into the kitchen, where she took the roast chicken out of the oven and carefully lifted it onto a platter, her eyes filling. She didn't know why the sight of her husband cradling Nathan's baby made her feel that Nathan would hate her, but she was as sure as if hatred had come from his body in a long, cold, unpleasant stream. He couldn't help it, she excused him to herself. She had separated him from his brother. "But it wasn't *my* idea," she said out loud, in a low voice. When she looked up, Hilda was coming in to help and Pearl wondered if she had heard. The table was set. Pearl had done everything before the others had arrived.

"Well?" said Hilda.

"What?"

"Are you cooking in here, or crying, or what?"

"I'm cooking." Pearl smiled with tears on her cheeks.

"What do you want me to do with these potatoes?"

Pearl handed her a bowl. "She's not so bad," she said, inclining her head toward the living room.

"Mrs. Levenson?" Hilda said. "She's practical. She comes to my house and gives Racket a bath. The baby slips out of her hands, and she shouts to her, 'Rachela, Rachela, come back, come back!' "

Racket sat on Nathan's lap during dinner, and he fed her bits of food she could suck on. Pearl marveled that she had ever imagined he might leave Hilda and the baby. Racket mouthed on a piece of boiled carrot, making loud sucking noises that convulsed Mike. The dinner was a success.

The doorbell rang as they were having coffee, and Mike went to answer it. He came back leading Ruby and Billy, whom he had never met. "Friends of yours," he said to Pearl, and the old suspicion, never far away, was back in place—friends who had perhaps helped her connive with his brother, friends who knew. Pearl wanted to reassure him, but she couldn't, and she *had* told Ruby she was in love with Nathan—only that, but still, too much. Now, as she introduced everyone, she was sure Ruby remembered that conversation. And Nathan would guess, and would hate her for yet another reason.

"I hope you don't mind," Ruby was saying. "You mentioned we could drop by."

"It's fine," said Pearl.

"This is Rachel," said Hilda, who was holding the baby now.

"She's cute," said Ruby.

"I didn't know there was a baby," Billy said, and he sank to his knees to be on Racket's level, waving his long fingers to get her attention. His eyes seemed even bigger and lighter than when he stopped at the office to call for Ruby and stood there looking as if he'd come in on a shaft of sunlight. Now his eyes seemed lit almost as if to give the baby something to stare at.

"Billy likes babies," said Ruby.

The kitchen was crowded. They barely had room for Nathan and Hilda and Mrs. Levenson, not to mention the baby, and now there were two more people. Billy remained standing after he stopped playing with Racket, and Mike brought in their only other straight chair for Ruby to sit on. Pearl had to wash her own coffee cup to serve them. She owned six cups and saucers and had never contemplated having so much company at once. Luckily there was enough cake. The kitchen was hot—the heat was bubbling up—and the window was steamy. Billy was wearing a sweater and he took it off. Pearl's chair was empty, but she'd have to dislodge several people to get to it, so she leaned back against the sink.

"We've been arguing about Spain," Ruby said, looking at Mike. "I brought Billy over because I thought maybe you'd talk to him."

"Spain," said Nathan, and he put down his coffee cup and looked steadily at Billy. "You're interested in Spain?"

"I'm very interested in Spain," he said. "I'm a student at City College, but I've been doing some organizing—rent strikes and that sort of thing. You have time to think when you're getting locked up every few weeks."

"I'm sure you do," said Nathan respectfully.

"I've been talking to some people about volunteering. The Abraham Lincoln Battalion—you know about that?"

"I know about that," said Nathan, with sad kindness. "I've been reading about the fighting at Jarama. A terrible thing."

"I think the Loyalists can win," Billy said. "It's an amazing chance—this is a true democracy that the military is trying to stamp out. The people of Spain—"

"Oh, what does a kid like you know about the people of Spain?"

said Mike suddenly, and he sounded angry, with all the anger of the last months, the anger against Pearl and Nathan, in his voice.

"What do I know?" said Billy quietly. "Well, I don't know much." He sounded good-natured. "Do you know a lot about Spain? I've been reading. . . ."

"Me?" Mike was disarmed, but still angry. "No, I don't know much about Spain. But I also don't know why a man would want to go fight in Europe if he didn't have to. I don't understand this Abraham Lincoln Battalion—I think they're a lot of crazy idealists."

"Hold it, Mike—not so crazy," said Nathan, and it was the first time Pearl had heard the old tone between them.

"How do you stop fascists by dying?" asked Mike, standing, his jaw tight and the muscles standing out. "Hitler's going to be impressed by the death count? And more impressed if the death count is a bunch of American kids?"

"Hitler?" said Mrs. Levenson. "War with Hitler?"

"They're talking about Spain," said Hilda.

"There are Jews in Spain, too," said Mrs. Levenson. "There are Jews everywhere. Everywhere Hitler will find them." She seized the baby and held her so tightly that Racket cried. "What a world we make for babies!"

Pearl had read about the dreadful fighting at Jarama. She had not known that Americans were already fighting in Spain until Ruby had told her. She hadn't known that the group of Americans was called the Abraham Lincoln Battalion. Ruby and Billy knew others who had gone—men who didn't know anything about being soldiers. Nathan had wished he could go, and Pearl realized that many of those going were men just like Nathan, like Nathan if Racket hadn't come along.

Some of them probably *had* babies. If it hadn't been for Spain and for the rally, she wondered what might have happened—or not happened—between Nathan and her. It was strange to think that Hitler had caused all this pain she'd been through—and the pleasure, too: the pleasure, even now, of loving Nathan.

Mrs. Levenson took her napkin and mopped her forehead. "It's hot," she said. Then she turned to Billy. "Tell me, young man," she said, "you have a mama? You have a papa?"

"Yes. In the Bronx," said Billy.

"And what do they think, in the Bronx, that you should go to Spain, maybe get killed—how does your mama like that?"

"I'm afraid she doesn't like it," he said. "I tell her, if I go, and the Loyalists win, maybe Hitler and Mussolini will stop trying to take over the world, maybe a bigger war won't have to happen. I have a little brother—maybe if I fight, he won't have to."

"This makes your mama change her mind?" said Mrs. Levenson. "Excuse me I should mind your business for you."

Billy blushed and looked at his shoes. "No, I'm afraid it doesn't make her change her mind," he said.

"And I can't do anything with him, either, Mrs. Levenson," Ruby said. She was sitting next to the old lady, her cake still on its plate on her lap, her fork in her hand. "I can't talk him out of it."

"You married?" said Mrs. Levenson.

"No, not married, but we'd like to get married. I'd like to have a baby," said Ruby.

"I wish you luck," said the old lady formally. "I wish you should have what you want." She sat back, fanning herself with her napkin, rocking sideways a little bit. Then she began to sing quietly in Yiddish.

"I've been working with a group that's raising money for Spain," Nathan was saying to Billy in a soft voice. "But that's all I can do. I'm a coward. I can't go over there and fight."

"You have a daughter."

"I don't know if I'd have the courage, even if I didn't have a daughter," Nathan said. "I do not find myself to be a particularly courageous person."

Pearl saw Billy staring at him and she knew Billy was falling for Nathan, too. Billy didn't believe Nathan wasn't courageous. "To tell the truth, he isn't," she said inwardly, thought it in words as if she were speaking to Billy. Nathan hadn't even had the courage to talk to her about whether or not it was his child she was carrying—yet she too couldn't help but forgive him. Even now, she liked handling plates and spoons he had touched.

Ruby and Billy apologized for breaking in on a family party, but Pearl was glad they'd come. The dinner had been going well, but if Ruby and Billy hadn't arrived just as the food was gone and the kitchen was getting hot, something bad might have happened. Mike might have turned on Nathan—though she couldn't quite imagine that. Mike was angry all the time but he didn't talk about Nathan or what had happened, as if he had lost the memory but kept the anger.

Or maybe Mrs. Levenson would have been difficult. Pearl assured Ruby, when they talked about it in the office on Monday, that her arrival had been welcome. But Ruby shook her head. Billy hadn't paid much attention to Mike, but he'd admired Nathan and said Nathan understood him. "It isn't your brother-in-law's fault," Ruby said quickly. "Billy would find a talking dog who'd agree with him, if nobody else came along."

Ruby was troubled, and a few weeks later she told Pearl that Billy really was going to Spain. He was out buying boots and a canteen at an Army and Navy store. And Pearl was about to stop working; she was too big now to hide her pregnancy. "I'm going to feel so bad," Ruby said. "May I come to your house sometimes? Just to talk? Will you be with me when he leaves?"

"Sure," said Pearl.

A few weeks later Billy did leave, on a passenger liner with a group of other volunteers. He'd explained to Ruby—and Ruby explained to Pearl—that it was all secret. The government had outlawed what he was doing, and his passport was stamped "Not Valid in Spain." The volunteers had to go to France, pretending to be tourists or students, and sneak across the border through the mountains. Ruby mustn't come down to the ship and wave.

She'd pointed out that if he were going to France to study, she'd go down and wave. "He said I wouldn't look so miserable then," she told Pearl, "but I'd look miserable, even then."

Billy insisted, but when he finally left, on a sunny spring day, Pearl and Ruby went to see the ship depart anyway. "We don't have to stand on the dock and look conspicuous," Ruby said. "We could just be passing by."

They had to walk many blocks from the subway station to the pier on the Hudson. They were shocked at the size of the liner. They could hardly see the passengers, far away, scurrying on the deck. They held back, the wind blowing their hair and blowing cinders into their eyes until Pearl didn't know whether Ruby was crying or whether she just had something in her eye. It was hard to understand that Billy was on the big ship. At last its horn sounded, and after a while they realized it was moving. It slid away from the dock, and water appeared. At the last minute another woman, who had been standing behind a pillar where they hadn't noticed her, rushed forward. "Leo!" she shouted. "Leo! Leo! Be careful!" Pearl and Ruby stepped forward, but they didn't rush toward the ship like the woman. They stood and waved, and Pearl was sure no one could have told them from friends of a departing tourist. The woman who'd called to Leo stumbled as she left the dock. She was older than she had seemed at first, and Pearl wondered whether the woman was Leo's mother.

Spring was easier for Pearl. She didn't have to go to the office anymore. They had less money, but she was careful. She didn't mind being pregnant—she thought she looked fine. She liked wearing maternity clothes. She was still unhappy about Nathan, but away from the office, and with Mike out of the house working, she was free to think about him. She avoided her mother, who wanted to come and visit often. Alone, Pearl could turn her mind into a little shrine to her brief happiness. She encouraged herself to do this because it was better for the baby. It couldn't be good for a baby if its mother was unhappy all the time. Pearl took herself for walks in the park and neglected the house and the cooking. At last she realized the time was close and she began to get ready. She cleaned the apartment and bought a crib and a layette.

Pearl had her baby on June seventh. Her labor was not too bad and the nurses joked with her, but Pearl was frightened. The baby would be born looking just like Nathan, or something would be wrong with the baby, a punishment for loving Nathan.

Mike was sent to the waiting room. Pearl lay alone, covered with sweat. She thought of Ruby's Billy fighting in Spain, and it was as if she were fighting in a war as well. Ruby had received a short letter from Billy. He had already made friends, and lost a friend who had died in battle. If Pearl and Nathan could have gone to Spain and given their lives for the Loyalists—perhaps she could have been a nurse—it would no longer be wicked that they had gone to bed together. The greater goodness would wipe out the lesser badness, at least if they died. She thought that maybe the same thing was true about having a baby. If she could bear the pain without complaining, she would be a good person who could be somebody's mother.

The doctor had told Pearl that when it was time for the baby to be born, he would anesthetize her, but when it happened, late at night, he wasn't there, and by the time he arrived the baby was coming. Pearl grinned at the doctor when he came into the delivery room. "I'm having a baby!" she said madly.

"Well, that was the idea, wasn't it?" he said.

One of the nurses laughed and the doctor frowned at her, as if only he and Pearl were allowed to laugh. Pearl didn't mind being naked below the waist, didn't mind that nurses were wiping blood and feces from her body. She wanted to send a message to Mike, but all she could think of to say was, It isn't what I thought it would be like. Of course, the nurses were too busy to carry messages. In another moment there was a great rip of pain—for a second Pearl thought that a stray bullet, somehow careening over from Spain, had hit her—and then came cries, a child's cry and the nurse's cry. "A boy, Mrs. Lewis, you got a boy!"

Pearl lay back exhausted. "Let me see him," she said, but her boy, Simon, was carried off. By the time they brought him back she was asleep, but she roused herself. "Doctor says you want to try breast-feeding," the nurse was saying to her. Pearl remembered now. She had said that—insisted. She reached for her son. His head was smaller than her breast, or not much bigger. She didn't know what to do. "Not many of the moms try," the nurse was saying. "Of course, I was breastfed. My mother can't believe women don't do it anymore. But she says it's bad for your figure."

"I don't care about my figure," said Pearl. She took the breast in her hand and stuck the nipple into the baby's mouth. The mouth was damp and flaccid around her nipple, and then it slipped off and Simon's eyes closed. Pearl poked him with her nipple some more. The third time, suddenly his mouth was muscular and busy, and Simon was sucking.

"Of course you don't have any milk yet," said the nurse.

"Well, he's found *something*," said Pearl with some excitement. She stroked Simon's head with her free hand and traced the outline of his body with her finger. He kept his knees drawn up and his eyes closed, like a small swimmer bobbing and floating, trusting her.

Home from the hospital, Pearl sometimes heard Mike's voice in the bedroom, talking to Simon as if he were an adult. The first time, Pearl thought that somehow someone had come along and gone into the bedroom when she wasn't looking. Mostly Mike's words were inaudible, but she heard, "how the hell anybody could think that would work," and she put down her knitting needles to listen, uneasy. Her mother had taught her to knit and she was making a sweater for Simon, but she found it tedious, and she couldn't remember to decrease for the armholes.

Mike had made love to her once during her pregnancy—wordlessly, almost brutally. He looked at her, red-faced, afterward, and Pearl wondered whether he had been trying to dislodge the baby from her womb with his penis. She didn't know if that was possible. She hadn't asked the doctor if it was all right to have sex when you were pregnant.

Hilda and Nathan came to see Simon the day after she and Mike brought him home from the hospital. They gave him a diaper bag fitted with baby bottles. Pearl wasn't using bottles because she was nursing, but she didn't say so. She was pleased. They stayed only a little while. At first Pearl couldn't look at Nathan, then she allowed herself—or forced upon herself—one long look when he wasn't looking at her. She noticed wrinkles on his face: he was beginning to look middle-aged. He seemed balder than he had been. He looked sad.

But she didn't think about Nathan as much. She was busy taking care of Simon. When Mike was at work, she put Simon into his carriage and took him down in the elevator and out into the street. In the hot weather, she walked with him in Prospect Park. Sometimes she passed a small, unpaved playground where, she decided, Simon would play when he was bigger. It was rather far from where they lived, but it had deep shade and a wading pool with a sprinkler in the middle. As she walked, Pearl talked to Simon, who was awake, lying on his back and looking up at her, about the playground and what fun he'd have there.

Twice when she looked into that playground she saw Hilda there. Once Hilda was reading on a bench, shaking Racket's carriage with one hand. The other time, she was crouching over the wading pool, and Pearl could see the baby, her arms flung wide. Simon was different from Racket, quieter and rounder. He liked being wrapped up, and lay with his arms and legs drawn up to his body even when he was unwrapped. He had radiant smiles. He fed eagerly at her breast.

One Sunday afternoon when she was nursing him, sitting up on their bed because the bedroom window caught a breeze and it was cooler in there, Mike came in and sat down on the bed. He watched silently for a long time. "I like that sound he makes," Mike said at last. It was true. When Simon nursed, he made a grunting noise. "Do they all do that?"

"I don't know," said Pearl hesitantly. He sounded friendlier than he had for a while.

"He's getting ready to be a musician," said Mike. "Maybe we'll start him on the clarinet."

Simon finished nursing and Pearl burped him and laid him on the bed between them. She looked at the baby and at Mike to see if they looked alike, but Simon just looked like a baby to her, not like Mike or Nathan, though he was dark like Nathan. Of course he was Nathan's, she thought, but maybe in some way he was Mike's as well.

"He's too nice," said Mike now.

"Too nice? What do you mean?"

"A baby should yell," said Mike. "This kid's going to be a pushover. You can't be like that. This world, you have to be tougher than that."

"He'll be tough," said Pearl, but she didn't want her boy to be tough. She didn't want him to fight with other children.

"You have to warn him," said Mike urgently, as if he were really criticizing Pearl.

"He's only a baby!" she said sharply.

"Right. Only a baby," said Mike, and now he sounded sarcastic. She was frightened, and it reminded her of the months when she'd been afraid of Mike.

"What do you mean?" she said in a low voice.

"I'm glad it's so simple for you," he said sarcastically. "I'm glad you think he's only a baby!" He had been happy, and now he was angry, and nothing had happened. Pearl was in her nightgown, though it was afternoon, and it was twisted around her hips, sweaty, smelly with breast milk. She pulled it down as she stood up and took Simon to his crib, but Mike wasn't watching her; he'd left the room.

Racket was a year old in August, and Pearl went to a toy store for a birthday present. The man in the store said that for a one-year-old, who would be learning to walk, she should buy a push toy. He showed her a rolling spool with a wooden handle. "Once she can walk, you buy a pull toy," he said. There was a yellow wooden duck on red wheels, which was pulled by a red-and-white string with a big blue bead at the end, and Pearl liked that much better. "But is she walking?" said the man. She didn't know, but she paid for the duck and put it into Simon's carriage.

Sure enough, she spotted Hilda crocheting on a bench under a tree. Racket was standing at her knees. Pearl pushed the carriage into the playground.

"How's Simon?" said Hilda, looking up.

"Fine," said Pearl. "I came to wish Racket a happy birthday."

"Thanks. I suppose we should go back to calling her Rachel, but I still like Racket."

"Does she still make a racket?" said Pearl.

Hilda nodded. Pearl took the toy from the carriage. "Look, Racket, I bought you a birthday present," she said.

"Nice of you," said Hilda a little huskily.

"I wanted to," said Pearl. "Can she walk?"

"She's starting. It's hard here because the ground is uneven. At home she can take three steps."

"The man in the store didn't want me to buy a pull toy unless she could walk," Pearl explained.

They looked at each other and laughed together. Racket fastened her mouth on the duck's yellow wooden beak. Hilda showed her how the toy could be pulled along, and Racket sank to her knees and pushed the duck back and forth on the ground. Then she began to crawl rapidly toward the fountain, leaving the duck.

"Not with shoes on," called Hilda. Racket was wearing new-looking white leather shoes—real shoes—and socks, and Hilda carried her back to the bench and took them off her. "I let her get her clothes wet," she said. "I bring extras."

Pearl took Simon out of the carriage and crouched on the edge of the wading pool with him in her lap. She dangled his feet in the water. He hung limply, then kicked and smiled.

"He likes it," said Hilda. Racket had seated herself in the water and was slapping it hard with her palms.

"Can she talk?" said Pearl.

"She has a couple of words."

"She's easier now?"

"Not really," Hilda said. But she smiled at Pearl, who had thought Hilda would never smile at her again. Pearl looked down at her easy baby.

"I've been wanting to ask you," said Hilda. "What happened to that boy? Billy."

"He's in Spain."

"He really did go? Oh, I hope he's all right! Things aren't going well for the Loyalists."

"I know," said Pearl. "I don't see Ruby so much, now that I'm not working." Ruby had come to see Simon and had brought him a rattle. She promised to come again, but she didn't.

Now Racket rolled over in the water. She was drenched and she began to cry. Hilda carried her back to the bench and took off her clothes. She pinned a fresh diaper on Racket, but when she set her down a moment to reach for her sunsuit, Racket began walking toward the pool, where Pearl was still sitting with Simon. She took one step, two, three, four. "Did you see that?" Hilda called, as Racket sat down hard in the sand and patted it, then rolled over to crawl once more. "Four steps!" Pearl nodded and smiled. Yes, she had seen the four steps.

She met Hilda in the playground twice more during the summer. Sometimes she looked for her but couldn't find her. She was afraid to suggest that they plan to meet, and Hilda didn't bring up the idea.

Pearl didn't know whether it was painful for Hilda to see her. Probably it was. Once when they met, Hilda was reading while Racket played, and she seemed to mind putting down her book. Another time they talked. Fall was coming, and Mike had a new job as a stenographer for the city department that heard workmen's compensation claims. Pearl wanted to talk about Mike's moodiness, about the hard things—and sometimes the friendly things—he said about Simon, but she didn't.

"You could come over and visit some day," Pearl said softly as they were preparing to leave the playground. She was lonely. Simon was no trouble but there wasn't much to do for him, either. Pearl had never been one for cooking and cleaning. She didn't have any friends, and her mother irritated her. It would be nice if Hilda and Racket would come over some afternoon. Racket could walk now, and she hurtled down the path toward the playground gate. Hilda got up to chase her. "I will," Pearl heard her say over her shoulder as she ran.

Hilda didn't come until the middle of November. Pearl had heard that she was sick. She met a neighbor of Hilda's in the street and the woman said, "Your sister-in-law's been sick with bronchitis." Pearl called Hilda to see how she was.

"I've been sick and Racket's been sick," Hilda said. "Now we're both really all right. I need to get out. Should I come see you?"

"You don't want me to come there?" said Pearl.

"I'm sick of the four walls."

"You're sure?"

"Of course." It was cloudy out. It looked like rain. Pearl was just as pleased that she didn't have to bundle Simon up and go outside yet—though she'd have to go later, because she needed milk and salt. She had forgotten to buy salt and had used it all up, even dumping the salt from the salt shaker into the water in which she was boiling potatoes last night. Even so, the potatoes had tasted flat, and Mike had asked for the salt shaker at supper.

She nursed Simon while lying on the couch looking over a magazine. She didn't think nursing was ruining her figure. Maybe it would make her breasts hang down too much. She experimented, holding Simon a little higher in her arms so as to push her breasts upward. But it was tiring. It was Friday. Friday seemed like a gray day of the week to Pearl, and she played with that idea to find out whether she really held it. She laid Simon on the living room rug and began gathering ashtrays and old newspapers. Mike always left his saxophone out with the case open on the floor and sheet music spread out near it, but she didn't move any of that.

At last the doorbell rang. Hilda was at the door with Racket in the stroller. "It didn't fit in the elevator," she said. "I had to pull it up the steps." She was out of breath.

"The carriage fits," said Pearl. "I'm sorry."

"The carriage is narrower," said Hilda, still gasping. She pulled the wicker stroller into the living room and sat down immediately. Racket climbed out. Pearl didn't know why Hilda hadn't left the stroller downstairs in the lobby. Maybe she was afraid someone would mind.

"Won't she fall?" she said, watching Racket.

Hilda shook her head. "She just learned to do that last week. She climbs out all the time now."

Racket walked over to Simon, who was lying on his stomach on the rug. She pushed at his face to turn it over. "Gently, honey, gently," said Hilda.

"You're still sick," Pearl said.

Hilda was still out of breath. "I guess it was stupid to come," she said.

"I'm glad you came," said Pearl.

"Well, I wanted to." Pearl helped Hilda take her coat off, and she put it in the bedroom. Simon was crying and she put him into his bassinet. Maybe he'd sleep. Racket's nose was running. "She's really still sick, too," said Hilda. "I hope Simon doesn't catch it."

"He's nice and tough," said Pearl.

"He's a pretty baby."

"Thank you."

Pearl made coffee. Racket got into Mike's sheet music and cried when it was taken away from her. Pearl gave her a magazine to play with, but she wouldn't be appeased. When Pearl brought the coffee into the living room, Hilda was trying to soothe her by showing her things out the window—a car, a man. Racket rubbed at her face and cried. "She needs to nap," said Hilda.

Pearl set the coffee cups on the telephone table. They'd make rings on the wood, and she saw Hilda looking, probably thinking that Pearl should use coasters. Pearl had coasters—her mother had bought them—but she didn't know where they were. She was squatting to put milk and sugar into her coffee, and she sat back on her heels, so her skirt touched the floor. She suddenly felt like a brave, interesting person. "I'm afraid of you," she said recklessly, happily—over the noise of Racket's whimpers. But although she didn't know how it could be, she knew that even though she was afraid—oh, my, how afraid she was—she was also not afraid. She was taller than Hilda and had an easier baby, and that made a difference even if it shouldn't—and she could do things Hilda couldn't do. Hilda couldn't say what Pearl had just said. And Pearl loved Nathan—even now. It was brave to keep loving him.

"I don't know why you're afraid," Hilda said coldly.

"Oh, you know why."

"Pearl, you can't possibly expect me to have still another conversation about all that from last year," she said harshly—as if they'd talked about it every day, Pearl thought. "I went through plenty at the time, but it's over, and I wish you'd forget it. You think the whole world operates differently because you and Nathan went through some foolishness."

It was harsh—there was nothing in her voice but harshness—and Pearl was more frightened than before, truly frightened this time. She was afraid she'd turned Hilda against her at last.

"I'm sorry," she said meekly. And yet she was glad it had come to this.

Hilda sipped her coffee. "All right." There was silence. Hilda had sounded disgusted with her, more disgusted for her foolish talk than for what she had done. Pearl wondered whether she had somehow done a greater wrong in talking and thinking about what had happened than in the thing itself. She still thought about Nathan all the time, and she was still sure that Simon was his. She never said anything about that to Mike now, and it was as if it were her fantasy —but it had happened.

Pearl looked down and kept herself from crying but Hilda said, "Would you stop it?"

"I'm trying," said Pearl. Then she got up and stood before Hilda. "You have to let me speak," she said quietly. "I injured you, and you have to let me say I'm sorry. I can't bear to lose you."

Hilda looked up at her. She was leaning forward, and she looked chubby but drawn, the muscles of her face still tight from illness. She coughed. "You haven't lost me," she said. "I'm—" It was hard for her to talk, Pearl saw. "I'm touched that you think about me." The last words came out haltingly, and Pearl nodded and turned away. Nathan had used that word. Touched. "I'm touched that you say you love me," he had said. Now it was important not to answer, not to cry anymore. They would talk about other things—indifferent things: babies, weather, bronchitis.

She tried. "Do you cough at night?"

"Sometimes," said Hilda. Pearl wished she could care for Hilda at night, bringing her something warm and soothing to drink. All this was true, even though she loved Nathan and he was Hilda's husband. Loving Nathan somehow made it more true.

She began to tell Hilda about Mike's saxophone playing and other things he was doing. She suspected she might have told Hilda some of this before, when they met in the park, but Hilda listened politely. Racket had quieted, but every few minutes she tugged at her mother and whimpered to be picked up.

Maybe this was the best she and Hilda would have. Pearl should seek a friend elsewhere, yet it seemed that Hilda was supposed to be her friend, almost as if they were more likely to be friends because they had loved the same man. People who loved the same country or the same song or child were more likely to be friends.

It was starting to get dark out. They had tried to put Racket down in Simon's crib, but she screamed and tried to climb out, and they found her hanging on the outside, clinging to the bars. She wouldn't take an arrowroot biscuit or a cup of juice. Hilda was worn out, anyone could see that. "I have to go to the drugstore," she said. "I have to get her prescription refilled."

"I'll go for you," said Pearl.

"Why should you do that? I have to go home anyway. Why should you go out if you don't need to?"

"I have to buy milk and salt," said Pearl. "I was planning to walk you home."

"Maybe it will be easier if you come," said Hilda.

"Oh, I know what," said Pearl. "I can take the stroller down the stairs. You go in the elevator with Simon."

Hilda was looking for her coat. Racket was screaming now. "Okay," Hilda said loudly over the screams. "I'll take Simon and you take Racket."

Pearl got her own coat and Hilda's and they dressed the babies. Now Racket was crying without a pause. "She's lost a lot of sleep because of her cough," said Hilda. The little girl was fighting everything—fighting the sleeves of her coat, fighting Hilda's hands when she buttoned it.

Simon's carriage was just outside the apartment door, and Pearl put Simon into it, then went back for Racket. She picked up her niece and kissed her. Her face was sticky with tears. Racket was still thin, and her legs never stopped moving, as though she were running in the air. Pearl put her into the stroller and held her there with one hand while she pushed the stroller out the door. Hilda took the carriage and pressed the button for the elevator.

Getting the stroller down the stairs with Racket in it was a struggle. The baby tried to climb out, and Pearl had to keep her hand on her all the way down. At last, after bumping her shins more than once, she reached the bottom of the stairs, where Hilda was waiting. Hilda held the outside door open and Pearl pushed the stroller out. They turned toward Flatbush Avenue, where the stores were. Racket was still crying, but she was lying down. Her cries sounded, now, as if she'd given up.

"If I go very fast," said Pearl, "maybe she'll fall asleep. It's worked with Simon. I'm going to run ahead."

"Where will I meet you?" said Hilda.

"Go to the drugstore," Pearl said. The drugstore was nearer than the grocery. "I'll go on to the grocery, and you meet me there."

"This is nice of you," said Hilda. "Maybe she'll sleep."

Pearl set out briskly, almost running. Sure enough, after a block Racket stopped crying, and when Pearl slowed down a block later and looked into the stroller, she saw that the baby was asleep. Racket stirred when Pearl slowed down, so she speeded up again.

It was getting dark and it was chilly. It felt like rain. Racket was warmly dressed, though. She'd be all right. Pearl passed the drugstore and glanced back. She thought she saw Hilda coming with Simon, about a block away. She had two blocks to go.

When Pearl reached the grocery store, she wasn't sure what to do. Racket was now fast asleep. The stroller probably wouldn't fit through the door of the store, which looked narrow. And if it did fit, the warmth and people and brightness inside would waken the baby.

There were people around. Racket would be all right, sound asleep outside the store for a moment.

Pearl stopped and waited for a long time to make certain Racket didn't wake up when the stroller stopped moving, but the baby lay still. Her breathing still sounded hoarse from her illness, and her nose bubbled. Sleep would do her good.

Pearl hurried into the store. Two people were ahead of her on the line. She had set the brake on the stroller, but she was nervous. She wished she could see it as she waited on line. Finally it was her turn, and she asked the grocer for the things she wanted. She was reaching out her hand to touch the brown paper bag in which he had placed her milk and salt when she heard sounds—people shouting, the sound of a car's brakes, a woman's terrible scream.

8 ❧

I COULD HAVE SAVED MY DAUGHTER'S LIFE IF I'D BEEN AT that corner a minute earlier. I didn't dawdle in the drugstore, and the man wasn't slow. At least I don't have to grow old thinking that if I hadn't stopped to look at nail polish, I'd have saved her life. I didn't stop to look at nail polish. No one saw Racket climb out of the stroller, walk to the curb, and step off except an old woman crossing the street toward her, who screamed but couldn't reach her in time—but when I got there, people were everywhere. I remember light, blinding light, but I don't know where it came from. It must have taken some time for an ambulance to come.

Everyone knew everything within an instant, it seemed—the policeman, the man who was driving the car, all the people gathered on the corner. Half of what they knew was wrong, but the rush of what they thought made it impossible to say. Everyone knew she was my child, and that I had left her outside the store. Pearl rushed out of the store just as I came along—as we all came along—as the man, who had leaped from his car, and the old woman collided with each other, reaching for my dead baby. In the light and screaming, Pearl took Simon's carriage and I received the angry comfort of strangers. Pearl was crying too hard to speak, and I don't think she thought about what everyone was assuming. By the time the policeman got around to asking me questions and writing down answers, which was at the hospital, where Nathan rushed in, looking like an old man, I had settled on the story everyone expected to hear: I had gone into the grocery store and left the stroller outside.

I could have done it. All my wishes and what little energy I had after the bronchitis, all afternoon, had been spent trying to put Racket to sleep, and once she was asleep, I too might well have just left her. Always before, when she fell asleep after crying for a long time—when she was exhausted—nothing could waken her. I've asked myself many times whether I would have left the stroller alone, and I think I might have. Over the years, when I've heard about other mothers who lost their children after a moment's inattention or neglect, I've felt sympathy, not outrage, as if I truly was the one who did it. Maybe I was.

As I was talking to the policeman, a nurse came in and quietly handed me Racket's shoes. They were leather shoes, not booties, because she walked so early. They weren't even new, or recently polished—just dirty white baby shoes with laces losing their tips. I kept them. I held on to them all that evening, although Nathan tried to put them away.

That night, as I stood there holding those shoes, I believe I thought that if I told anyone it was Pearl who left the baby alone, she would have been prosecuted for murder. I don't know why I thought that; I was in turmoil, of course. With my baby dead, I wanted to die, and if someone was going to be prosecuted for murder, it seemed best that I be the one. Pearl had Simon to care for. I knew that there was another reason to go along with everyone's mistake. I knew it was better if Nathan thought that I, and not Pearl, had let Racket die, but I didn't think that through for a long time.

My mother-in-law sat *shiva* at my house. I don't know if Nathan and I would have done it otherwise. We never went to synagogue and I didn't know the rules for mourning. For a week, we sat on low benches that the funeral home had lent us. I remember my mother-in-law sitting there, solid and square, rocking and sobbing, then suddenly stiffening and screaming as if she was the old woman who saw Racket hit, or as if the car had hit *her*. Pearl and I had never called our mother-in-law Mama, but now we did. Pearl and Mike were with us most of the time. Mama screamed for Simon, her remaining grandchild, and when he was brought to her it seemed to comfort her a little. She held him on her lap and rocked forward, pressing him between her breasts and her lap. He lay still and let her as her granddaughter never had.

"It was my fault," said Pearl, in terror, the first time we were alone.

"I don't want you to talk about that," I said firmly, and she obeyed. I had forgotten about her and Nathan, I noticed at one point. It hardly mattered, considering what had happened. They were formal with each other, as if they didn't know each other very well, as if they were the only two of us *without* a reason to be close—for I'd always been at ease with Mike, and it seemed that Pearl and I could never push the thought of the other completely aside. Sometimes I thought that maybe they *didn't* know each other very well, maybe what had brought them together was formality, unfamiliarity, mystery.

Mike cooked. He spoke little, and never managed to offer condolences, though he said, "Hilda, Hilda," to me, over and over again. Every day he cooked supper for us, then led Pearl and Simon off to their apartment as Nathan and his mother and I sat down to eat. Mike could make canned soup with cheese sandwiches, French toast, or hamburgers with baked potatoes and canned peas. We had those three meals in order for many days, until finally I told him I could go back to cooking, and Mrs. Levenson stopped staying at our house all day and even overnight.

We'd had Racket for only a year and three months, but it was impossible to remember how to live without her, or to start that life up again. After Mike and Pearl had gone back to their regular life and Nathan was teaching again, I was alone in the apartment all day. There were days when I would lie on the couch in the living room, and it seemed that there was no reason for me to have legs except to go into the bedroom to pick up Racket, no reason to have arms except to hold her. I could remember the exact feel of her weight, her restlessness. My arms would ache so hard for her that I would rub them and sob, rub them and sob, until the slipcover was soaked. Then on other days it was anger that gripped me. I had *told* Pearl that Racket had learned to climb out of the stroller. I had told Pearl, and she had seen Racket climb out, but she had not remembered, or not thought it mattered, or not cared about Racket the way she'd have cared about her own child. Sometimes my jaw worked as I lay face down on the couch, sobbing, and I wanted to bite Pearl.

One day, two or three weeks after Racket had died, I thought I was feeling a little better, and I took a shower and put on clean clothes. I began to think about Pearl, and although she had been humble and scared the whole week after Racket's death, as if she too thought she was going to be prosecuted for murder, I thought of her as uncaring and indifferent. Of course I knew she couldn't mind as much as I did, and it made me angry that the world did not mourn my child as I did, but had gone on without a pause, except that the old woman who'd seen her die had come by one day with Italian cakes and tears, and the wife of the man who'd been driving the car called me and told me her husband cried at night.

I was angry with Pearl, and I thought my anger was merely going to propel me out, maybe into the park. It would be good for me to go for a walk, just a short walk in the cold air, and then I could stop at the store and buy bread for breakfast and a few other things. I had not done any shopping since that day. Mike or Nathan had done it all.

But I walked straight to Pearl's house. I hoped she was not going to be there, although as I walked along, with tears not quite shed, feeling like someone in a play, playing the part of a woman walking along a street, I also did want her to be there. When I reached her building, I ran up the stairs. I felt strong. It didn't make me lose my breath to run. When Pearl opened the door, I stepped in, and to my own surprise I began hitting her. "I came over," I said, but as I was speaking, I was swinging my arm in my coat and glove, reaching up at her face. She stood there, shocked, looking down at me. I slapped her, not hard, because something was making my arm heavy so that I could hardly move it, and I couldn't get any force behind it. The air pressed it back. But after I slapped her I began pummeling at her face and pummeling with my other hand—my pocketbook slid off my wrist—at her arm and her body.

"Hilda," she said, and closed the door behind me. I could hear Simon crying somewhere. Pearl didn't try to stop me. At first my blows were like a baby's, weak, but then my strength returned and I hit her sides and back. I threw myself at her and hit her shoulders and legs. She backed up and somehow I pushed her down. I was ashamed, but I couldn't stop. I was sobbing and beating my sister-in-law, still in my gloves, but as hard as I could now, beating her sides and buttocks and legs. I bit her arm through her blouse. I was on top of her.

I could feel her stir at last—it took a long time—and finally she made a pass at my wrists, and then she put both her hands on my wrists and held tight. I felt relief, as if I wanted to be stopped. She held my wrists and I sobbed against her breasts. We were both lying on the floor, on our sides now, sobbing. At last I felt Pearl, who was stronger and bigger than I, release my wrists and put her arms around me, drawing me closer to her. My stockings were torn and I had heard something else rip. I think my heel had got caught in the hem of my skirt.

At last I sat up. Neither of us spoke for a long time. We were both out of breath. "Go and wash," Pearl said at last.

I took off my coat and my gloves. The fingers of my gloves were split. I went into the bathroom and washed my face and hands and combed my hair. When I came out, Pearl was sitting in the living room nursing Simon, her blouse unbuttoned, a diaper thrown over her shoulder for modesty. Her hair was disheveled and there was a red mark on her cheek.

I sat down, ashamed.

"The hem of your skirt is hanging," she said. "You'd better fix it. My sewing box is in the bedroom."

I went for a needle and thread. Then I took off my skirt and sat down opposite her and hemmed it. Most of the hem was down.

"I haven't told Mike I was the one who really did it," said Pearl. "You told me not to talk about it."

"I haven't told Nathan," I said.

"Why didn't you say right away?" she said. "I thought everybody knew it was me, until later."

"I was confused," I said. "Then I wanted them to think I did it."

"I shouldn't have left her outside," she said. "Everyone knows you can't do that."

"I know," I said, "but I might have done it."

"I don't think so."

"I don't know what I would have done."

She moved Simon to her other breast, but didn't drape the diaper over her shoulder this time. "Nathan already hated me before," she said, stroking Simon's dark head. He was an industrious eater and he made a noise when he nursed. I hadn't watched Pearl nurse him much. At our house she'd taken him into the bedroom.

"No, he doesn't hate you," I said. "He certainly doesn't hate you." But I thought that maybe he did. He'd hated himself since he'd gone to bed with Pearl, I knew that, and maybe he hated her, too.

Nathan had never asked me for a detailed explanation about

Racket. He didn't want to talk about what happened, or to talk about her. Pearl had gathered most of Racket's clothes and removed them from the house, and Nathan had arranged with the super to store her crib in the basement. I'd put her shoes and a few other things away in a drawer. Already it was almost as if she had never been.

It took me a long time to hem the skirt. We didn't say anything more. Pearl finished nursing Simon and he fell asleep. She sat and held him on her lap for a while, and then she stood up gracefully and carried him into the other room. I made myself watch her, not letting myself think all the obvious thoughts—how it could have been me carrying a baby into the other room, and so on. In fact it hardly ever was me, not that way. Getting Racket to sleep was always a battle. I never glided along with her the way Pearl did with Simon. I don't glide, anyway.

Pearl had kept her hair short after she'd cut off her braid, and she looked young. Her neck looked long. I didn't know whether Pearl would think I was crazy or be mad at me forever for hitting her, or whether she'd just be so embarrassed that it had happened—our lying on the floor crying and me hitting her, wearing my gloves and shoes—that it would be impossible even to talk. I felt meek, let me tell you, sitting there hemming that skirt under orders.

I heard Pearl go into the bathroom. She was in there a long time, and I realized she was taking off her makeup and putting it on again so she could cover the red marks. When she came out she was wearing a fresh blouse and her hair was combed and her face looked nice. She sat down next to me. "I'd give anything to bring Rachel back," she said. "I hope you know that."

"You wouldn't give Simon," I said cruelly. I was angry because she'd said Rachel. She hadn't called Racket Rachel for months.

"No," she said, and stood up and went into the kitchen. Finally I finished hemming the skirt and I put it on. I followed Pearl into the kitchen. I think I wanted to see whether she would point out how unnecessary that last remark had been. I remembered the way it had felt when she held my wrists to keep me from hitting her any longer, and I think I wanted to see whether she'd do something like that again. But she didn't say anything. She was washing her lunch dishes. I went and put on my coat and took my ruined gloves and my purse and let myself out of the apartment.

After that when I felt like going out I didn't go to Pearl's house. I walked. Sometimes I'd meet a neighbor, and she'd bend her head and speak to me inaudibly. "I beg your pardon?" I'd say, but nobody ever said anything to me that I could hear.

I had very little to do. I read many library books. Sometimes I read a whole book in a day, and later it would be hard to remember that I didn't live in those characters' lives. I never forgot about Racket, though, even while I was reading. Her death was always there.

That winter, the Loyalists were doing badly in Spain, and the American volunteers were retreating with the rest of them. Nathan went to meeting after meeting, and came home shaking his head, saying little. It seemed to be the only thing that could distract him, hearing about the troubles in Spain, hearing people give speeches about Marxism, about economic justice, about the Soviet Union. He read a lot, too—difficult books about economic theory. I wondered how he could pay attention, but I think the books helped him, the way a different man might have been helped by climbing a steep mountain or swimming miles.

Once or twice I went to a meeting with him. I was not tempted to go more often, though the meetings were more interesting than I expected. Nathan said less than he had before about his political opinions. He said less than he had before about everything. We hardly ever spoke. When I think of that winter, I remember silence and grayness. One day Nathan told me he'd heard that Ruby's boyfriend, Billy, had been wounded at Teruel. He didn't know how badly, or where Billy was. He knew a friend of Billy's, and had run into him handing out leaflets.

The next day I called Pearl. She'd seen Ruby. "Ruby wants to visit you," she said.

"Why?"

"She feels bad about Racket."

"She has better things to do."

"Hilda, why do you talk like that?" said Pearl.

"I don't talk like that."

Pearl went back to talking about Ruby and Billy. Billy had been wounded in the hip. His hip had been shattered, but he was alive. Ruby was happy that he was alive, but worried about him. He was still in Spain. She didn't know much.

"Tell Ruby she can come see me," I said.

Ruby came a week later. "That sweet baby," she said as soon as she walked in. "I couldn't believe it when I heard about that sweet baby."

"Thank you," I said. I made coffee for her. I got her to talk about Billy. Billy had had to walk across the Pyrenees. He liked the Spanish people. He'd stamped on grapes with Spanish peasants in the Guadarrama mountains.

"His letters aren't really unhappy," she said, "but he keeps writing about men who died. I'm supposed to visit their mothers. He sends me their names. Not the names of the mothers, thank goodness. He wants me to look in the phone book and see if I can figure out who the relatives are and go visit them. Can you imagine?"

I shook my head.

"It would be so hard," said Ruby, "I don't know if they'd want me to come. I didn't know if *you* wanted me to, and we'd met before."

"It was nice of you to come," I said. It might have been the first friendly thing I'd said to anybody since Racket died. She had died on November 19, 1937, and this was probably late February or early March. That's a long time to go without saying anything nice. It made me like Ruby, because I'd said something pleasant to her, that little lie. Of course I hadn't wanted her to come, any more than the grieving mothers of the boys lost in Spain would I tried to figure out whether their pain would be worse than mine, whether it made it better or worse that your child had lived for years and you'd gotten to know him, whether it made it better or worse that he'd died for a good cause instead of in a stupid accident. I imagined Ruby going from house to house, making the grieving mothers lie about wanting her to come, and making them feel better because they'd been nice to somebody, dopey little Ruby who still looked about fourteen— well, maybe by now she looked sixteen—and the thought of it seemed funny.

Then I realized that nothing whatever had seemed funny since the day Racket had died. I kept talking to Ruby—"Are you able to write to Billy?" I asked, and she said she kept writing but she didn't know if he always got the letters. She had her hat on her lap and she kept turning it around and around, a little wool hat. But I was thinking different thoughts: I was trying to remember something funny from the months that had passed since November, something funny in the papers or on the radio. We still listened to the radio now and then, and I remembered that we used to laugh at many of the programs, but now I couldn't recall anything funny at all. I suppose we'd stopped listening to the funny programs without even talking about it.

It really wasn't a funny year. Even in the worst parts of the Depression, funny things happened, silly things, just because everyone was so poor. I remember my father offering me his old socks, thinking there must be some use to them when they couldn't be darned any longer, hating to throw them away, and how I'd laughed to think of a time in which a gift from a father to a daughter was used socks. I'd taken them, too. I used them for dust rags or something.

But 1938 wasn't a funny year. Maybe people who didn't lose a baby found something to laugh at, but Nathan and I didn't. I wondered whether he laughed at school. Being with young people—now there had to be funny moments there. Now I was really grateful to Ruby for coming. She had made me think. I gave her more coffee and then she left.

That night I asked Nathan whether anything funny ever happened in his school. He looked out from under his eyebrows at me. He stared as if he had trouble seeing me, and I wondered whether he'd wept away his eyesight. Later it did turn out that he needed glasses. But then it seemed as if he was looking at me through fog and smoke.

"Yes," he said. "There's a little girl. Evelyn Grossman. She's very funny. She's a natural comedienne."

"Do you laugh?"

"I laugh." He was reading the paper, and he looked down at it again. Then he looked up. "You think I shouldn't laugh?"

"No," I said. "I'm glad there's something to laugh at. Tell me something she said."

But he couldn't remember. "Maybe you need to get out of the house," he said.

I thought that was true, and I began to think about getting a job. I'd thought about it right away, right after Racket died, when I realized how little there was for me to do at home. But I'd buy the paper and forget to read the want ads, or I'd sit down to read them without a pencil, and be so tired—from nothing—that I couldn't stand up and go for a pencil to circle the promising ones. Then when I finally had some numbers to call, so much time had passed that I was sure those jobs had been filled.

Now I began to think about a job. They were easier to find than when I got the job at Bobbie's. I didn't want to go back there. Everyone would talk about Racket. I wanted to take a job with strangers, and not tell them I ever had a baby. The only way I could get better was to let events cover her up. I began to know that I wouldn't always feel as bad as I felt then. For a while I'd thought I'd feel the same way for my whole life. But when I thought about the mothers who had lost sons in Spain, I thought that maybe in ten years those women would feel a little better—and then it occurred to me that maybe *I'd* feel better in ten years, too.

I decided I wanted to work in a store. It would be simple. Somebody wants shoes, you give her shoes, she gives you money, you put it in the till. I could be nice to people without too much trouble. I thought about all this for a few days, and then I dressed up a little and took the subway into New York and went to the big department stores—Lord & Taylor's, Altman's, Saks. I got a job at Macy's, which pleased me because it was the biggest even though it wasn't the fanciest. I wanted to be on the first floor where the crowds swirled around, but after I'd filled out an application and taken an arithmetic test and been trained for two days, they put me in Misses' Sportswear. I liked the training. Someone had figured out everything and all I had to do was learn it. There was a procedure when a package was to be sent, a procedure for everything. I had to put the number of the department in a box, the date in another box. Each time I learned a new procedure, it made me feel better.

When I got out on the floor, it was harder than I expected. I had to stand all day, and the first day there, I wore holes in my shoes. I went home and soaked my feet. They were red and blistered. Nathan was shocked.

I made mistakes at work, and then tears would come to my eyes, as if I'd simply reached my limit in hard things before I got to that store. Making a mistake and having to get permission to void a sale and start over, I cried, but I didn't let the woman in charge see me. Sometimes I just had to count things—skirts on a rack, or blouses folded on a shelf. I liked that. I couldn't possibly do harm to anyone, counting skirts. After all, Pearl had left Racket outside that store, but I'd let Pearl push Racket's stroller.

I liked being able to help people. One customer didn't speak English. I don't know what language she was speaking, maybe Italian or

Spanish. I kept smiling at her, and she smiled back and patted my arm. Finally I patted her arm. We got to be great friends. She went into the fitting room and I brought her skirts until she found one she liked. She could let me know what she liked and didn't like, and I smiled and even clapped my hands. We rejoiced together. She had a wedding ring on. I wondered whether she also had had a baby who died. It could be true. She was in her thirties, and there were no children with her. Not speaking each other's language, we didn't have to talk about these dead children. We were able to rub cloth between our fingers and pantomime how much we liked the cut of the skirts.

It was good to be bringing money home again. I'd thought money didn't matter, even though Nathan didn't make much, but with money we had possibilities. I used my employee discount to buy a new chair for the living room. It was the color of mustard, with a fringe on the bottom. When the chair was delivered, I looked at it, and thought that it had nothing to do with Racket, it was a place where she had never been. It made me know we had to move, and after a few months, I began looking for another apartment. I walked up and down the streets on Sundays, looking for signs in windows advertising apartments for rent. At last I found one, just a few blocks away from our old apartment, but far enough to have different neighbors who didn't know us. It was similar to our old apartment, a little bigger—but it felt different. You turned to the right when you walked in the front door, instead of to the left. Moving out, I felt as if I was leaving behind my daughter, who was buried under the floorboards. I felt worse than I had expected to feel. She had been dead for almost a year by then.

It was after Nathan's disillusionment with the Communists. I had found him slumped over, one day, listening to the radio. Stalin had signed a nonaggression pact with Hitler. Nathan continued to go to meetings for a while after that, and some of his friends tried to reassure him. They said that Stalin knew what he was doing, that he should trust Stalin—but he couldn't. Once I found him crying. After a while he stopped going to meetings. Then we moved, and we were busy in the apartment. We had to buy new things. I shortened our old living room curtains and put them in the bedroom, and bought new drapes for the living room.

At work I was moved to the first floor and sold pocketbooks. I watched the crowd and marveled that I didn't know any of these people. Sometimes elegant women in suits and dark hats walked by, talking to their friends, looking like characters from a play about the upper classes. Once a line of schoolgirls in uniform marched past me, speaking French. I had no idea who they were or how they'd got there. It was easier to sell purses than sportswear—I didn't have to walk around so much. And it was one more move away from my old self, not just the self who still had a daughter, but even the newly bereaved self who cried when she made a mistake.

Now I chatted with customers and directed people who were lost. I could even direct people to the baby clothes department. It was good that there were still babies. Maybe someday I'd have another one. The first time someone asked me the way to baby clothes—not a mother or a grandmother but a man in a fedora—I watched myself to see if the question would break me, but I was all right.

I liked giving directions. I wanted to help people even more, and during the slow times, when I was supposed to look busy, rearranging and straightening the stock, I planned what I'd do if someone took sick and collapsed near my counter, how I'd rush around to catch her under the arms and lower her carefully to the floor. I didn't make friends, or at least, I didn't go beyond a certain point with the friends I did make. I liked my work friends. Sometimes I worked side by side with a woman for a long time and never learned her first name. I was Mrs. Levenson and she was Miss Bradley or whatever. I had friends with whom I'd never sat down, whom I'd never seen seated. We would talk, of course, when things were slow, but often about the store. The other women told me about the departments where they had worked, the advantages and drawbacks of each one.

This may seem cold but it was not cold. With each month that passed I felt stronger. Sometimes I let myself remember good times I'd had with Racket, rocking her or playing with her. When she was alive I hadn't thought of myself as a good mother, but now I could see that I'd been a good mother. I'd loved her. I never learned how to make her stop crying, but I was on her side. I got angry when she cried, but not at her—angry at the setup that made us strangers. I wondered what she would have been like if she'd lived. She had just been starting to speak a few words, but of course they didn't really sound like someone talking.

Nathan and I didn't talk about her. Losing her had brought him closer to Pearl and Mike, though—or at least closer to Simon. He was stiff and formal with Pearl, stiff and subdued with Mike, and I thought he was afraid, after Stalin had signed the pact with Hitler, that Mike's main subject from then on was going to be "I told you so." And of course, being Mike, he couldn't help but give us some of that. "I don't suppose you're surprised?" he said.

"Yes, I'm surprised, Michael," said Nathan.

"I could have told you."

"You could have told me Stalin was going to sign an agreement with the Nazis? If Stalin is on the side of the Nazis, why did he go to all that trouble in Spain?"

"Beats me," said Mike. "I never thought any of those guys had any brains."

"Some people think it's a trick."

"And you?"

"I'm not a tricky person, Michael."

"Oh, yeah?"

This was in the lobby of the hospital, of all places. Mrs. Levenson was in the hospital. She'd always had a bad heart, and now it was worse. We had met at her bedside. Now we were leaving together.

"So where's Simon?" Nathan said, changing the subject. He needed Simon. I'd been afraid Simon would be too much of a reminder, but Simon was everybody's comfort. He was a quiet, bright little boy. He'd run to Nathan and beg to be picked up and swung in the air. Nathan didn't swing too hard or too high and that was what Simon liked.

"He won't let me do it," Mike had said, the first time Nathan had played this way with Simon. "He cries when I do it."

"You're rough with him," said Pearl. "It scares him."

"Who's rough? I'm not rough."

Now Pearl offered us a ride home with them. We still didn't have a car. She suggested that we stop at their house to see Simon. He'd been left with a neighbor. All the way home, we talked about the coming war. We were all watching it come, those months. I couldn't remember ever thinking so much about faraway places, even though

I was married to Nathan and we'd always talked about politics and current events. Now it was hard to remember that anything else mattered except Hitler being handed Czechoslovakia and marching into Poland. But at least it gave the four of us something to talk about that didn't make anybody run and hide. Pearl was the most upset, to my surprise, the most insistent that Roosevelt should bring our country into it.

"What if there's a draft?" I said. "What if Mike has to go?"

"Nathan could go, too," she said.

"Well, yes, I suppose so." Nathan was wearing glasses by now. He'd finally had his eyes checked, and it turned out his vision was very poor. "You are a menace, Mr. Levenson," the eye doctor had said in a friendly way. "It's not safe to have you moving among us without glasses." I didn't think the army would want somebody like that.

"I don't want Mike to have to go," Pearl said now. "Don't think that. For God's sake. But Hitler's going to take over the world if we're not careful." She had brought Simon home from the neighbor's and was taking off his coat. She seized him and kissed him as if Hitler were coming up the stairs. Simon ran to Nathan as soon as he was freed and squeezed between his knees. "Want up," he said.

Nathan began to play with him. I saw Pearl watch them with a light in her eyes, and I wondered whether she still thought about Nathan, was even still in love with him, or whether it was Simon she was thinking about now. She was standing in the doorway, about to carry Simon's jacket to wherever she kept it, but standing still, she turned back, looking quite young and unaware of herself or of me looking at her. I was sitting in the chair where I'd hemmed my skirt after I beat her up, after Racket died. It seemed like a long time ago. Simon had been an infant, but babies grow into children quickly. Looking at Pearl, I felt something rather sweet and new come over me—despite all the fear and misery of worrying about war, which seemed to have replaced my grief, or to have gathered my sorrow into it. I forgave Pearl, that was what it was. I was embarrassed when the word came into my head. It didn't seem like something modern people did, forgiving. I wished I could say it, but I knew I wouldn't, certainly not in front of the men. I would have stood and touched her shoulder and said, "Pearl, I forgive you." Of course the men would have thought I meant something else.

Whenever I saw Nathan's mother, for two years, she wailed. She never stopped rocking back and forth. She never quite stood up straight after the death of her granddaughter. She'd ask, "Why didn't God take me instead? Why not me?"

I'd get angry with her. "How should I know?" I'd say to her.

Then when she had gone, I'd cry and ask Nathan, "Why does she do that to me?"

"She doesn't mean to upset you."

"Then why does she bring it up over and over? How should I know why God took the baby instead of her?"

"She doesn't really think you'll answer her."

"I don't know what to say when she asks that."

"I know."

Of course the suggestion made me angry because I'd have been delighted to give her to God instead of my child. It wasn't as if God had suggested the exchange and I had refused. I couldn't agree with her out loud, though.

But it also angered me because it was too flattering to her. If such a thing were possible, if there was a God and He needed a certain number of us to keep up the troops in heaven, I knew that this grumpy old lady would never make a suitable substitute for my lively daughter. But I didn't believe in anything like that—I couldn't comfort myself with the picture of Racket wriggling for God in heaven.

"Leave me alone," I shouted at her once. "It's harder for me than for you."

I thought she'd be angry with me forever, but she only shouted, "Of course harder for you. Who said not harder for you? God forbid I should think not harder for you."

Then suddenly one day she died of heart failure. Mostly we were surprised. She wasn't particularly old and although she had been in the hospital twice, she didn't act sick. She would clutch her chest when she came upstairs, and we wouldn't have handed her a heavy package to hold, but we assumed she'd go on that way for a long time. When she died I thought that at least she would no longer come into my living room and wail, and I wondered whether she had died of a broken heart.

God didn't give Racket back even though He had now decided He could use Mrs. Levenson after all. He must have wanted them both. "So send her back!" I found myself shouting at my dead mother-in-law one afternoon when I was alone in the apartment, my arms in the dishpan full of suds.

"I should have screamed with her," I said to Pearl one day.

"About Racket?"

"Yes. Remember how she used to scream?"

"Of course. I don't think it made her feel any better."

"I don't know," I said. It occurred to me now that I might have asked Mrs. Levenson whether she wanted me to answer her question about God. "What do you mean, answer?" she'd have said. "How should I know from answer?"

"I'm sorry she died," I said to Pearl.

"Me, too," she said. "I think I mind more than Mike does."

"Nathan minds," I said.

"Maybe Mike does too," said Pearl. "It's hard to know what Mike really thinks." We were in the playground where we'd sometimes met before. It was a Sunday, and I'd gone over to her house with a knitting pattern she had wanted to borrow. It was the summer of 1940 and Racket had been dead for two and a half years. Simon was three. When I'd reached Pearl's house, she was about to take him to the playground, and she asked, a little hesitantly, if I wanted to go along. Mike stood by sullenly and watched us talk. I didn't know if something particular was bothering him or not.

"Mike is like a boy," I said now, while we watched Simon play. I pictured Mike zipping up his jacket and tucking his face down, putting his hands in his pockets the way boys do. Even when he wore a topcoat and a hat instead of a cap he kept his head down, looking at the ground and whistling. "He whistles," I said.

"Yes," Pearl said. "Boys whistle."

"There are things he doesn't seem to talk about," I went on. I wondered if he ever talked about Pearl and Nathan. Well, we didn't;

why should he? But I thought he thought about it. He spoke to Simon as if it was in his mind.

I suppose Pearl thought it would still be painful for me to go to the playground, but it wasn't. I'm not made like that. Or everything was painful. Once, the summer after Racket died, I'd gone and sat in that same playground, the unpaved one with the trees, the one we'd liked. It was late in the evening, almost dark, and no one was there. I cried quite a bit there, but I cried quite a bit everywhere that year.

As we talked, Pearl stood next to the slide, and whenever Simon reached the top and started down, she would go over and crouch, waiting to catch him. He hadn't yet learned to put his feet down when he reached the bottom, and he was afraid to slide down unless she was there. When we left, Mike had said, "Don't baby him, Pearlie."

When I said there were things Mike didn't talk about, Pearl didn't answer because she had gone over to the bottom of the slide once again. She was wearing a dark green skirt and when she crouched, it touched the ground. She laughed at Simon, who was working up his courage at the top of the slide. "Should I come now, Mommy? Should I come now?" he called.

"Now would be fine, darling."

"Would *now* be fine, too? How about *this* now?"

"This now would be fine, too."

At last he came down, and she caught him and kissed him. She put him down and shook the gravel off her skirt.

"Mike thinks like someone in a room without doors or windows," she said. "He just goes around and around."

251

"So he never changes his mind?"

"Never," said Pearl. "He never changes at all. No, that's not true. He does change. He wears out a path on the floor and then things change. It's different."

"What's different?"

"Well, the floor has a slope," she said. We both laughed.

I looked up at the leafy trees. It was the time of summer when the leaves seem widest. I've always wondered whether they get narrower later. I looked up to see whether the trees were going to help me or whether I was going to be sorry for what I was about to say.

"Has he forgiven you for your—for that unpleasant experience with—"

"No, Hilda," said Pearl. "It was very pleasant. It wasn't unpleasant until later. Sorry."

So she could talk about it more easily than I. Of all things. It silenced me for a minute. Simon had wandered off, watching a bird. Then I said, "I wanted to know whether Mike is still angry with you."

"In a way he'll always be angry," she said, after a pause. "But he's worn a place on the floor. Anger's different when it's a habit."

"He'll never understand it," I said.

"Understand it?" Pearl's voice was tremulous.

"The way I do, I guess," I said.

We had moved to a bench and Pearl had taken out her knitting, but now it lay untouched in her lap. "So how do you understand it, Hilda?" she said, not looking at me.

I thought about it. "It was selfish," I said.

"Yes."

"On the part of both of you."

"Yes."

"But selfishness isn't a capital crime," I said. I turned on the bench to talk to Pearl, though I was also watching the trees behind her. The leaves moved a little, up and down. "I don't want to spend my whole life listening to people apologizing to me," I said. "It's insulting."

"How is it insulting?" She stared at me. "I don't understand why it's insulting."

"I don't either," I said. Then I added, "It keeps you and me from knowing each other."

"Catch me, Mommy," Simon called now. "Catch me!"

"I've thought about that," she said to me, ignoring him, "but I thought it was mostly Racket."

"Well, Racket, too," I said. "Of course."

"How could you like me?" she said.

"And if I hate you?" I said. "How am I better off?"

She shrugged and picked up her needles. "I don't know how you're better off, Hildie. Heaven knows I'm not better off if you hate me."

"Catch me!" called Simon again, running past us. This time she stood up and ran over to where he was waiting and picked him up. Then she wiped his nose with a handkerchief she took from her skirt pocket. Then she decided it was time to go home for lunch, and we should pick up Simon's toys. On the way home she talked about other things.

After a while we began to see each other all the time again. We'd have each other's family to our houses for supper. The men were quiet, but they didn't protest. Or we'd go shopping. Pearl bought a new winter coat that fall, and I went along to watch Simon in the stores while she tried coats on. Pearl was always hungry. I didn't remember that from before. She was always suggesting that we stop at Schrafft's or Child's. We had pancakes at Child's when we went shopping, or we went to the Automat for baked macaroni and cheese or tongue sandwiches. We usually went shopping on Saturdays. I'd been in the store at work all week, but I didn't mind. We found things to laugh at, somehow, on those days.

Simon loved to put nickels in the machines at the Automat and be picked up to open the doors and take the food out. I remember how intently he worked the machines while I grasped his firm waist. Even though Racket had lived such a short time and had been dead for so long, it was always a surprise to me that Simon didn't kick and struggle when I held him.

One day in the Automat we met Pearl's old friend Ruby. She was married now, she told us. She still worked at Bobbie's. Billy had mostly recovered from his injuries. "He walks stiffly," she said. "He's afraid it will keep him out of the army."

"He wants to go again?"

"He still wants to fight Hitler. Billy thinks if he doesn't get Hitler, nobody will."

"So he thinks we'll be at war soon?" I said.

"We should have been at war long ago," said Ruby.

She had lost Pearl's address and we all wrote down addresses. Then a week or so later I came home from work and heard voices in the living room, and it was Billy talking to Nathan. I was glad to see him. He'd grown up a lot. He had been like a child when we met him. I remembered him shyly standing in Pearl and Mike's kitchen, trying to deal with so many strangers. Now he was more confident, but still quiet. He was telling Nathan how sorry he was about the death of Nathan's mother. I wondered whether they had already talked about Racket. Of course they had, I thought. I walked into the room to say hello and to see whether Nathan had offered him anything to eat, and Billy stood up and came toward me. He lurched when he walked. He pumped my hand for a long time. Then he took my shoulders gently between his fingers and leaned forward to kiss my cheek, aiming the kiss very carefully. "Hilda," he said.

"It's good to see you," I said. "Are you all right?"

"I'm fine," he said. "You're the one who's had troubles."

I went to bring a fruit bowl. He was talking eagerly to Nathan about his experiences, about the friendliness of people in Spain. Old women had kissed him and cried over him.

"The winter was rainy, yes?" said Nathan.

"Rain. Then heat. Oh, boy."

I left them and went to start supper. After Billy left, Nathan followed me into the kitchen and stood watching me quietly. "Do you know what he said, Hilda?" he asked me. "He said Ruby wrote him about Rachel, and he dreamed about her for weeks."

"There in Spain?"

"Yes. He said when he has a daughter he's calling her Rachel. He said he fell in love with her when he saw her."

"I remember that he was nice to her," I said.

"I didn't even remember. I just remember him talking about getting killed, with that light in his eyes."

I was tidying up while the meat loaf cooked. They'd eaten oranges, and I gathered the peels and threw them away. The breakfast dishes were still in the sink. I was washing them, knowing that Nathan was standing behind me. Then he came closer and put his hands on my shoulders just the way Billy had, not wrapping the whole palm over the shoulder but taking my shoulders between his thumbs and fore-fingers, the way one would pick up a dress. When Billy did it, it made me feel as if he thought I might break, as if the loss of my daughter had shriveled me until I was brittle. Nathan's fingers felt different, more definite. I turned off the water and he pulled me around and looked down into my face. Then he kissed me hard on the lips.

Nathan had kissed me many times in the years since he had gone to bed with Pearl and since Racket had died—two events I thought of together now—but if he kissed me in the kitchen it was to comfort me because I was crying. He kissed me in bed when he made love to me, but his lovemaking had been perfunctory, almost embarrassed, as if someone behind him were saying, "Now kiss her."

But that evening in the kitchen he kissed me like my young lover, and groped at my clothes as though he had never seen me without them. I was wearing a blouse and skirt and I laughed at him as he unbuttoned the blouse slowly, from the top down. "Now what's got into you?" I said.

"I don't know. It's a good time, isn't it?"

"Don't you want to have supper?"

"When will it be ready?"

The meat loaf had half an hour to bake.

"That'll do, I guess," said Nathan. I laughed and turned down the oven.

We went into the bedroom, me with my blouse still hanging open. I hadn't had time to make the bed in the morning and it was still unmade. Nathan undressed quickly and I took off my clothes, too, sitting down to unroll my stockings.

"I love to watch you do that," he said.

"Do what?"

"Roll your stockings down. You do it with the bottoms of your fingers, not the tips."

"I don't want to start a run."

"You're a kind person, Hilda," he said, a little sentimentally.

"Kind to my stockings?"

It was pleasant to take them off and to wiggle out of my girdle. Nathan hadn't watched me get undressed for a long time. He'd seen me, of course, night after night, but he hadn't seemed to be watching me. Maybe he had been, all along, if he looked forward to seeing me take off my stockings. I felt free and as if my belly was a pleasant thing, for once.

I got into bed. He was hard—he had been erect the whole time I was undressing. I wanted to give him everything, all the warm circles of excitement gathering in my body. My breasts seemed to reach toward him when he stroked them.

I thought he was murmuring "little one" when he entered me. I wasn't certain and didn't want to ask. The words I thought I heard moved me. I hadn't been anyone's little one for a long time. "My big girl," my father used to say, when I would cook a meal after my mother got sick. I had learned how to be big. I didn't want to be little forever, but I wanted to be little for a while.

"Sweet," Nathan was saying. "Good." He made love to me vigorously and even a little brutally, as if there was *no question* it was going to happen, and could be no question. I loved it. I hadn't thought about how every gesture, before, was a question, but now I saw that that was how it had been. And he laughed. He gnawed at my shoulders and neck, and laughed as if he were a gigantic, outrageous pet let loose on me. I felt young, a girl, a beautiful girl.

He kept saying endearments that didn't make sense, as if he had never learned, and had to make them up. "Sweet little," he said, "sweet little."

When we were finally still I said, "Aren't you hungry?" Then I said, "That was lovely."

"It was lovely," said Nathan. "I'm starving. What happened to dinner?"

"I was going to boil potatoes to go with the meat loaf," I said. "I didn't even peel them."

"Well, we'd better peel some potatoes, then," he said, but he put his arm around me and pulled me closer, as if I was his girlfriend and he was a sailor and we were walking on the boardwalk, and I leaned my head into the crook of his shoulder and neck, there in bed. I began to be cold, and pulled the covers around us.

"I want you to be like that all the time," I said.

"All right."

I didn't want to ask questions, but after a few minutes he began to talk. "Billy talked and talked about the baby," he said.

"You said that."

"And about you."

"About me?"

"He talked about Spain," Nathan said. "How sometimes what a

man did led to something terrible happening. Once he and a friend were talking, and then the friend got up to take a piss. It was the middle of the night, and they were lying under some rocks, trying to get some sleep. They knew the rebels were around them. His friend was shot on the way to the ditch they used as a latrine."

"He got killed?" I said.

"That's right," said Nathan. "Billy said he kept thinking that if he'd said one more thing, to delay the man, it might not have happened, or if he hadn't talked at all, the man might have gotten up sooner, and it might not have happened."

"I understand," I said.

"He said it must be like that for you. I don't know if it is."

"Like what?"

"Do you torture yourself—blaming yourself for—for what happened?" he said.

I considered. I felt close to him. "No," I said. "I did for a while." And that was true. There was the moment when I let Pearl take the stroller while I took the carriage—how about that moment?

Nathan was silent for a long time. Then he said, "Hilda, please don't take this wrong. I miss Rachel every day. I feel terrible about losing her. But sometimes I think, if you hadn't done that, I couldn't have lived. If you hadn't made a mistake—after. After my mistake."

"You'd have lived."

"I'd have been in awe of you all our lives."

I turned and sobbed into his chest, and then I wiped my eyes and we got up and put on our robes. We peeled the potatoes together.

9 ❧

"Did you worry when Frances was fifteen months old?" said Pearl. She looked over her shoulder as if she thought someone might hear us, but we were on a bench at the Central Park Zoo and behind us were plants and the lion house, no people.

"I've never worried about Frances," I said, as if I didn't know what she meant. Frances, my daughter—the new daughter who was born five years after Racket died—was about two, and she was walking near us in pink overalls, not exactly chasing pigeons but following them, following one for a while as it clucked and tottered along the cobblestone path, then following another.

"I held my breath the whole time Frances was fifteen months old," Pearl said. "And that was months ago. I couldn't even mention it until now." She stood to get a better view of Simon, who had gone to watch the seals across the cobblestone walk in front of us, and had momentarily disappeared. Pearl never let her hair grow. She looked more regal than when she was younger, tall and now broad-shouldered, in a straw hat, frowning judiciously and tilting her head and chewing on a piece of fruit or a peanut.

"He loves those seals," she said.

Now Frances sat down on the ground and put something into her mouth. I called her to me and took it away and gave her an animal cracker. I was at peace with Frances. She reminded me of myself. People say that's the baby mothers have trouble with, but I'm on good terms with my own practical nature, and Frances was a practical baby, waking when she was hungry and eating until she was full, falling asleep when she was tired. I thought she approved of me. I didn't worry that she would die. I don't think the thought ever crossed my mind, which is silly, because any human being may die, but that's the way it was. There was a trace of sadness about Frances from the first, and I sometimes wondered about that, but I didn't worry. I had not particularly thought about her being fifteen months old. She was quite different from Racket. She didn't learn to walk until she was fourteen months, and so she was barely toddling around at fifteen months.

That just isn't the way I think. Pearl thinks differently from me. It's often interesting to see what thought will have crossed her mind.

I knew she wanted to say more, but I didn't feel like encouraging her. Now Frances came over and put her hands on our knees, one hand on mine and one on Pearl's. She had brown hair, and the curls were just coming in. She'd been bald for a long time. Pearl took her finger and followed the curve of one of Frances's curls, against her scalp. "Funny to think she's a woman," she said.

"A small woman."

"Someday she'll get her period. Do you think she knows about growing up?"

"Of course not," I said.

"I think she does," said Pearl.

"How could she know? She can hardly talk."

"She's always known."

"Has Simon always known about growing up?"

"Not the way Frances does."

I looked at her. "What are you *talking* about?"

"Don't yell at me," said Pearl. "I guess I mean knowing what it's like to be grown up. The way things hurt, but you get used to them. Now, Racket would never have learned that."

"I still don't know what you're talking about."

"Sometimes it drives me crazy that we'll never know Racket as an adult," said Pearl. "If there was anyone on earth I wanted to know, it was that kid."

"She was just a baby."

"She wasn't just any baby," Pearl said.

"She was difficult."

"No, I don't mean that," said Pearl.

Now Simon came over to us. "I have to go to the bathroom," he said.

Pearl stood up. "Now where am I going to find a men's room?"

"I think they're near the cafeteria," I said.

"Will you go by yourself?" she said to Simon.

Simon looked at his shoes. "Do I have to?"

"Well, I can't go into the men's room," said Pearl, "and you can't go into the ladies, can you?"

"I don't want to go alone," said Simon.

"Well, maybe I can find some nice man to take you," said Pearl. The two of them set off. I picked up Frances so she wouldn't follow them. She was chubby, a solid child. Her overalls had ruffles and she had on a little short-sleeved blouse. It was summer. I smoothed her curls, mostly to touch them, and set her on her feet again, and she took off after another pigeon, but only a few steps from me.

Her blanket was beside me on the bench, a thin flannel receiving blanket from which she could never be parted for long. She came back between pigeons and leaned over to rest her face on it for a moment, as if to draw something from it—comfort or courage; maybe she was a little afraid of the pigeons. It was a pink blanket, almost white from being washed so many times. I had to wash it at night and dry it on the radiator. She was upset if she woke up in the morning and didn't find it in her crib, yet sometimes it had to be washed.

After a while I looked up and saw Pearl coming back. I didn't see Simon for a moment; he was lagging behind. I remember looking at Pearl as she came back toward me. She must have found a nice man to take Simon to the bathroom, because she was walking with him. The strange thing was that he looked like Nathan, so like him—the way he held himself and moved more than the way his face looked —that for a startled second I thought it *was* Nathan, coming toward us in the Central Park Zoo for some unfathomable reason in the middle of a school day when I knew he was teaching summer school. Of course it was not Nathan, but a somewhat younger man. Pearl fit well beside him, because of her height. She looked blond and happy, like a bride. The man turned in the other direction now, toward the polar bears, with a wave, but Pearl still smiled, swinging her arms as she came toward me. Simon was walking a little behind her, looking elsewhere. Following his glance, a stranger wouldn't know which adults he belonged to.

A little while after that the children tired of the zoo, or maybe we did, and we went out into the park. Frances walked slowly, and sometimes she wanted to be carried. Pearl and I took turns, though I think Pearl carried her more than I did. It was getting cloudy, but I knew Pearl was happy to be in the park and didn't want to go back to the subway, and it seemed that if she was willing to carry Frances I should let her do what she liked. We went down to the lake and the children watched the ducks. Simon walked carefully around the rim of the lake, and Frances tried to imitate him. I would have carried her off someplace where there wasn't a lake to fall into, but Pearl was willing to walk with her and hold her hand.

The park was full of people, but not too many people. It was wartime, and everything had a certain look that I'd come to think of as "the war"—things looked brave, I guess I'd have to say. It looked brave for a child's collar to fly up near his neck when he rode his tricycle: the wartime tricycle looked flimsy and the child seemed to be riding into uncertainty, right there on the walk with his mother ten steps away, looking brave herself, in a skirt that the wind pulled tight to her body. Everything bright looked like a scrap of a flag. Yet I'd had enough. I wanted to go home and make supper.

Pearl led us away from the lake on one of the paths. She was looking for something she thought she remembered. There were fewer people now, and Simon and Frances began to roll on the grass. We sat down and watched them. Pearl lay down on her back. "Those are storm clouds," she said, shading her eyes with her hand and looking straight up. She reached out and pulled me down so I could see too—pulled me by the back of my neck.

I lay and looked at the clouds, though I'm not the sort of woman who lies on her back on the grass in the park. They were big, spiraling, dark gray clouds. "We'd better head for the subway," I said, but we didn't, not yet.

I could see people walk by now and then. They probably thought we were unconventional. I knew that bits of grass and possibly ants would work their way under my stockings and into my underwear. I yanked my skirt down so no one passing could see up my legs, but there was no one passing. Frances came over and rested her face on my face and I was overwhelmed by the sweetness of her smell.

Frances ran off again and I sat up to watch her. Pearl, still lying on her back, ran her finger along my arm, reaching it lazily just as far as it would go, then moving it up and down over my elbow.

"What?" I said.

"I felt a dro-op!" She sang *drop*.

We called the children and by that time it was raining. Then I saw lightning and there was thunder in the distance. We began to hurry down the path, first running slowly with Frances between us. Then Pearl snatched her up and we went faster.

The path curved. It might not be the shortest way back to the subway after all—we were quite far from the subway. A little earlier, we'd walked through a tunnel under a road, and now we came to the tunnel. It was raining hard and it kept thundering. Two young men were already taking shelter in the tunnel. We hurried inside. On the way through before, we'd stopped to call hello and hear the echo. Now Simon tentatively said, "Hello? Hello?" The thunder was strange in the tunnel.

All at once Frances began to cry. "Bank! Bank!" she wailed. It was her word for her blanket, and with actual panic I realized that I didn't have it. I was carrying a handbag and a diaper bag. The blanket had been in the diaper bag along with our lunch and a couple of bottles. I reached into the diaper bag but I knew the blanket wasn't there. The bag wasn't full enough. I'd taken the blanket out and let her hold it while we looked at the animals, but I had it when we sat on the bench. I might have left it there, or I might have left it on a bench near the lake.

Frances was crying hard, and Simon was looking at me with terrible concern. "You didn't lose Francie's blanket, did you, Aunt Hilda?" he said soberly.

"I hope not," I said. I looked up at Pearl.

"I'll get it," she said in an instant, before it even occurred to me that there was anything we could do. Pearl handed me her pocketbook and her straw hat and took off into the rain, running back the way we'd come in her tight skirt and high-heeled open-toed shoes.

"Where's Mommy going?" said Simon.

"Pearl, don't be silly!" I called.

"She'll be struck by lightning," he said. Frances had sat down on the dirty ground in the tunnel and was still crying. Rivulets of water were running in, and puddles and streams were forming, the rain was so sudden and hard. The two young men turned and looked at us, but didn't say anything. I crouched with the two handbags and the diaper bag to pick up Frances, and stayed low, holding her on my knees, to talk to Simon.

"She'll be all right," I said, though I was worried too, and I thought he could probably tell I was worried.

"No, you don't understand, she could get hit by lightning," he said.

I knew that people did get struck in Central Park, it wasn't just a silly fear. "Not so close to the big buildings," I said, though. "Only in the other part of the park. It won't happen."

But I was worried, and Simon wasn't convinced. "It could happen," he said. He walked closer to the end of the tunnel from which Pearl had run, and stood with his hands in his pockets, watching the sheets of rain and waiting for her.

Frances sobbed and I held her against me. Finally I put the bags down on the muddy ground. Every time there was a clap of thunder now, Frances screamed. Simon came over and held on to her foot. "The *thunder* can't hurt us," he said, and when she didn't answer, began shouting it again and again, "The thunder can't hurt us! The thunder can't hurt us!" His voice echoed and bounced and the two young men stared. I rocked Frances, her muddy shoes kicking against me, and used one hand to stroke Simon's back and shoulder.

At last, suddenly, Pearl was behind us—she'd come from the other direction—soaking wet, laughing, holding out the soaked blanket. Frances stopped crying abruptly and took it, then wriggled out of my arms and sat down in the mud, holding it to her face. I felt terrible that I could not do for her what that scrap of flannel could do. Simon, who did not like to hug his mother, crouched near her and began wiping her shoes with his hands.

"It was in the zoo," Pearl said. "On the bench in the zoo. You noodle. You left it on the bench in the zoo."

It was as if she was proud of me. Her hair was flat against her head, which made her nose look large and her chin jut out. Her blouse and skirt were translucent, clinging to her body.

"Are you all right?" I said, and put out my arms to her, and Pearl made a funny sound; I wasn't sure whether it was a combination of laughing and being out of breath or whether she was crying.

"What is it, Mommy, were you afraid?" Simon said.

Pearl came into my arms and put her head close to mine. "I wasn't afraid," she said, "but I'm so cold." She pulled my arms closer around her. "I don't know why I did that," she said. "It's not going to rain forever. We could have waited. It wasn't going away."

"I don't know why you did it either," I said.

"Now I'm so cold," she said. I held her until the rain dwindled and stopped, and then we walked—wet and dirty—to the subway.

When Frances was four I got a sore throat, then a bladder infection. I was sick all spring, and finally Nathan said I should go away for a week or two. Someone he knew suggested a place on Long Island, a sort of rooming house on the beach. I took Frances with me. There was no one to take care of her when he was at work, and I'd have missed her. And I took Pearl with me to help take care of Frances. She deserved a vacation, too, we told her. She was working in an office but they gave her some time off. It was early June and we spent about ten days on Long Island. Some of the guests in the rooming house lived there all the time, or all through the warm months, but others came for a week or two. Meals weren't served but you could leave your groceries in the refrigerator and cook for yourself. Pearl was worried about leaving Simon with Mike. "He has no patience with Simon," she said. But Simon was still in school, so we couldn't take him with us.

Mike drove us out there on a Saturday with our valises. Simon came along and at the last minute I thought Pearl might not stay. Simon was nonchalant, though. Mike helped us carry our things in. The landlady wasn't home, but she'd asked one of the other guests —a young woman who'd lived there all winter—to show us our room. "I'm Gussie," said the young woman. She asked Frances, "Do you want to see my bird?"

"Where is it?" said Frances. She probably thought Gussie had a bird in her pocket that might fly out at any moment. She pulled back.

"Upstairs. I'll show you later." She walked us down the corridor and we all went into our room. It was large, with a threadbare dark red rug and a plank floor around it. A big bed was in the middle of the room and a crib was in one corner. There were four windows, all in a row, and outside were pine trees. The windows were open and I smelled the trees and the salt water nearby.

"She's sorry there isn't a cot," Gussie said. "You asked for a cot."

At home Frances had a bed. I think I'd expected that she would sleep with me and the cot would be for Pearl.

"Can you go in there?" Gussie said now to Frances, leaning over to talk to her. She was skinny, with dyed blond hair. She was probably thirty, but she seemed like a girl. She was wearing a bathing suit, though it wasn't hot out.

"Is there a bird in there?" said Frances.

"No, honey, no bird. Let me show you." She picked up Frances and put her into the crib, shoes and all. I thought she'd object but she lay down. It wasn't much longer than she was. She lay on her back, arms and legs spread, her skirt up so her underpants showed. "Where's the bird?" she said.

"She forgot to tell you," Gussie was saying to me, shrugging, apparently in the direction of the landlady's room. "Someone else is using the cot."

"It's all right," said Pearl, and that was when I was afraid she'd say she wasn't staying. Simon was looking out the windows into the trees. Mike stood holding the suitcases.

"You'll be all right with him?" said Pearl to Mike, moving her chin in Simon's direction.

"Of course," said Mike. "Why shouldn't I be all right? Come on, Tiger, we'll head back to town. Got a long drive ahead of us." He put down the bags.

Pearl seized Simon and kissed him, but he wrestled away from her and followed Mike.

"I think maybe it's better when I'm not there," she said, after they were gone.

"He looks like a nice kid," said Gussie.

"He's a good boy," Pearl said.

"Can I show her around?" she said to us. "What's your name, honey?"

"Frances Levenson," said my daughter.

"Okay, Fran, let's go," said Gussie. I didn't think Frances would want to go off with Gussie, but she did.

"Do you really have a bird?" I said as they left.

"A canary. His name is Rosie."

"Rosie is a girl's name," said Frances.

"It's short for Franklin Delano Roosevelt," said Gussie. "I had another one called Eleanor, but she died."

When they were gone, Pearl kicked off her shoes and lay down on the bed. I opened my suitcase. "Do you mind if I take this dresser?" I said. There were two.

"Whichever you want."

"Is this all right?" I persisted.

"Why shouldn't it be all right?"

"You don't mind sharing a bed, do you?"

"I don't mind," said Pearl. After a while she stood up and un-packed her own clothes. I was putting my underwear into the first drawer, my blouses underneath, and so forth, but she just filled one drawer randomly, then the other.

When Gussie brought Frances back she offered to show us around too. I wanted to go exploring by ourselves but Pearl said yes. Next to the house was a big shady lawn with a hammock and picnic tables. A young couple was lying on a blanket in a sunny place at the end of the lawn. A small cottage was near the house and Gussie said more guests stayed there. "We all get along," she said. "We have good times."

She pointed us toward the beach and said she had to go wash her hair, and Pearl and Frances and I set out by ourselves. It wasn't far, just down a dirt road past a store where you could buy snacks and suntan lotion during the season. Past it was the beach, covered with rocks and pebbles. Long Island Sound, which was gray, stretched into the distance. Little, overlapping waves made a low, steady noise reaching the shore. Far away I could see a boat. I liked the smell, and the sound of the gulls mewing. The beach went as far as I could see in one direction, but in the other, a dune cut off our view. We began to walk, while Frances came behind us. She picked up shells and carried them.

"She's nice," said Pearl.

"Gussie?"

"Uh-huh."

"I don't know." I thought she was too eager to make friends. I wanted to be alone with Pearl and Frances.

That night Gussie said she was cooking fried chicken and it would be silly for us not to have some. Besides, we had no food. We had thought there was a store within walking distance, but it turned out you had to get a ride with the landlady, and she went when she went. We were glad to have Gussie's fried chicken that night, and after that she suggested that we share food and it seemed easier. She had a car.

The third or fourth day Gussie and Frances and Pearl went down to the beach. I was reading and didn't go, and as soon as they left, I was sorry. I lay on the bed, with the breeze blowing in, and played with the tufts on the bedspread. Then I fell asleep. They were still gone when I woke up. I had a dry mouth, and I went into the kitchen to find something to drink. No one was there. The house was big, but only a few people were staying there just then. The landlady went into town a lot. She worked part-time at the post office.

I made coffee and went back to our room. I was annoyed with Pearl for going off without me, even though I could have said something at the time and I didn't. I remembered a time when Pearl had just married Mike and they were living with us. I was angry with her for being young and pretty, for finding her way so easily into the household. I wanted her to suffer, I think. I'd get angry with her for no reason and she'd just take it. I'd confuse her on purpose.

I heard them coming back. Pearl came into the bedroom, eating something out of one hand. "Where's the baby?" I said.

"She's asleep. I was carrying her and she fell asleep in my arms. I put her down on the living room couch."

"What are you eating?"

"Crackerjacks. Frances is fine, Hilda."

"You kept her out awfully long. No wonder she's tired."

"We got to talking," Pearl said.

"I don't know what you and Gussie find to discuss for so long," I said.

"Nothing," said Pearl. "Are you angry with me?"

"No. Why should I be angry? I have no reason to be angry."

"Just checking," she said.

That night all the guests gathered in the living room and played charades. It was Gussie's idea. It was a good idea, I had to admit. I resisted it because I was starting to dislike her. But the charades got funnier and funnier, at least so it seemed. Pearl crawled on the floor, pretending to be a mouse, and Frances shrieked with laughter. Gussie guessed everything before I'd even started to think about what it could be.

That night I couldn't sleep. I tried to keep still but I kept shifting around in bed. My arms and legs felt cramped. I thought Pearl was asleep but at last she sat up. "What is it?" she said.

I didn't answer.

She sat there for a long time. Moonlight made boxes on the blanket and half-lit her in her pajamas. "Hey," she said, the way Mike would say it—awkwardly.

Then she drew me into the curve of her arm and lay down close to me. I was embarrassed, but I put my arm around her. Then I was so happy I tried not to breathe, as if she might think that the pressure of my chest moving in and out was a signal for her to go away. I wanted time to stop.

After that some things were different. I noticed that all three of us took off all our clothes without going into the bathroom. Every day Pearl and I went for a walk on the beach, usually with Frances. Gussie never came with us, but sometimes Frances stayed behind with her. "You two should be in pictures," Gussie said to us when we came in laughing from the beach one day.

"In pictures?" I said.

"The Something Sisters. Hey, you're sort of sisters, aren't you? What's your last name again?"

We explained that we had different last names even though our husbands were brothers, that Mike had changed his name years ago. "Oh, I remember," she said. I was confused; I didn't remember even telling her our husbands were brothers. Then I realized Pearl must have told her. "Pearl Lewis and Hilda Levenson," Gussie said. "The L Sisters." Her voice was slightly bitter.

Gussie thought we should sing, and somehow plans for singing began to be made. Harold, the man of the young couple, said he

knew lots of good songs. He brought out a guitar and it turned out
he could sing Woody Guthrie songs about electrical dams and power
stations and we gathered in the evening to sing. One night somebody
made popcorn. We were singing union songs when I went out to
check on Frances, who was asleep, and when I came back Pearl and
Harold were singing a duet, and then he kissed her. His wife wasn't
there that night for some reason. I think if she had been, it wouldn't
have seemed like anything.

After a while Pearl said "I'm sleepy" and leaned against me. I
stroked her hair, but she stayed only a minute and then said quietly
to me, "Let's go for a walk." We walked out onto the lawn. It was
a warm night, but I was chilly, and Pearl said she'd get sweaters and
check on Frances again. While I waited, I sat down in the hammock,
leaned back in it, looking at the moon, which was past full by now.
The hammock felt rough under me. It was stiff canvas, not very wide.
I pulled my feet in and tucked them under me. When Pearl came I
didn't get up, and she tossed me my sweater, which I spread over me
like a blanket. Pearl tried to climb into the other end of the hammock, but she spilled me out, and I fell on the ground. We both
laughed.

"Stop it, they'll come running," she said, and this time we held
hands and lowered ourselves carefully into the two ends of the hammock, and pulled in our legs one at a time. "Okay, right leg," said
Pearl. "Now my left. Now your left." When she pulled in her second
leg the hammock was crowded and swayed hard, like a boat in a
storm. We held on to the edges. The moon had gone behind a cloud
and it was dark.

"I'm glad I came along on this vacation," Pearl said.

"You gave Harold quite a kiss."

"I wondered what you thought."

"It's none of my business."

"I'm not going to fall for Harold," she said. "Don't worry. I'm inoculated."

We rocked back and forth. "Did you ever get over Nathan?" I asked at last.

"Really get over him?"

"Yes."

"No, I didn't," she said. Then after a moment she said, "But I'd rather have you."

"You can have me trouble-free," I said.

"Yes. Nobody cares."

I was silent for a while. "I care," I said.

"That's not what I meant. You know that's not what I meant, Hildie."

The next day was the last day of our vacation. On the beach we were alone. Gussie told Frances she was going through her old clothes and Frances could try them on and pretend to be a princess. They treated Frances a little like a princess there, in fact. She was always being singled out. I thought it made her shy, but she wanted to stay with Gussie.

Pearl and I walked slowly down to the beach. It was a chilly day and she was wearing striped pants—green and white stripes—and an old brown jacket. She leaned over for some shells and began sorting them. I looked out at Long Island Sound. It was gray and foggy, and I couldn't see very far. "My father brought me to a place like this once," I said. It had just come to me.

"Around here?"

"I don't remember where it was."

"Was your mother alive then?"

"Yes, but she didn't come. It was just my father and me. He carried me on a beach. I remember that the stones hurt my feet."

We walked for a while. "I forget how old you were when your mother died," said Pearl.

"Fourteen."

"It must have been terrible."

"By then I knew she'd die," I said.

"Was she sick for a long time?"

"A year." I thought I'd told her before, but I was pleased that she asked. I felt like talking about my mother. "I remember one of the last times she took care of me," I said. "She was in bed, and she called me to come to her and sat up a little so she could brush my hair and braid it. But it was funny, I'd been braiding my own hair for a while by then and I didn't like the way she did it. You know how when you braid someone's hair from behind, the braids go down the back. Well, I thought it was more grownup the way I did it myself, down the sides."

"I remember," said Pearl. "I had braids, too."

"Of course. That long braid." I remembered when she had cut it off. I started to laugh at her. "That must have been so much trouble, cutting it off. You were such a fool, Pearlie."

"I remember you thought so at the time."

"I thought I'd have to go picking up after the two of you all my life."

We had turned back. When we reached the house we stopped for

277

Frances and then we all took a nap together. I was a little sunburned, though it had been cloudy on the beach. The skin of my face and arms felt tight and a little gritty. I lay happily in the lumpy soft bed between Pearl and Frances, who both fell asleep. I stretched my toes out, reaching down to rub away the sand that had caught between them.

But there was one more night. We bought a big chicken and invited everyone. We hadn't been cooking with Gussie for several days. She'd made different excuses. That day she said she'd be sure to come, but she didn't. The rest of us ate together at the big table, and we had a good time. Gussie came in when we were nearly done, but she said she'd eaten. After dinner we all went into the living room and Harold took out his guitar and began to play, but it was as if someone had asked us to restage one of our other nights so it could be looked at. His wife seemed upset and I thought they might be having a fight. There was an older woman staying there then, Mrs. Engel, and she sat and crocheted and smiled at everyone, but insisted she couldn't sing. "I'm a good listener," she said.

Frances was still up. She kept asking for "Take Me Out to the Ball Game" and at last we sang it. We were Dodger fans, being from Brooklyn, but Gussie was a Yankee fan. She teased Frances about it, although Frances barely understood. Frances knew she was for the Dodgers, and she knew the song, but I'm not sure she knew what the Dodgers were, although Nathan often listened to the game at home.

As we sang "Take Me Out to the Ball Game," Gussie leaned over to where Frances was sitting cross-legged on the floor, and said, over and over again, "Yankees, Yankees, Yankees," and sure enough, when we reached the line "Root, root, root," we all sang "for the Dodgers" and Frances and Gussie sang "for the Yankees." Frances noticed what she had said and looked startled; then I saw that she was crying.

"It doesn't matter," I said, leaning over to talk to her. "Gussie's just teasing you. It's just a song."

When the song ended Pearl said to Gussie, "Don't you think you overdid that a bit?" She sounded angry.

"Fran's my buddy," said Gussie. "You don't care, do you, honey?"

Frances shook her head, but she still looked blubbery.

Then Gussie said to Pearl, "What do *you* care, anyway? She's not your kid." I turned around. Gussie was looking at Pearl, her eyes sharp and cold. "Or is she? Or can't you keep it straight, who's who in your family—who are the husbands and wives, who are the men and who are the women?"

She said it in an ugly voice, and Harold turned and looked at her. A moment later he asked whether there was any popcorn and said he was finally going to learn how to make it. Mrs. Engel continued to smile and look around her. I stumbled out and went for some toilet paper to wipe Frances's nose. Then I picked her up and said over her protests that she had to go to bed. Pearl came in ten minutes later.

"What did you tell her?" I said.

"Now or before?"

"Both."

"I didn't tell her anything. I've just been sitting there. I talked to Mrs. Engel."

"But before," I said. "You didn't say anything to Gussie about—about things that happened in the past?"

"Of course not," said Pearl. "Why would I do that?"

"You must have."

"But I didn't."

But of course she had.

Frances was eight when we began going away for a month in the summer, not to Long Island but to a bungalow colony in the Adirondacks. Many people who stayed there were Jewish teachers. We went back every year. Frances learned to swim in the lake. Nathan half relaxed—there were people he could talk to. It was the start of the McCarthy years, and from the first, I think, he knew what was going to happen.

At a hotel near where we stayed, fund-raisers for the Teachers Union were held, and everyone would load up in a couple of cars and go. Folk singers sang old European songs and the political songs we'd grown up on.

There was some tension at the bungalow colony. People whispered about one person or another. The manager of the place was a charming bachelor whose name wasn't Jewish. People said he'd changed it and even that he was some sort of spy for the Board of Education, which had begun investigating Communists in the schools.

There was some suspicion of Mike, too—maybe even one or two people who remembered his taking notes at Party meetings years before. Or maybe it was just because Mike argued with everyone he met. "That's *ridiculous*," I'd hear him say from across the beach, the pitch of his voice rising. He and Pearl and Simon would come for a week every summer and crowd in with us. Pearl and I would stay up late talking as if we didn't see each other all the time at home.

The spring before Nathan lost his job, I thought he was trying to slow time. He'd come home later and later each afternoon, and then not change out of his suit. There was always chalk dust on him, as if he wanted to save it. I thought I ought to gather it in an envelope, the way I'd saved Frances's baby teeth and, earlier, Racket's small white shoes, which were still in my bottom drawer; sometimes, searching for an old sweater, my fingers would touch the paper bag I'd put them into. The paper was old and soft, and when I felt it I wouldn't remember for a moment what it was.

When the term ended in June of 1953, Nathan was somber, and I could sense that each thing he did—mark the grade reports, fill out the forms teachers fill out at the end of the year—had taken on a sacred quality. He'd be back in the fall, but it might be his last June as a teacher—and in fact it was. "What will you do—" I tried to say. He shook his head. He had no idea what he'd do if he lost his job. I knew he thought he should have a plan, out of prudence, but he didn't.

I didn't want to worry Frances about Nathan's job. I didn't want her thinking Nathan was some sort of criminal. I didn't know what a child would think. She was eleven. Most of the time she seemed busy with her friends and dolls. Sometimes she was quiet. Once I found a sheet of loose-leaf paper that had fallen from her notebook. "Ways to Help Mommy and Daddy" she had written at the top. She'd numbered ten lines but had written down only two ways: "I. Help with the dishes. 2. Don't say things that remind them of things."

One night when Pearl and Mike were with us at the lake, Pearl and I sat up talking. Everyone was in bed except the two of us. We were sitting on the steps of the cabin. It was the only place we could be alone, and there we were bitten by mosquitoes, but Simon was asleep (we hoped) on the screened porch behind us; we couldn't go there.

"You should tell her," said Pearl. She was eating a peach in the dark, and I could hear each bite.

"What do you mean, tell her? What do you want me to say?"

"Tell her the whole story. Tell her about Nathan and the Party, in the thirties, and what's happening now."

"Oh, she knows all that," I said.

"I don't think so."

"I don't want to worry her."

"Hilda," said Pearl, "Frances worries. She worries all the time anyway. Can't you see that?"

"What does she have to worry about?" I said.

"She thinks about everything," Pearl said. "One day she asked me if I'm happy."

"She did?" I said. "What did you say?"

"I told her I'm happy about some things, unhappy about others."

"Why didn't you just say you're happy?" I asked her. I suddenly wanted her to make a speech, to say she was happy, that she loved Mike, that she didn't love Nathan anymore, that she had long ago stopped thinking about whether Simon was Nathan's child. And for a second I was afraid that she had sat herself down and told Frances everything.

"Why should I tell her I'm happy?" Pearl said.

"Because she's a child."

Pearl said, "Oh, Hilda, stop it!"

I couldn't say what had passed through my mind. I kept wondering if Simon was awake, listening. Finally Pearl said, "Let's go to the rec hall."

Walking down there, I asked, "Do you talk to Simon about— different things?"

"About what?"

I didn't want to go into it. "The things that come up," I said. "Do you and Simon talk?" Simon was sixteen—I didn't know what it would be like to have a sixteen-year-old son.

"About some things," said Pearl. We walked in silence and I could feel Pearl deciding what to say. Then she said, "When he's twenty-one, I'm going to tell him that Nathan is his father."

I didn't answer right away. "But Pearl," I said finally, "maybe Nathan isn't his father."

"Oh, Hilda, look at them. Just look at them."

"People look like their uncles," I said. But as we walked down the dirt road in the quiet, I could hear my voice in my mind, and it didn't sound sure.

The rec hall, a big room near the beach, was empty. Pearl picked up a Ping-Pong paddle and slapped a ball with it. Neither of us knew how to play but we tried hitting the ball back and forth. We had to run for it so much we were out of breath in an instant. We sat down on folding chairs at the side of the rec hall. "I want you to be happy," I said.

"Well, keep playing Ping-Pong with me, then!" she said.

"I can't."

"Neither can I." She slapped my leg. "Frances knows plenty," she said. "Never mind."

"Well, that's what I think."

"I look at her sometimes," said Pearl. "She's looking past us. She understands this stuff about Nathan's job better than you or I do. She probably knows everything—all about Racket and everything."

"All about Racket?" I hadn't been thinking about Racket. I still didn't like talking about her. Now and then Pearl wanted to talk about her and I tried to let her. "Well, she must know some things about the baby," I said. In fact, there was something I wanted to ask Pearl. "Do you and Simon talk about Racket?"

"No," said Pearl. "That's not on purpose—I meant to. I don't know what I was going to say. But when he finally asked me, it was at some awful moment. I think we were in the basement, and I was taking clothes out of the dryer. Maybe other people were there. And he said, just like that, 'Did Aunt Hilda ever have another baby?'"

"What did you say?" I said.

"Well, I lied," said Pearl. "I said, 'She had a miscarriage once, a late miscarriage.'"

"Why in the world did you say that?" I had assumed Simon knew about Racket—almost as if he might remember her.

"I guess I didn't want to frighten him," said Pearl. "Simon's—you know what he's like. This was a few years ago."

"But how could you do that?"

"Well, do you want me to tell Simon everything?" she said, turning and facing me.

"No," I said. "No." I was amazed at the lie she had told about my baby. But that's what it's always been like with Pearl. I never could predict her.

"I mean, we could sit them both down and tell them about Racket," she said, standing up and walking around. She was looking for something to eat, I thought, but there was nothing. She stood at the Ping-Pong table and fingered one of the balls as if she might bite into it. I watched to see if she'd crush it.

"Don't be silly," I said. But it made me picture myself sitting across a table from Frances—my kitchen table at home—saying, "You had a sister. She never stopped kicking, fighting me. . . ." And maybe Frances would say, "Oh, I know all about her. Don't you remember—you said this, you said that?"

Pearl and I kept talking, but about other things. "Mike will wake up and not know where I am," she said. "He'll yell and wake up the whole house." Yet she stayed where she was, leaning against the Ping-Pong table. I thought of Mike asleep on the daybed in the cottage living room, then waking and missing Pearl, pounding the mattress as if she might have slipped into a hole in it. He would think the same twelve thoughts over and over. There were things Mike would never think and would never say, and so he had to shout very loudly. "He'll yell at you in the morning," I said. "He'll say you were up late and so you'll sleep late, and you'll miss a beautiful summer day, and how many summer days do you get? He'll wake you up to say that."

"I know it," she said. "He'll say, 'You talk to Hilda enough at home—here you should go swimming.'"

But after a while we got tired, and we started up the hill to the cottage. Pearl laid her hand on my arm as we walked, as if to get my attention, but she left it there. I wanted to hold hands with her, to walk swinging our joined hands like a couple of girls in kindergarten. Then I saw someone coming toward us as we walked: a thin figure in a light shirt—Simon. "He heard us!" said Pearl, joking.

"Good evening, mother and aunt," he said, coming up to us. "Are you planning to wander the premises all night?"

"We were just going back," I said. "You're still awake?" He was dressed.

"I am a fitful sleeper," said Simon. "If I ever join the navy, I can take a watch in the middle of the night."

"The navy!" I said.

"Don't say things like that," said Pearl. "He said it to me once, too. That he might join the navy."

"Better that than Brooklyn College," said Simon cheerfully. "Better that than Brooklyn." He did a little dance step. He was trying to do a hornpipe.

"I don't think they do much dancing now," I said.

"The navy's a lot better than it used to be," said Simon. "Though I don't know about anti-Semitism in the navy. Do you ladies know anything about that? How I'd do with a Jewish name?"

"Lewis isn't a Jewish name," I said.

"Oh," he said lightly, and brushed his mother's shoulder with one hand, as if what he was saying was really meant for her. "I'm thinking of taking the name Levenson. Taking it back. What do you think, Mom?"

"Levenson," said Pearl.

"Well, it's our *name*, after all," said Simon. "I don't know why Dad changed it. Cowardly to change it."

He stood there smiling at us, just as tall as Pearl now—smiling down at me. For a second I thought he might be walking in his sleep; the conversation felt like one in a dream. He didn't come back with us right away. He said he wanted to walk down to the lake, and he kept going when we went back to the cottage. I lay awake until I heard him come in a little while later.

The next day Pearl and I went shopping together at the Grand Union in town. When Pearl was visiting, she didn't seem to mind spending some of her short vacation doing the shopping, even though I offered to go alone so she could be at the lake earlier. I guess she liked picking out food.

I drove. I hadn't had my license for long, and I liked driving Pearl places. I drove slowly through the grounds of the bungalow colony and out onto the highway, while she sat beside me talking. I was tempted to keep driving through town. "We could go someplace exciting," I said.

"Grand Union will do."

She went back to what she'd been saying. "Do you and Nathan fight?"

"Yell and scream?"

"Well, sort of."

"No," I said. "Nathan won't. And I guess I won't."

"You fight with me," she said.

"Now and then." When Pearl and I had an argument neither of us could leave it alone until it was settled, and we'd talk—usually on the phone—until it was over. Once we talked until three in the morning. We'd been arguing about whether people were basically good or bad, I remember. It had started with Hitler and ended with our children. At the time she was trying to defend Mike for punishing Simon. "It will teach him, I guess," she said, but then she cried.

"He doesn't need to learn, he already knows," I said. I always liked Simon and worried about him.

In the store, now, I took a cart and started down the aisles. I needed hamburger meat. "Do you mind frozen french fries?" I said.

"No, that's fine," said Pearl. "Let's get some fruit."

"Of course." In the fruit and vegetable department, she couldn't be stopped. "Look at the cherries," she said. "Really nice cherries. And the plums."

"Let's get some plums," I said. I was already putting cherries into a brown bag.

Pearl leaned over the display of plums. It was July and they were those tart, dark red plums with yellow flesh. She reached out an arm for a brown bag and began selecting plums, fingering them lightly and putting them into the bag or letting them be. I stood behind her with my cart, waiting.

She was so familiar: the curve of her back, her narrow back and big hips. That chopped-off blond hair. She weighed the plums and then went in search of a clerk to mark the bag. I'd lost Racket, I suddenly thought, I could never tell Nathan the whole story—but I'd kept Pearl. The clerk, in his white apron, seemed to point toward the front of the store—and beyond, to the mountains—and Pearl looked too, and they nodded together. It was a hot day, they were probably saying. They chatted a moment. She nodded again.

And she came back to me, waving her bag like a prize. I'd lost something and I had something, and that was true for her, too. My eyes filled but I turned away so she wouldn't see. Pearl took the front of the cart and pulled it down the aisle, looking at the other fruit with interest.

"I already have bananas," I said.

"I know, I ate one for breakfast. There are three left."

"I'll be back."

"We eat a lot."

"That's all right. I want you to eat a lot," I said.

Then when we left the store I didn't go straight home after all. I kept driving past the entrance to the bungalow colony. "I'm carrying you away," I said.

"I notice."

I didn't know where I'd go, then I remembered a stand up the road that sold antiques and pottery, and I pulled in there. "I want to see what they have here," I said.

There were no other customers, and the old woman who ran the place was inclined to talk. She guessed we must be from New York. "You look Jewish," she said. When we began looking around, she showed us a few things. "You like antiques?"

I said I didn't know much about them, and she showed us old washstands and ladles and devices to warm a bed in winter. There were rows of cups and saucers and spoons and glasses in all sizes and colors.

I was thinking that I might buy Pearl a present, but I didn't see the purpose of a glass or a cup. It would just be something to dust. She came toward me carrying an old picture frame, carved dark wood. There was a photograph in it, an old-fashioned baby in a long white gown. She handed it to me. The baby had startling dark eyes, and I knew what she meant, but I fingered the wooden frame.

"Do you like the frame?" I said.

"The picture reminded me . . ."

"It could be any baby," I said. I put the photograph down and we went out to the car.

"I like places like that," said Pearl.

"For a few minutes," I said.

We drove back to the bungalow colony. Next to me on the front seat, Pearl was silent. When we got there, we were both hungry. The cabin was quiet, and I thought all the others were at the lake. There were crumbs on the table, and in the refrigerator a bowl of tuna salad with waxed paper over the top. They had come up from the lake and had lunch and gone down again. We put away the groceries. "Tuna fish okay with you?" I said, and Pearl took out the bread. I made instant coffee. We ate, talking about Mike some more. "At least he still thinks I'm good-looking," said Pearl.

"Yes, I think he does," I said. I was going to say she *was* good-looking, too, but I heard a sound, and Frances came into the kitchen, barefoot, her index finger holding her place in a book.

"I thought you were down at the lake," I said. She was in her bathing suit. She was getting chunky—she had that solid look little girls have before they grow breasts.

"I was down there this morning," she said.

"Aren't you going back?"

"I guess so."

"Did you eat lunch?"

She nodded. "Can I have a cookie?"

I gave her a cookie and she sat down at the table, as if cookies required formality. Pearl and I were sitting there with our instant coffee, and Pearl took a cookie, too. "Where did you go?" said Frances. "I wanted to go with you."

"Just to Grand Union," I said. "You were here when we left."

"I like Grand Union."

"Oh, don't be silly," I said. "It's just a store."

"It's a little different," said Frances.

She took another cookie and I put the box away. "Are you coming to the lake?" she said.

"Yes," I said. "I just want to straighten up. You go ahead."

"I'll wait for you," said Frances.

"It's hot," I said. "Go down there and swim. You're swimming so well."

"Were you telling secrets?" she said.

"Secrets?" I said. "Of course not. We don't have secrets. Stay and walk down with us if you want to."

But Frances put on her sneakers and went down to the lake. I wiped off the table and put the dishes in the sink while Pearl put on her bathing suit, and then she talked to me while I put on my suit and my terrycloth jacket. Pearl always strode down to the beach in her suit with nothing over it.

"Let's take the plums," she said. She washed them and dried them and put them back into the brown bag. I took my knitting and we walked down to the lake. A few people were there. Nathan had been swimming—his hair was wet. He was leaning back in an Adirondack chair looking tired, his glasses beside him on the arm. Simon was dressed in his city clothes. He had brought a bathing suit but he wouldn't change, much less go into the water. Yet he went to the beach every day and looked out at the lake. He stared and stared.

"Is a mermaid going to come along and tell you something?" I said to him, but he didn't answer.

Frances was swimming back and forth. She was allowed to go where the water was just over her head, and that was where she was. Her swimming had improved, but she always seemed to hoist herself out of the water when she stroked with her left arm, as if she needed to check, every few seconds, to see where everyone was. She saw us and came out and ate a plum, and then she wandered off into the little stand of trees for a while.

I knitted and watched her. I could just see her, sitting under a tree near the water. When she was little, she had talked to herself in a low voice, on and on. Once I'd caught something she said and answered her, but she was angry. As I watched her from the beach, I realized that even though she was bigger now, I was still listening for the sound of her voice, as she sat there on those pine needles—partly to make sure where she was, the way I did when she was little, and partly to hear what she'd say. After a time she came back to us and went into the water again, and then she sat on a different rock, just a little way into the lake. I listened to the men talk. Pearl had a conversation with a couple of women from other cabins, and then the others went back to their cottages. Nobody but our family seemed to stay at the lake for long. I liked looking out and seeing the light change as the sun went down. I liked watching Nathan, his chest hollow and skinny, lying back in the chair, defenseless and yet, it seemed, content. I even liked watching Mike, who was restless— smoking, stubbing out his cigarette and going to take a boat out, then smoking another cigarette, shouting at Simon to become different. Pearl didn't swim, but wanted to be near the water. I took my own short swim and wrapped myself up again until I was warm. I sat in the sun and after a while it made me sleepy.

"I think I might be ready to start back," I said, not in a very loud voice.

Pearl heard me. "A nap might be nice," she said. We stood up. I reached for my beach jacket again. "Take the plums," said Pearl, as I turned to catch up with her. She was waiting for me, squinting into the sun, her hand shading her eyes, her long arm graceful. I reached back for the brown paper bag. The belt of my jacket dragged in the sand, and I pulled it up and brushed it off and tied the jacket closed.

"Give me a plum," said Pearl

ACKNOWLEDGMENTS

Maria Guarnaschelli's faith called this book into being; Claire Wachtel's determination and brilliance rescued it and its author many times. I'd like to thank those two past and present Morrow editors and the many others at Morrow and HarperCollins, especially Jen Pooley, who've been kind to me and my work. Thanks also, for helping me finish this book and supporting it after it was written to my agent, Zoe Pagnamenta, to the corporation of Yaddo, to Susan Holohan, and in particular to my mother, Rose Eisenberg.